GOOD

AS

DEAD

GOOD AS DEAD

A NOVEL

SUSAN WALTER

LAKE UNION
PUBLISHING

Published by Lake Union, Seattle

www.apub.com

Amazon, the Amazon logo, and Lake Union are trademarks of Amazon.com, Inc., or its affiliates.

ISBN-13: 9781542029025
ISBN-10: 1542029023

Cover design by Rex Bonomelli

Printed in the United States of America

Lying is a delightful thing, for it leads to the truth.

—*Fyodor Dostoevsky*

PART 1

HOLLY

Three months ago

I woke up from a thick, dreamless sleep, and for several seconds I had no idea where I was. I didn't panic, not at first. It's happened to me before, at my grandparents' on their pullout couch, on our trip to Big Bear in an unfamiliar motel room. *Where am I? Oh yeah, now I remember.* Those confusing first few seconds when I wake up somewhere other than my own bed, they're not scary. Not usually.

But this time was different. When I opened my eyes, all I saw was white—the walls, the sheets, the stiff synthetic pillow under my knee. *What is wrong with my knee?* I closed my eyes. *Think, Holly . . . think.* In the darkness I heard hushed whispers, the hollow scraping sound of curtain rings on metal rods. There was a nauseating smell. Antiseptic, with undertones of death and dirty diapers. I knew that smell. I hated that smell. Last time it meant an emergency C-section, lucky to be alive.

Suddenly I knew. A second before I didn't, but then I did. It hit me like a sucker punch. I cried out. The pain was unbearable. Like a thousand hands twisting my skin until it tore off the bone. I knew I was howling, but I couldn't stop. Because I remembered.

I remembered everything.

CHAPTER 1

The first thing I noticed was the flowers. There were thousands of them, in every color, making graceful S curves along the front of the house. I wondered if they were the kind you had to replant every year. I made a mental note to find out.

The house was bigger than I expected. I was glad they didn't let me choose it, I would have been embarrassed to pick one this nice. The front door was tall and painted bright red. Above it, a pair of matching gables stared out into space like big eyes with pointy eyebrows. It had a circular driveway, so you could go in and out without turning around. Instead of plain old asphalt, it was paved with chalky gray bricks arranged in a pattern that looked like zippers unzipping. I couldn't decide if it was pretty or just made me dizzy.

Evan came around to my side and opened the car door for me. I didn't say thank you. I never said thank you to Evan. The accident wasn't his fault, but that didn't mean I had to be nice to him.

Savannah, my teenage daughter—and the only reason I didn't take all the Vicodin they gave me at the hospital in one swallow—refused to come see it. She said she was tired, but I knew the real reason she didn't want to come. I didn't want to see Evan, either, but we had all agreed to this, so there was no point putting it off. Besides me, Evan, and Evan's evil boss, Savannah was the only one who knew why I was here, looking at this beautiful house. A house I could never afford but would be mine with a simple nod of the head.

"What do you think?" Evan asked before I even got all the way out of the car. If I'd had to guess, I would've put him around my age. Maybe a bit older. Forty at the most. I wondered if he was married. He didn't wear a ring.

"I like the flowers," I told him.

"Aren't they magnificent? You'll have a gardener, of course."

Of course. Evan said that a lot. *We'll take care of everything, of course. If you have questions, you can call me anytime, of course.* On the weekends, he sometimes wore a faded blue baseball cap with a *Y* on it. For Yale. Apparently he went there. I wondered if he'd majored in kissing ass, because he was really good at it.

I started toward the front door. My knee was stiff, but I tried not to limp as I walked up the uneven stone path. I'd finished my eight weeks of physical therapy, but Evan said I could do more sessions if I wanted to. *Of course.*

He followed me onto the front porch. Not a porch really, just a covered entryway, so you could open the door without getting rained on. There was a little wooden bench by the door. It looked brand-new. I wondered if it came with the house, or if Kiss-ass put it there.

Evan offered me the key. "Do the honors?"

He smiled at me. I wondered what he was thinking. I didn't imagine he felt sorry for me, not anymore. He probably thought I was the luckiest bitch on the planet. When you have enough money, everything is for sale. I proved that.

I took the key from him and unlocked the door. The bolt was heavy and made a loud thunk when it retracted. I don't know how wide the doorway was, but I remember thinking you could roll a piano through it—not the kind they have in bars, the pear-shaped kind that they have at fancy hotels and inside Nordstrom.

The knotty wood floors were cinnamon colored, *to match the smell of the place*, I thought. The creamy vanilla walls and gingerbread curtains made me feel like I was walking into a chai tea latte. My eyes welled with tears at the perfection of it all. Happiness mixed with shame mixed with grief, it was damn near overwhelming.

I slipped off my shoes and padded through the grand entryway, under a wagon wheel chandelier with bulbs the size of tennis balls. I wondered where you bought bulbs like that. And how on earth I would change them.

The dining room—*it has a dining room!*—was straight out of *Downton Abbey*, with a thick wooden table and eight high-back chairs. Four additional chairs—*dinner for twelve, anyone?*—stood guard beside the lowboy buffet. I wondered if there was china inside. I didn't dare look.

I continued on to the kitchen, which had an island you could sit at. There were only three stools, but room for twice as many. Not that I would need more than three. It was only Savannah and me, and I didn't plan on having any guests for breakfast. If we were a normal family, we would probably eat in the nook, which was enclosed by walls of glass with rugged pine trees just beyond.

There was a formal living room I would never use, and an office with built-in bookcases I likewise wouldn't need. They would look silly if I didn't fill them, so I'd either have to keep the door closed or take up reading.

The stairs to the second floor were carpeted, but I took them slowly. My physical therapist had told me not to baby my knee, my leg needed to get stronger, I should push through the pain. But I still leaned on the railing a bit, noting how smooth and wide it was under my palm.

There were three bedrooms upstairs. The first two were regular-size, except that they had bathrooms and balconies, which made them feel grander. The master was at the end of the hall. I pushed open the double doors and stood at the threshold.

I knew they had to furnish it with a king-size bed—the space would have looked ridiculous with anything smaller. But I'd never had a king-size bed in my life. It felt at once both lavish and cruel.

There was a quilted storage chest for blankets at the foot of the bed. Just past that, a shabby chic sofa faced a fireplace lined with little glass rocks that looked like what happens when a windshield breaks. It was more like an apartment than a bedroom, and I wondered what I was supposed to do with two walk-in closets now that I wasn't a "two" anymore. *Will my allowance be enough to fill them with new clothes? And what do I need with new clothes?*

I sat on the bed and looked out the double french doors leading to the balcony—more like a porch, really—which was decked out with a grass mat and twin lounge chairs. The view was all trees and sky. I couldn't help but wonder . . . *Dream house? Or private prison?*

There were certainly plenty of secrets to keep locked inside.

EVAN

Three months ago

A small crowd had gathered on the sidewalk. It was a narrow residential street with boxy single-story homes sprinkled between aging stuccoed apartment buildings. A pair of sneakers hung on the power line over my head. Someone once told me that meant "drugs sold here," but I don't know if I believed that. I mean, if that guy knew it meant drugs, surely the DEA did, too?

I parked my Range Rover a safe distance away and walked toward the scene. I inventoried the lookie-loos: a bare-legged couple dressed for jogging, an elderly woman gripping a shopping caddie, a woman in a sundress and sandals with tattoos up her arms, three teenage boys who probably should have been in school.

A few more spectators gazed out at the street from front porches and stoops. I counted nine in total. One of them, a dark-haired man in a shiny tracksuit, had his phone pointed toward the wreckage, probably hoping to earn some Twitter love with his livestream of the carnage. Though I didn't peg him as an influencer, I knew this kind of stuff could go viral, so I kept my distance.

I eased my way toward the uniformed police officer standing guard at the scene. An ambulance was parked diagonally a few feet behind him, rear doors open to receive. And then I looked down.

Nausea bubbled up the back of my throat. I understood then why they covered the dead. No question the man was killed on impact. His head was indented like a partially inflated basketball, and the way his legs were bent made him look like a Muppet, with limbs of cloth instead of bones.

I tripped over my own feet as I backed away, nearly falling on two paramedics loading a woman onto a stretcher.

"Sorry," I mumbled. The woman's shirt was ripped, and I could see her bare breast. One leg was wrapped in bandages at the knee. Her head was bleeding through a brick of gauze at her hairline. Her eyes fluttered a little, like she was going in and out of consciousness. One hand flexed open and closed as if she were trying to grab on to something that should have been there, but inexplicably had been taken away.

"Excuse me, Officer," I said to the uniformed cop closest to the body. My voice shook, but not for the reasons he probably thought. "The woman, I . . ." I paused. I didn't want to lie to a cop, but I needed information he wouldn't give to a stranger. "I think I may know the family. I want to help if I can." Part of that was true. I did want to help someone. I never said it was the victim. "Please, can you tell me her name? I just want to be sure before . . ." *Before what? Jesus, where am I going with this?* "Before I reach out."

The cop looked at me. He wore a brass name tag that identified him as Kellogg—a fitting name—his rosy cheeks and upturned nose made him look like a live-action Snap, Crackle, or Pop. I thought about the kids from my high school who wanted to be cops. Not exactly academic superstars. But they still had the power to make my life miserable, I had nothing to gain by pissing one off.

"We'll alert the family," he said brusquely, and turned away from me. And I knew I had a problem. Because I couldn't take control of the situation if I didn't know her name.

Click-clack! Behind me, two paramedics raised the stretcher like a giant accordion. They were about to wheel the woman into the ambulance. I started to panic. The situation was getting away from me.

"Where are you taking her?" I asked the female paramedic as she started pushing the woman toward the truck. "What hospital?"

"Tarzana Presbyterian," she replied, then asked me something that caught me off guard. "You want to ride along?"

The question was so unexpected I almost flubbed it. "No, I'll follow in my car," I said, riding her assumption that I knew the victim.

"You want to take this for her?" She reached under the sheet and produced something so miraculous, if there were such a thing as angels, I was sure they would be singing.

"Yes, thank you," I said. I held out my hand, and in the most glorious stroke of stupidity she handed me the woman's purse.

And my first problem was solved.

CHAPTER 2

"I took the liberty of having it furnished," I told Holly as I handed her the key. "I wasn't sure if what you had would work in the space." I felt nervous, but I had no idea why. In my ten years working for Jack, I'd hosted senators and movie stars and even a crown prince—people with much more discerning palates than Holly Kendrick. Yet it felt like someone was pounding a drum between my ears.

"Did you decorate it yourself?" she asked without looking at me. The question struck me as strange.

"No," I said. Of course it was a lie. I didn't want her to know I spent hours at Ethan Allen, comparing fabric samples, opening and closing dresser drawers to make sure they felt good in your hand. She already thought I was a pussy, I didn't want to make it worse.

"Can I go look around?" she asked.

"Of course. It's your house." I could have left it at that, but I added, "If you like it, that is." I had no doubt she would like it. Why wouldn't she? It was in the heart of the fancy Calabasas neighborhood she requested, on one of the best streets. Compared to the sad little apartment she was coming from, this was frickin' Buckingham Palace. Still, I wanted her to feel like she had some choice in the matter, that if she didn't like this one, we could just go out and get her a different one. Which we could.

She stepped up to the candy-apple-red front door and put the key to the lock. Her silhouette—tiny waist with sumptuous, perfectly round hips—was from a different generation. Born fifty years earlier, she could have been a pinup girl. From the front her heavy makeup and dark roots around her hairline made her look trashy, but from the back those bleached-blonde waves completed the fantasy—a fantasy I had to force myself to push away.

"I'll wait outside," I said to the silhouette. I wanted to go with her, watch her run her fingers over the polished stone counters and gleaming stainless steel. See her face light up knowing it was hers, all hers. Mostly I wanted to see her smile. In the three months I had known her, she had never cracked a smile. At least not for me.

"Take as long as you need," I said to the back of her head. The door closed behind her with a decisive thump.

It was a glorious summer day. Bright sunshine with a crisp breeze. Growing up in New Hampshire, days like this were so rare that if we got one, we would beg our teachers to have class outside. They were so starved for sunshine they often would oblige.

I didn't go back to New Hampshire anymore. Nothing and no one to go back to. Which was fine. I found my own version of family here in sunny SoCal. The Beach Boys were right about California girls. It had taken me a while to accept a sports bra as a top you can wear out on its own, but now I just said thank you.

I sat down on the wooden bench I bought for ninety-nine dollars at Home Depot and immediately realized why it was so inexpensive. I silently chided myself. Usually I'm much more discerning. And I settled in to wait.

Across the street a man worked in his garage. In his saggy Levi's and vintage Chuck Taylors, I took him immediately for a movie industry guy. This neighborhood was full of them. Men who never grew up. Call me old-fashioned, but I can't relate to a man whose idea of work attire consists of a rock band T-shirt and sneakers unfit for any type of athletic activity. He saw me staring and waved. It felt wrong to wave back, but I did. He'd find out soon enough that I didn't live here. Hopefully that's all he'd find out.

I startled when the door opened. I'd expected her to take longer, to savor the details. I couldn't help but feel disappointed.

"Please tell whoever decorated the place they did a good job," Holly said without the slightest hint of a smile. I was sure she had a beautiful smile. I doubted she'd ever show it to me.

She walked toward the car. I noticed she was limping.

And suddenly I knew no matter what we did, it would never be enough.

ANDY

Three months ago

Fuck, fuck, fuck! Why didn't I leave earlier? I know why. Because an hour should be enough time to go sixteen fucking miles. But this is LA, where driving sixteen miles can take longer than traversing the face of the moon. And I'm a stubborn ass who refuses to accept that.

I took my anger out on the steering wheel, squeezing it until my knuckles turned white. I could feel sweat trickling down my vertebrae, bumping its way toward the crack of my ass. I hadn't moved more than ten feet in the last ten minutes. Even in an apocalypse, with everyone taking to the streets at the exact same time, a log jam like this would seem hyperbolic. And yet here I was.

I looked at the clock, did a quick calculation. *If I get off at the next exit and take surface streets, I'll probably add five miles to the drive, but at least I won't be just sitting here, marinating in my own body fluids.*

Decisions, decisions... I cranked my neck out the window. It was cruelly hot for May, with relentless sun and not even a hint of a breeze. On the other side of the freeway guardrail, a row of towering palms loomed like prison bars, mocking me with their dogged uniformity. Once upon a time, palm trees conjured images of mai tais and tropical beaches, but now, in their maddening stillness, they just pissed me off.

I contemplated my phone. I thought about calling to say I was going to be late, but then if by some miracle I got there on time, I'd look like a nervous Nellie and just annoy them. But if I didn't call, or called at the last minute, they'd think I was rude. *Ugh, why didn't I just leave earlier?*

I dialed my agent's office. The assistant picked up. "I can't believe I'm saying this," I started, "but I think I'm going to be late." There was a beat of silence, like he couldn't believe it either.

"You want me to call them?" he asked, not even trying to hide his incredulity.

"Wait!" I said, my iron grip on the wheel giving way to hope. "I'm moving again!" I eased my foot onto the accelerator. "Don't call them, I think I might make it, sorry! Thanks!"

I said a silent prayer to the gods of traffic *(please keep moving, please keep moving!)* as my car shifted into second gear, then third. *If I continue at this pace, I might just get there on time. As long as there isn't a wait at the gate, and the walk from the parking structure isn't too far.* Studio lots can span ten city blocks. If the parking wasn't close, I was sunk.

I pulled up to the guard gate with four minutes to spare. There was no line to get on the lot *(halle-fucking-lujah!)*, but the parking situation sucked. There were six soundstages between the structure and the executive bungalows, and I cursed myself for not wearing sneakers. I parked illegally, in a spot reserved for "Vanpool Only," willing to risk that I might get towed. And then I ran.

I arrived at the meeting pink-skinned as a pig, with blisters already budding on my big toes and heels. The assistant to the assistant offered me "Something to drink? Sparkling water, cappuccino?" but after my full-out sprint, I didn't trust my stomach.

"Just water, thank you," I said, hoping she didn't notice the sweat beading on my hairline. My agent worked really hard to get me this meeting. I don't want to name-drop, but this guy I was seeing was a huge deal—what in Hollywood we called a triple threat: actor, producer, and even sometimes director. He didn't meet with many screenwriters, but he apparently liked that script I wrote for Clooney, and if the meet and greet went well, I could be his guy for his next big thing.

There was a plexiglass barrier walling off the reception area from the inner sanctum. Inside the brightly lit terrarium, shiny millennials sat at cubicles, staring into computer screens or otherwise trying to look busy. Just beyond them was the boss's office. I knew it was his office because I could see him, silhouetted against a big bay window overlooking the lot. I don't know why this gave me a thrill, it's not like I didn't know he worked there. But seeing him in his element, knowing in a matter of minutes I'd be sitting across from him, breathing the same air, made my new blisters momentarily stop throbbing.

"Here you go." The assistant to the assistant handed me a glass of water. Nobody gave out bottles anymore, for fear of being perceived as an environmental terrorist. She also handed me a napkin, which, once she turned her back to me, I used to mop my brow.

I limped across the cowhide rug to wait on a dimpled leather settee the color of money. I gazed at the wall of movie posters *(five of them, all huge hits!)*, feeling silent exhilaration that the legendary multihyphenate who could put both my kids through college with a nod of his head was right on the other side. And he wanted to work with me! All I had to do was not be an asshole for the fifteen minutes he allotted me, my agent had said—easy enough, even for an asshole.

Ten minutes passed, then ten minutes more. I had only been three minutes late—*a miracle!*—certainly that wasn't enough to make him change his mind about meeting me? Another five minutes passed. I was about to take out my phone to call my agent when the assistant's assistant approached. Her expression was pained. "I'm so sorry," she said. "Something's suddenly come up. This meeting is not going to happen today." And my exhilaration popped like a birthday balloon.

I glanced toward the big boss's office as I was escorted through the reception area, but he had closed the blinds, so I couldn't see who he had chosen to meet with instead of me. Not that it mattered. I was still getting tossed out on my ass.

My phone lit up as I walked back to my car. It was Laura, my agent. Wanting to know how it went, no doubt. I pressed "Ignore." A moment later the phone buzzed again. This time it was Libby, my wife. I needed this job. *We* needed this job. I let the call go to voice mail.

Walking across the lot, between the soundstages and star trailers, I recalled an episode of *The Brady Bunch*, my favorite show when I was a kid. One of the "bunch" wanted to wiggle out of a date without hurting the boy's feelings—must have been Marcia, because Cindy was an infant and nobody wanted a date with Jan. After spending act one agonizing about how to let him down easy, Marcia said the exact same thing about something suddenly coming up. It was the first and only time I ever heard that phrase—until ten minutes ago. Marcia's date knew, as anyone with half a brain would, what it really meant: *I'm not into you.* I don't remember how the episode ended, just that I felt really bad for the guy, and ashamed of Marcia, who was the nicest of the three sisters and should have known better.

I finally reached the garage. My feet were killing me. The blister on my left heel had bled through my sock, staining the inside of my cap-toed Oxford. Mercifully, my car was still there. I limped over to it, got in, and in the privacy of the darkened shell, I kicked off my bloody shoe and, though I'd never in a million years admit it, I cried.

CHAPTER 3

"Did you meet the new neighbors?" Libby asked, hands on hips, from the threshold of the garage. It was more of an accusation than a question. I could read the annoyed subtext in her perfectly sculpted brow. *Why didn't you introduce me?* if I did. *Why didn't you go say hello?* if I didn't.

"I waved to the husband," I said, recalling the man on the little wooden bench, how he sat with his knees splayed wide, his six-foot-and-then-some frame too big for the narrow wooden slats. "They seemed like they were in a hurry," I lied, hoping this would spare me from an onslaught of *Why didn't yous.*

"They've certainly had a lot of deliveries," she said, as if it were odd for people moving into a new house to get new things. "By the looks of it they got all new furniture!" She was right, there had been a steady stream of delivery trucks over the past few days—bedroom furniture from Ethan Allen, rugs from Z Gallerie, a washer and dryer from Best Buy. I wasn't sure if a middle-aged couple getting all new everything was unusual or just annoying—we hadn't so much as upgraded our TV in over a decade. I pondered the possibilities. *Newly married? Newly successful? Or simply from so far away it didn't make sense to bring anything?*

"I wonder what they paid for the house," Libby thought out loud, and I wondered why she wondered these things. "The more the better," she added. We hadn't talked about selling our house, but I suddenly realized she'd been thinking about it. All this time I'd thought she had dragged me to look at "the updated, traditional, three-bedroom gem" when it was for sale and open "just for fun."

I fiddled with the Shop-Vac, hoping she would get the hint and go back inside. Turning the garage into a woodworking shop had been an accidental stroke of genius. I got to be out of the house without using up my allotment of "me time." I'm no master carpenter, but I enjoyed my little projects—bookcases for the girls, a step stool for the pantry. I even redid all the crown molding in the dining room. I stretched that project out to four glorious weeks. And in the rare instance that we actually used the dining room, I got to brag about my handiwork.

"What kind of people are they?" Libby asked. If I hadn't known her for fifteen years, that might have seemed a vague question. But I knew exactly what she was after. *Are they fancy? Are they connected? Could it be useful to know them?* This was LA, after all. And I was in the movie business.

"I have no idea," I answered truthfully. "He wore a suit." Of course that could have meant any number of things. Lawyer? *Already have one.* Agent? *Have one of those, too.* From across the street, I couldn't tell if it was a nice suit or just some Men's Wearhouse two-for-one. Maybe he worked at a shoe store.

"Well, if they can afford that house at what they were asking, they must be doing pretty well." And she could have stopped there, but she couldn't help herself. "Better than we are."

And there was the bitch slap. She was right, of course. We could not afford that house. But luckily our house was just fine. Our marriage . . . not so much.

I've often thought about the life cycle of a marriage. The fairy tales I read to my daughters, they all end with the wedding. The courtship is long and tortuous, filled with obstacles and evil stepsisters trying to keep prince and princess apart. And then it's "happily ever after." Fairy tales aren't interested in what comes next. Do they assume it's smooth sailing "till death do they part"? Or do they know marriage is an order of magnitude more difficult and simply not suitable material for fairy tales?

I remembered when I couldn't get enough of my wife. I loved slipping into familiar conversations, a familiar bed, familiar sex. I loved her laugh. I loved that she used it freely and often. Most of all, I loved her optimism. I was in this highly speculative career of writing movies, and she thought it was so cool, and knew beyond a shadow of a doubt that I would make us rich. We were not rich. And she quickly learned there is nothing cool about not knowing when your next paycheck is coming.

But things changed when I stopped making money. The stench of failure followed me everywhere I went, burrowed its way into every *good morning*, every *good night*, every *what's new?* As disappointed as my wife was in me, I was way more disappointed in myself. I walked around with an ominous feeling that something was about to break. One of us was going to say or do something that pushed the other over the edge. I tried to distract myself by making step stools and perfect miter joints, but I knew I couldn't hide forever. Eventually I would have to face my failing marriage, and accept that our best days were probably behind us.

I thought about Belle and Cinderella, sailing off into the sunset with their handsome princes. If this was happily ever after, somebody should tell the evil stepsisters they got the last laugh.

HOLLY

Three months ago

I don't text and drive, but once I park, I sit in the car and check my phone. It's stupid, really. I don't know what I'm hoping happened in the handful of minutes since I left point A and arrived at point B, but I always check before I get out. Except for that one time my boss emailed me to ask if I could come in an hour early to rebill some clients, I never got time-sensitive emails. I didn't care if there was a sale at Wayfair, and it's not like they email you if you win the lottery. Plus I don't play the lottery. Like I said—stupid.

We had a spot in the garage under our building, but my husband had lent it to a neighbor whose sister was visiting from San Diego *(In her brand-new Camaro! How could we say no?)*, so we parked on the street. Today was hot, so I kept the engine running. The Cherokee was old, but the air-conditioning still kicked butt, and I wanted to enjoy every last second of it. We had an AC unit in the apartment, but we tried not to run it all day because it was costing us a fortune—and it wasn't even summer yet.

My husband walked around the front of the car and tapped on my window *(c'mon!)*, and I held up my index finger *(one sec!)*. He opened the door for me, as if it would will me out of my seat. He still wore his hair high and tight from his military days. He used to get it cut every other week. I told him, *What a waste of money. It's the easiest haircut in the world. Let me do it!* So he bought me clippers. He taught me how to bend back his ears to get the tiny hairs between his temple and his jawbone. It was probably the only place on his body that I hadn't already explored. I suddenly felt jealous of his past barbers, that they had been there first.

"That damn phone is going to be the death of you," he teased as he swiped it from my hand.

"Hey! I was reading an email from Savannah's school!"

"Savannah's school can wait five minutes," he scolded. Of course it could wait, but I still wanted to read it.

He reached for me. I remember his grip on my arm. Firm but not aggressive.

I remember getting pulled out of my seat by hands so familiar they felt almost part of me.

I remember tussling over my phone, how he'd held it at arm's length, making me swat at it like a kitten pawing at a loop of yarn.

I remember his laugh, playful and sweet, as he slipped the phone into his back pocket.

I remember how he shimmied away from me as I groped his backside like an awkward teenager at her first high school dance.

I remember the violent jolt in my shoulder as he was ripped from my grasp with inhuman force.

I remember the grinding shriek of the car door exploding off its hinges like a thousand champagne corks popping all at once.

I remember a massive hunk of metal slamming into my knee, then spinning me like a top to the pavement.

I remember how hot the asphalt felt against my cheek, knowing it was burning my skin, wanting to lift my head but not remembering how to do that.

I remember time seeming to slow down. Nowhere to go. Nothing to do.

Except maybe die.

CHAPTER 4

Moving day came too soon.

I knew it made no sense to bring my dead husband's stuff to the new house, but I couldn't leave it behind. Evan had offered to "take care of it," but I didn't want that man touching my husband's things. Besides my memories and our child, those worn leather belts and puffy sweatpants were all I had left of him. So I boxed them up.

"Where would you like these?" the mover asked me, standing over one of the boxes. Unlike the boxes filled with toiletries and bedsheets, which were carefully labeled to indicate the contents and intended destination ("dish towels/kitchen"), I didn't know what to put on a box containing a dead man's shoes, so I just left them all blank.

I thought about the closets—one for him, one for her. But putting his stuff in one of them seemed morbid and a little insane. "Just put them in the garage, please," I told the mover.

"Welcome to the neighborhood!" I must have jumped, because my new neighbor immediately apologized. "Sorry if I startled you. I live across the street. Andy."

He extended his hand, and I shook it. "Holly."

Shit. I hadn't thought about what I would say to the neighbors. I took in his droopy jeans and faded AC/DC T-shirt. *Is that how people dress here? Like wannabe rock stars?* I was suddenly afraid I'd misjudged the neighborhood. I thought Calabasas people were snooty and kept to themselves. *And what is this guy even doing home in the middle of a workday? Doesn't he have a job?*

"Congratulations on the house. It's really beautiful. We—my wife and I—walked through it when it was for sale," the jobless rocker said brightly, as if there was nothing creepy about him having been in my bedroom. "Are you new to the area?"

My heart was pounding. *How long will it take him to realize that I am a fraud? Does he know already? Surely he must be wondering what a woman wearing jeans from Target is doing in a house as nice as this one.*

"Thank you." I tried to smile. Even that was fake.

"Where are you moving from?" he pressed, and my heart beat faster. *He knows you're from north of the Boulevard, where the apartment dwellers live. He just wants to hear you say it.* I hated him already.

"Not far," I said. *How's that for coy?* I was learning from my teenager.

"Well, let us know if you need anything," he said cheerfully. "My wife has a line on all the good shopping in the area." He winked at me. I tried not to bristle. *Do I look like a woman who likes to go shopping? Or needs to go shopping? Probably the latter.*

"That's kind of you, thanks."

"Mom!" Savannah called out, coming to my rescue. I felt a flood of relief at an excuse to cut this short.

"That's my daughter. I'd better go. Nice to meet you . . ." *Shit. I forgot his name already.*

"Andy."

"Andy. Sorry."

"Don't worry about it. Holly, right?"

He had to one-up me. "Yeah."

"See you around, Holly." He waved and walked across the street. My house was definitely nicer than his.

And I had no idea how I was going to explain that.

EVAN

Three months ago

The nurse finally looked up at me from her post behind the counter. Her Pepto-pink scrubs were faded and stained. I felt like an asshole, standing there in my $1,800 suit, clutching a pleather purse from Payless. Needless to say, my shoes didn't match my purse, and I wondered if she'd picked up on the obvious incongruity.

"Can I help you?" she asked.

I had a burning feeling in my chest. *Guilt?* I had no right to be there. I was a fraud and a charlatan. *Fear? Shame?*

"Holly Kendrick?" I said as if I'd been saying her name my whole life, when, in fact, this was the first time. I was careful not to identify her as a friend or a relative or anyone who would give a shit that I was there.

The nurse studied me a beat. I cursed my suit and the rich-guy vibe it gave off. I probably looked like a funeral director. *Who the hell comes to the emergency room wearing a suit?*

"Are you a family member?" she asked. I was prepared for this. I opened my mouth to spew my lies, but before I could get a word out, a bloodcurdling scream shocked the room into silence. I took a gamble.

"That's Holly," I said with feigned certainty.

The screaming intensified. There was a flurry of activity. Nurses, physicians' assistants, and a bleary-eyed intern dropped what they were doing and hurried toward the source. Words of comfort wafted out from the ward. Screams turned to sobs. She was keening.

"Please," I begged, a little surprised at how genuinely distressed I felt. I didn't think I'd ever heard a person cry like that, and for a second I got scared I wouldn't be able to go through with this.

The nurse finally broke. Maybe it was the purse that convinced her. "Last bed on the left."

I tipped my head as she buzzed me through. The ward was mostly empty. I passed an old man on a respirator who looked frighteningly close to death. A few beds down, a little girl with her leg in a splint played on a phone. Her parents nodded to me, and I returned it with a solemn smile.

I finally reached the end of the row. The curtain that curved around Holly's bed was closed, and for a moment I didn't know what to do.

"You can see her, but she's sedated now. Didn't want to scare the other patients," a woman in a white coat said, and with a whoosh she pulled back the curtain.

And there I was, standing at the foot of Holly Kendrick's hospital bed. I knew from her driver's license that she was thirty-seven, but in her tattered state I couldn't have guessed that. A tuft of bleached-blonde hair plumed out from a thick white bandage wrapped around her head. No one had bothered to remove her heavy eye makeup, which had smeared into her eye sockets, making her look like a cross between a raccoon and a sad clown. Her lips were dry, and the corners of her mouth curved down like a dead fish. Her eyelids were pinched closed, like they were squeezing back a bad dream. Gazing upon her in her most vulnerable state made me feel like a Peeping Tom, but in truth I was something much worse.

I knew there was no way I could close things up in one visit, but I couldn't leave without at least making contact. I had my spiel rehearsed and ready. I even had special business cards. I have cards for every occasion—"litigator," "real estate specialist," "liaison"—I'm a corporate Jason Bourne. I didn't know how this would play out, so I had them all at the ready.

I would have to lead by acknowledging the death of her husband. I wished I could say *My thoughts and prayers are with you*, but I couldn't. I don't believe in God. I don't pray. I have no one and nothing to pray to.

My brother's first child died of SIDS. Sudden Infant Death Syndrome. He found the baby, cold and stiff in her swaddle. Doctors had no explanation. Apparently it's something that just happens. My brother was inconsolable. He asked God, *Why me? What did I do wrong? Please, if I could just go back in time, I'll be a better dad, a better husband.*

God didn't send him back in time. Yet through it all, he never lost his faith. If anything, the tragedy made it stronger. He had to make sense of what happened. His daughter must have died for a reason. Maybe not to punish. Maybe to teach. Yes, that must be it, God killed his kid to teach him something. I suggested maybe what he should learn is there's no such thing as God. I could see in his eyes that he felt sorry for me.

So what to say to this woman who just watched an SUV shatter her husband's limbs and drive his skull into the pavement with so much force it looked like someone took an ax to it? *I'm sorry for your loss?* Why do people say that? The loss is the least of your problems. It's the pain that follows we should be sorry for. A loss is an event, a moment in time. But grief is relentless—a simmering flame that can be stoked by a whisper. It burrows down in the deep recesses of your heart, then surges up like bile, filling your lungs until it hurts to breathe. My own mother died six months after I graduated from law school. I couldn't breathe for a year.

I placed the purse at Holly's feet—there was nowhere else to put it—and contemplated my next move. I knew coming to the ER was aggressive, but I couldn't risk waiting even a few hours. I thought about waking her up. When you're in the hospital, people wake you up all the time—to take your vitals, give you meds, draw your blood. It wouldn't be unusual. But I had no idea what they'd given her, if she'd even be coherent.

"Can I help you?" a stern female voice asked. I turned, expecting to see a nurse or candy striper. I was surprised, but not ill-prepared, to see someone much more important.

"You must be Savannah," I said, being careful that it didn't come out as a question. I recognized her from her eighth grade graduation photo, which I had found online on my way to the hospital.

"Who are you, what do you want?" Her tone was hostile. Young people are like wild animals, in tune with their instincts, able to sniff out predators. Clearly she sensed I was a threat. And, of course, she was absolutely right.

I answered without hesitation. "My name is Evan, and what I want is to help you."

Her mouth curled into a snarl, and for a second I thought she might strike me. "You a lawyer?"

I sidestepped the question. I was, of course, but I wasn't sure I should reveal that. So I answered her question with a question. "Why, do you need a lawyer?"

But my belligerent teenage adversary revealed nothing. "I think you'd better go."

I looked at her, in her tight jeans and boots, needing braces her mom couldn't afford. I knew from my Google search that she was fifteen and almost done with tenth grade. Years of public school in tough neighborhoods probably made her marginally street smart, but she had no idea how the world worked. Or so I thought.

"I have important information for your mom," I said. Which was partially true. I did have information for her mom. But more than that, I needed information from her: How much did she see? What did she remember? And what was she planning to do about it?

The girl crossed her arms in stubborn defiance. "She's going to want this information," I pressed. I had to talk to Holly. I wasn't going to be sent away by a combative teenage girl.

"I have all the information we need." She waved her iPhone. I must have looked confused because she clarified. "My mom's car had a dash-cam. It recorded the whole thing."

Her punch took the wind right out of me. I just stood there with my mouth open, too stunned to speak.

If what Savannah was saying was true, then I would need another miracle.

I suddenly regretted that I didn't pray.

CHAPTER 5

"So do I own the house? Like, is it in my name?" Holly thumbed through the contract on the table in front of her. I understood wanting to know what you were signing, but she was on the receiving end of a $2 million house. What the hell was she so worried about?

I explained that the house was in a trust, that she was the beneficiary and I was the trustee. I explained how this relieved her of having to pay property taxes—the trust would take care of that. I explained how the trust would also provide her an allowance and continue to pay all expenses related to the accident. I don't know if she was satisfied, or just overwhelmed, but she signed.

I slid one last paper in front of her. As she read it in the dim evening light, I realized my knee was bouncing under the table. I put my hand on it to stop it.

"NDA? What does that stand for?" she asked.

"Nondisclosure agreement."

She nodded slowly. "That means I don't tell anybody why you are paying for everything." I nodded. We had discussed this already. "And Savannah has to sign it, too, right?"

"That's right."

"Savannah!!" she shouted, then shook her head. "I'm not used to such a big house. I'll go get her."

She pushed her chair back. I noticed how she hesitated before putting weight on that left knee. A wave of shame surged through my body. But we had a deal, there was no going back now.

Alone in her kitchen, I looked around. Worn dish towels hugged the handles of her shiny new appliances. The Caesarstone counters had been buffed until they shone. She had laid place mats around the table in the breakfast nook. They were round with cheerful yellow flowers.

I recalled my childhood kitchen growing up in rural New Hampshire. My mother had bought these rectangular, laminated place mats with paintings of famous European cities on them. I ate every meal gazing upon the Eiffel Tower, the Colosseum, the Basílica de la Sagrada Família. It was the closest to Europe I ever got as a kid. I'm not sure I even knew they were real places. I have no idea where my mom—who, as far as I knew, had never left the state of New Hampshire—bought them, or why. Maybe she wanted to spark my curiosity about the world. Or maybe she just thought they were pretty. I don't know if it was because of those place mats, but upon getting my degree from Yale I got as far away from New Hampshire as I could, as soon as I could.

"You know I'm only sixteen, right?" Savannah appeared in the doorway and glared at me in her confrontational teenage way. She'd had a birthday since the day of the accident. Sweet *(ha!)* sixteen. As Holly reappeared behind her, I couldn't help but notice Savannah was built completely differently than her mom—hard and athletic to her mother's gentle curves.

"We'd still like you to sign it," I told Savannah. "You're named in the trust. It's important that you understand the terms of it." The truth is, I wanted to scare her a little. Having her signature on the contract signaled she knew she was getting paid off, which would hopefully compel her to keep it to herself.

I offered her a pen. As she took it from me, I noticed she'd gotten her nails done. They were painted pale gray, with electric-blue party nails on each ring finger like my socialite ex-girlfriend used to do. She was adjusting to her new affluent lifestyle nicely, which was a good thing. The more luxuries she enjoyed, the less she'd be willing to disrupt the arrangement.

She wrote her name in perfect cursive, then slid the paper across the table at me. As I was tucking it away, the doorbell rang. We all looked at each other like we'd been caught robbing a bank.

"Are you expecting someone?" I asked Holly, and she shook her head. We both looked at Savannah.

"Don't look at me!"

"The only person who knows we live here is you," Holly said, eyes on me.

"Did you give the police your new address?" I asked, trying to suppress the rising panic in my voice.

"They would know how to find us," Savannah interjected. "They're the police."

My car was in the driveway. I could slip out the back door, but if they'd noted my plates that would only make things worse. Any investigation of me would lead them to Jack. And then it would only take one smart guess for this whole thing to blow up in our faces.

The doorbell rang again, followed by the rap-rap-rap of knuckles on wood.

"Should I answer it?" Holly asked, and I reluctantly nodded. All the lights were on. No detective worth his paycheck, even a meager one, would believe no one was home.

I held my breath as Holly headed for the door. Savannah and I stayed back as she peered through the peephole, then opened the door for four smiling faces.

"OK, we know this is corny, but our daughters made you cookies," a man said. It was the hipster from across the street with his wife and two kids. I was relieved Holly's twilight visitors weren't LAPD, but letting the neighbor see me on the premises for a second time was downright irresponsible. Our eyes met and I waved, cementing me to this family and this house.

"Andy," Holly said to her neighbor, not really as a question, but not quite sure either.

"That's right. And this is my wife, Libby, and our girls, Tatum and Margaux."

The little one hid behind her mother as Holly smiled at her.

"We know you must be beyond exhausted," the hipster's wife said. "We don't want to be a bother, we just wanted to say hello and let you know we're here if you need anything."

The wife looked to be about forty, but well maintained, with bouncy, blown-out hair and toned arms. A man's Rolex hung loosely from her wrist. *An heirloom, maybe?* Whatever the case, it was immediately clear that appearances were important to her.

"That's so kind of you, Libby," Holly said, taking the plate from her outstretched hands.

"We didn't put nuts in them, because you never know these days," Libby said, glancing at Savannah.

"Oh, it would have been fine if you did, but thank you." Holly looked expectantly at her daughter.

"Yes, thank you," Savannah echoed.

"That's Savannah," Holly offered.

"Hi, Savannah," the wife said. Then suddenly Holly's new neighbors were looking at me. We hadn't anticipated having to explain my presence, so I just said, "Evan." I had come straight from the office, so once again I was in a suit. At least I'd left the jacket in the car. And removed my tie. I would have preferred not to have looked so much like a lawyer, but there was nothing I could do about that now.

More waves and smiles, and then they were gone. But the damage had been done. I had been seen with Holly and Savannah, inside the house my boss had bought for them. There was only one degree of separation between Jack and this family, and that was me.

"What do you plan to tell them about me?" I asked Holly as the foursome headed back across the street.

"Nothing," she replied. Her tone was defensive. Obviously she wouldn't tell them I was her literal partner in crime. At least not on purpose.

"We have to be prepared if they start asking questions," I pressed.

"Well I'm not going to lie," Holly said. "I've done enough of that."

I got an uneasy feeling in my stomach. They would figure out that Holly was unmarried and unemployed sooner or later. Questions were bound to follow. This was an expensive house. And the wife had clearly taken note of that.

Holly must have sensed my unease, because she added, "People in this neighborhood are rich and snooty. They'll forget all about me by next week."

I looked down at the cookies, arranged like a pinwheel on a thick ceramic plate. The plastic wrapping was wet with condensation. They were still warm.

"I trust you," I said, wishing it were true.

I watched the neighbors disappear into their house. Holly was wrong. They'd be back. They'd left their plate. And they'd have questions that would rattle even a skilled liar like me.

ANDY

Three months ago

I probably needed therapy, but anyone who's seen *Good Will Hunting* knows people who become therapists are the most fucked-up of all of us. Plus who the hell has the time? Yes, I was depressed, but it was no great mystery why. It had been almost a year since my last paid writing job, we were broke, and I had zero prospects. That is categorically depressing.

I used to be an investigative journalist. The money was atrocious, but I didn't do it for the money. I wrote about fascinating people—a teenager falsely accused of murder who read law books in jail and proved her innocence, a septuagenarian who scaled Everest, a father of three who faked his own death. I trafficked in facts. But bullshit was the currency of the movie business. And I'd damn near had enough.

I'd busted my ass to get to that meeting. It had been set for five weeks. I'd prepared like I was interviewing a source, memorizing details that even the devil himself didn't know. And then to show up just to be dismissed because "something suddenly came up"? *What the actual fuck?*

I cursed myself for the pity party I was having. If I were more evolved, I would have seen the bright side. I had a foot in one of the most competitive industries in the world. I had a powerful agent who gave me access to all the big players and made me believe I would soon be a player myself.

But so far it hadn't happened. I had been in Los Angeles for almost eight years, and I still felt like that kid at the aquarium—staring at all the brightly colored fish with his face smooshed against the glass. I tried to fall in love with the sprawling freeways *(don't call them highways!)*, the endless summers, the Dodgers, but they all felt like friends of friends, never wholly mine.

My career never felt wholly mine either. There was a lot of money in Hollywood, but access was guarded by a network of gatekeepers whose most practiced skill was stringing you along. The Hollywood elites took care of their friends. As a relative newcomer from an outside industry, I was treated more like someone's tolerated plus-one than a cherished invited guest, allowed into the room but not permitted to feast.

But Hollywood needs wannabes like me, because without outsiders there can be no insiders. And so occasionally the gatekeepers throw us a bone, to keep us salivating at the door. And we hungrily snatch up their table scraps for an opportunity to play, and the bragging rights that come with getting a deal. There were thousands like me, pawing at a door that would let in only a few. In the end, only a tiny handful of movies ever get made. As a (barely) "working writer," I was part of this big machine that never stopped churning but produced almost nothing.

So why didn't I just quit? The game of schmoozing and pitching was addictive. Every time I wanted to give up (e.g., now), a carrot (e.g., interest from this mega-multihyphenate) was dangled so close I could *(almost!)* reach out and touch it. The Eagles nailed it: Hollywood is the Hotel California. You can try to check out, but once the business gets its claws into you, it's impossible to leave.

Lying in bed that night, I thought about my future. The *New York Times* would probably have a job for me, but going back to writing for a newspaper felt like a step backward. Print journalism was a dying industry. The money, the glory, the ability to reach people in far corners of the globe— that was in the movie business. I wanted my stories told in surround sound, with sweeping music and stunning images and performances that would blow your heart wide open. Besides, I couldn't just call my old boss and ask for my job back. I'd need a reason—a story that had to be told.

I had no intention to go looking for one, of course.

But sometimes stories had a way of finding me.

CHAPTER 6

"You want to know something strange?" Libby asked as I joined her at the breakfast table. She was dressed for Pilates, in smooth Lululemon leggings and a high ponytail. I was still in my sleep attire, boxers and a white Beefy tee.

"Sure," I said, indulging her. Libby had a different standard for strange than most people. She thought tea with milk was strange, despite the fact an entire nation of people who probably shared a fair amount of DNA with her drank it every day.

"The Kendricks aren't listed as the owners of their house. I checked the public record." *What is strange,* I thought, *is that you checked the public record.* But I played along.

"Huh," I said noncommittally. "Who owns it?"

"Some company called Happy Accident Enterprises, LLC," she informed me.

"Maybe you should go over and ask them about that?" I deadpanned.

"You're the investigative journalist," she quipped. *Yeah, but I don't care,* I thought, but kept it to myself.

"Have a good class," I said dismissively.

She flipped her ponytail and trotted out to her car. I had to admire how she stuck to her rituals, even in hard times. She never missed her exercise class, did her makeup just to go to the grocery store, made inventive meals that even our finicky girls would eat every single day. She got irritated during my periods of unemployment, but she never let it get her down. She was resilient where I was porous, confident to my self-loathing. We were living proof that opposites attract. One might argue she got all the desirable qualities. At this point, my biggest achievement was probably lassoing her.

I pulled on some sweats and headed out to the garage. Margaux needed a new desk, so I'd decided to build her a custom one that would fit under her loft, which I had also built. As I opened the garage door to let in some sunlight, I spotted Holly Kendrick in her front yard, wrestling with the wooden bench on her stoop. I jogged over to her.

"Hey there, need a hand?" I offered.

"Oh, hey, Andy," she said. Her cheeks were flushed. She was wearing a tank with a scooped-out neckline, and I couldn't help but notice she had an incredible body—full breasts and a tiny waist. I tried not to stare. "This stupid bench is a hazard. Every time someone sits on it, it nearly falls over. I was going to tighten the screws, but I don't have any tools."

I inspected the base and immediately diagnosed the problem. "The screws are fine. You're missing a support brace. That's why it wobbles." I pointed, and she bent over to look. Her cleavage was so close to me it was like the beginning of a bad porno movie. I forced myself to take a step back. "I can fix it if you like. I have all the materials. It's kind of a hobby."

"I wouldn't want to trouble you," she said.

"It's really no problem," I insisted. She seemed hesitant, so I added, "Or if your husband needs tools, I could lend them to him?" Her lips pinched like she'd bitten into something sour. I suddenly realized the blatant sexism of my suggestion, so I added, "Or I could show you how to do it?"

And then something unexpected happened. She started to cry. One minute she was sparring with a bench, and the next minute she was sobbing like the jilted heroine in a tragic telenovela.

"I'm ssss . . . sorry . . . ," she stuttered between sobs. Big, sloppy, wet tears rolled down her cheeks and disappeared into the abyss of her cleavage. I wanted to guide her over to the bench to sit her down, but given its fragile state I thought better of it. She snuffled, and a string of clear mucus slid down her upper lip. If only I were my grandfather, I could have saved the day with my handy pocket square. But alas, I was just me.

"Please, don't apologize," I said. "I'm the one who should be sorry. I didn't mean to upset you, I was only trying to help—"

"My husband's dead," she blurted. And I was confused. Because I literally saw him two short days ago, sitting at their kitchen table. She must have sensed my confusion because she helped me out. "Evan's not my husband. He's just . . ." Her voice trailed off. *A friend?* She kept me in suspense for a beat, then, "Someone who's helping Savannah and me."

I found her turn of phrase strange—and not in a *tea with milk* way—but I let it slide. "Why don't I take you inside?" I offered, suddenly wishing she wasn't so beautiful given that my wife was already obsessed with her and would be back home soon.

Holly nodded, and I opened the front door for her and followed her into the kitchen. I found a napkin on the island and handed it to her as she slumped down into a chair.

"I can't imagine what you must think of me," she murmured as she smeared the mucus across her face.

"I think you must be in a lot of pain," I said, taking the seat across from her. As a reporter I had interviewed a lot of people in distress. I knew how to get people talking. And I was more than a wee bit curious now.

"I still can't believe it. It was . . ." She hesitated, as if not sure how much she should tell me. "Sudden," she finally offered. *Does she want to talk?* I wasn't sure.

"Do you want to talk about it?"

She looked down at the floor. She reminded me of a source with sensitive information—wanting to spill, but nervous about revealing too much. I pressed as gently as I could. "I can't imagine how devastating that must have been for you."

She wiped her nose, then blotted her face with the back of the napkin. "I'm sorry. I didn't mean to dump on you." She stood up. *Nope, doesn't want to talk about it.*

"I'll grab the bench on my way out," I offered, and she nodded. It felt weird just leaving her like that, all tears and agony, but hugging her would have been even weirder. So I waved a little wave, then left her there.

Walking back to my garage with that bench under my arm, I started to think maybe there was something strange about my new neighbors.

I cursed my reporter's curiosity, and my plethora of free time.

HOLLY

Three months ago

They moved me to a private room. Savannah said it had a nice view, but I really couldn't tell you. They rolled a cot in for her, but mostly she slept with me, curled up against my good side, head nestled under my chin. Having her close to me like that, her shiny hair pressed against my cheek, reminded me of those first few months after she was born, how I used to sleep with her tucked under my arm like a football and breathe in her marshmallow-sweet smell. Except back then she was the helpless one, and I was the protector. Now it was the other way around.

The doctor told me I had suffered a concussion and needed surgery on my knee. Savannah stood over me as I signed my consent, nodding and assuring me it was going to be all right. She brought me Jamba— Peach Perfection, my favorite—to soothe my throat made raw by the breathing tube. She kept track of my meds, ordering the nurses to taper off the painkillers so I wouldn't become a crackhead like my dead brother.

A few people from the dental office where I worked came to see me, bringing flowers that Savannah arranged and tended. As my strength returned, panic set in. I was living like a queen on colorful smoothies and sandwiches from Bristol Farms, in a hospital room that cost more per day than my rent for a month.

I tried to tell Savannah we couldn't afford to keep me here, but she brushed me off. "Don't worry, Mom. Just get well. I need you, you're all I have left." Her complexion had dulled—she was as pale as chalk—and I knew that smile she put on when she tended to me was a lie. So I lied for her, too, ate the food she brought me, and weaned myself off the Vicodin, requesting Tylenol instead.

After about a week, she showed up with my makeup. I thought she was just trying to help me feel human again, so I let her smooth foundation over my blotchy bruise and sweep my eyelashes with mascara. When she was satisfied, she leaned back to examine her handiwork, then announced, "There's someone I need you to meet."

I pulled on a robe, and she wheeled me down a series of lifeless hallways to the hospital chapel. We were not regular churchgoers—Sundays were for pancakes and grocery shopping these days—but I certainly would have understood if she wanted a word with God.

She rolled me up to a pew toward the back, where a man in a suit was sitting. *A clergyman? A funeral director?* He stood up as I approached.

He was tall—at least six inches taller than my husband—which would have put him around six feet four. His suit was indigo blue and a little bit shiny, with tapered legs and strong creases. He had the face of a star quarterback, with a square jaw and dimpled chin, and his skin was so smooth I wondered if he shaved right before I got there. I always liked a close shave. My husband said it was a sign of discipline—a man with a close shave probably made his bed and balanced his checkbook. *Don't trust a guy who can't make time to shave,* he always said.

"Mom, this is Evan," Savannah said flatly. He offered his hand. I was still in the wheelchair, so I had to reach above my head to shake it.

"Hello, Holly," he said with a smile as fake as a January tan.

"He's paying your hospital bills," Savannah announced. And the man did not contradict her, just stood there like a statue. *Maybe he is from the military,* I thought, *an old buddy my husband never told me about?* I had heard stories about marines taking care of the widows of their fallen platoon mates. I had thought the stories were exaggerated, but maybe it happened more than I thought?

"He also paid for all the food I brought you and said he would buy us a house," Savannah continued. The statement was so absurd I almost laughed. But her expression was as somber as the crucifix tacked to the altar behind her. I waited for the man to correct her. He didn't.

"I . . . I don't understand," I said, not really to anyone. I looked up at Savannah, at her skillfully winged eyeliner and perfectly curled eyelashes. She had adopted such a grown-up facade, sometimes I forgot she was still just a child.

"He's helping us," she said tentatively, as if she wasn't entirely sure. I sure as hell had my doubts. I would have believed a GoFundMe page or a few catered meals, but a house? She must have misunderstood. I had never in my life had a house. My grandparents did. My brother and I would spend hours in their pool—every house in their Northeast Bakersfield neighborhood had a pool—practicing swimming the whole length without taking a breath. We thought traveling great distances *(thirty whole feet!)* underwater made us invincible. Five years later my brother was dead. So much for invincible.

"What happened to you and your husband was a terrible accident," the man said, with enough emphasis on the word "accident" to make my scalp tingle. I never doubted it was an accident—my husband and I weren't important enough to be targeted, I didn't need some Brooks-Brothered goon to rub it in my face. People with more money than you love to state the obvious, like something isn't true until it comes out of their mouth.

"Even if you knew who was driving the car," he continued, "there's no guarantee of a settlement."

The word pierced the air like the tolling of a bell. Paired with that shiny suit and a face so emotionless it looked carved from stone, that word—"settlement"—and the stink that wafted from his mouth as he spoke it told me he had to be one of two things: an insurance man or a lawyer. I braced myself for the blizzard of bullshit I knew was coming.

"It's best if you can find a way to move on," he continued. "I'm here to make that possible."

I had been off the heavy pain meds for two full days and was clear enough to know "helping" me was not his priority. I looked at him and his Barbasol-fresh shave, suddenly second-guessing my husband's assessment of what made a man trustworthy. "Why?" I asked. "Why do you want to help me?"

And then Savannah said something so frightening that for a moment I forgot how to breathe. "He knows who was driving the car, Mom," she whispered. "He works for him."

Heat rose up the back of my neck. I felt my cheeks grow hot. The pieces suddenly fell into place—the suit, the hospital visit, the promise of a house. My voice shook when I spoke. "If that's true, then you need to tell the police."

But he remained stone-faced. "Savannah and I thought there was a better way to handle it," he said matter-of-factly, as if we were talking about a naughty kid who stole a candy bar instead of a reckless murderer. "We'll compensate you very generously, no lengthy court case needed."

And there it was. The bribe laid out in terms even a simpleton like me could understand. I was a call girl and he was my pimp. My sex act was silence, and if I kept my mouth shut, his client would pay big. I was so disgusted, if I could have stood up, I would have slapped him. I was about to shout—*No deal, no fucking way!*—but he continued. "I had the surgeon who did your knee flown in from Stanford, he's the absolute best."

I growled at him. "Who told you to do that? I never told you to do that!"

And then he did something damn near satanic. With the pop of one eyebrow, he indicated Savannah.

I looked at her in disbelief. Her face flooded with fear. "The ER doctor said you might never walk again," she said. "I didn't know what to do!" Tears welled in her eyes. "Please don't be mad," she pleaded. And suddenly I was the adult again.

I looked at my daughter. People always said she took after her dad, with those wide Norwegian cheeks and perfect straight nose. Some days, when she smiled or blew me a kiss, I saw the resemblance, but today all I could see was my baby girl, innocent as a fawn still teetering on wobbly legs.

My heart broke open. "It's going to be OK, baby," I assured her, though I had no idea if it would be. It was going to be months before I could walk again. And even once I was healed, I could never support us on my measly bookkeeping job. We had no savings, and no safety net. We lived paycheck to paycheck on two incomes, and now that my husband was dead, we barely had one. If things could have been worse, I had no idea how.

"I'll explain everything when you are well again, not here," the man said. "In the meantime, your rent has been paid, and all the bills from your stay here will be sent to me."

And then I realized we had already accepted his gifts and his terms. We were bought and paid for.

I looked up at the face of a man who just might well be the devil, and I shuddered.

Because right there, in that barren hospital chapel with God as our witness, we had just made a deal with him.

CHAPTER 7

"Don't be mad," my daughter cooed as she walked in the room, "but I bought you something." She pulled her hands from behind her back. They were cradling a crisp shopping bag the size of a couch cushion. Normally when someone gives me a gift, I feel excited. But rather than lift me up, the surge of emotion I felt had a heavy, downward pull. I knew the money was ours, and that we had every right to spend it, but that didn't mean I felt good about it. I had convinced myself we had no choice—the hospital bills alone were more than I'd made in my entire life, Evan had made sure to tell me that. I was damned if I took the deal, dead if I didn't. I was starting to regret that I'd chosen damned.

I took the bag from Savannah. Inside the shopping bag was another bag, as thick and creamy as a vanilla milkshake. It had a drawstring and fancy lettering on it: *LV*. I had never owned designer anything, but even I knew what *LV* stood for. I glared at Savannah.

"It's Louis Vuitton!" she said, as if I didn't know.

"I don't need a Louis Vuitton bag," I said, not that it mattered, because now I had one.

"Yeah, you kind of do," Savannah corrected me. "Because we live here now!" She made a grand, sweeping gesture with her arm. "And you need to look the part. Open it!"

I slid the bag out of the duster—I knew that's what they called it, because I used to shop for Louis Vuitton on eBay. Not to buy, just to dream. I never had the guts to walk into the store on Rodeo Drive and face the snooty sales clerks, who—let's be honest—probably lived in my old neighborhood. But no one could scorn me for window-shopping online, which I sometimes did in the wee hours when no one was watching.

Somehow Savannah knew the exact one I liked, the checkered Sperone in white and gray—*maybe someone was watching after all?* The backpack-style bag had delicate straps and a sneaky side pocket. *Perfect for sneaky people like us.*

"It's beautiful," I said, and it was. And I never in a million years imagined I would own one. "Thank you for getting it for me." I was touched that my daughter had gone out and shopped for me, but this sudden flood of nice stuff filled me with shame. Surely my husband's life was worth more than a designer handbag and a three-bedroom house? I knew I deserved nice things as much as any Real Housewife or two-bit movie actress, but it wasn't fun to get them like this. I imagined my husband looking down at me, shaking his head in disappointment that I chose money over justice.

"I got one, too!" Savannah announced, producing another shopping bag. I must have looked alarmed because she added, "Don't worry, it's not the same one as yours."

I was worried, but not about that. "We shouldn't be too conspicuous," I said, and she frowned.

"It would be conspicuous *not* to have a designer bag in this neighborhood, Mom." She was probably right. I wanted to live in Calabasas for the clean air and good schools, but walking around in Old Navy activewear surely would have raised some eyebrows. As for what any friends from my old neighborhood would think of my lifestyle upgrade, Evan instructed me to tell them my husband had a big life insurance policy. It wasn't uncommon, he'd said. Not that they were coming around. I told my Friday-night-Zumba friends and the handful of moms from Savannah's school who had texted and called that we were moving, and we said our goodbyes and "good lucks" over the phone. I didn't have to worry about my family nosing around, since my only brother was dead and my parents had basically disowned me when I got pregnant before I was married.

As for my husband's family, he didn't have much—just the grandparents who raised him when his mother couldn't be bothered. Gran and Pop-Pop moved to Arizona after he joined the military, and if they'd wanted to keep in touch, they never let on. We never even got a Christmas card from them, so there was no point in sharing our change of address. We were kind of an island, Savannah, my husband, and me. Which was sad before, but now rather fortunate.

"Please be careful," I cautioned Savannah, taking in her pebbled leather Neverfull tote. "There are limits on how much we can spend." I wasn't tracking her spending, but I saw a lot of shopping bags cross through the front door, and I thought it was about time I said something. I knew she was trying to shop away her feelings, so I didn't want to admonish her, just maybe slow her down to create an opening to grieve more honestly.

But Savannah just shrugged. "If you ask me, they got off easy. We could have asked for way more."

I tried to imagine what "way more" might look like. *A boat? A beach house? A private jet?* I guess there were always things to want, holes to fill, people to compare yourself to. But I'd never longed for a fancy life. I never watched those makeover shows or fantasized about prancing around in designer shoes. They had already given us more than I knew what to do with.

"It's a very nice bag," I said. "Thank you." I wanted to say more, tell her how proud I was of her for being strong for both of us, but I couldn't find words. It was like there was this thick fog between us now, and every time I opened my mouth, I choked on it. Our little island had endured its share of storms—a missed curfew, a bad grade, a pair of stolen gold hoop earrings—but we had always been able to talk things through. But the accident had cast us out to sea. My daughter was drifting away, and I had no idea how to navigate the ocean of space between us.

I watched Savannah as she arranged her things in her oversize tote—notebooks, makeup, phone, wallet. I wanted her to have nice things, but I also wanted her to learn the value of hard work, to know the sense of accomplishment that came from saving up for something.

Christmas was coming. I usually started shopping for her right around the start of the school year. I loved snooping around for clues about what she might like, then surprising her with a gift she'd think was beyond our means, but that I'd found at an outlet mall or online. That look on her face when she unwrapped it was always my favorite gift. As I watched her tuck the last few items into her $2,000 tote, I wondered why rich people bothered doing Christmas at all. *What's the point when you can just buy whatever you want?* Maybe it was selfish, but it made me sad to think I had nothing left to give her.

"Look!" she exclaimed. "Everything fits!" Sadness balled in my throat as I thought about what values—or lack of values—I was imparting to my daughter. Yes, Savannah had agreed to this arrangement when I was on a breathing tube, but I could have stopped it. I could have told Brooks Brothers to fuck off, that we'd rather live under the freeway than take his blood money. But I didn't. Because I was too scared of what would happen when the checks bounced and the food ran out and Savannah and I had nothing to live on but grief and regret.

I remembered my Sunday school teacher talking about how so many things in life are both a blessing and a curse—how mountains do not rise without earthquakes, how the tragedy of the original sin gave us the blessing of free choice. Even the crucifixion of Christ himself was both—he was murdered! But his death allowed him to rise and live forever as our savior.

I thought about what my life had become. A bottomless bank account was a hell of a blessing. But living a lie was the worst kind of curse.

My personal blessing and curse pulled at each other like two pit bulls tearing at a bone. I had a sour feeling in my stomach that was growing more putrid every day. It was only a matter of time until those warring dogs pulled me to pieces.

But in the meantime, I had Louis Vuitton.

EVAN

Three months ago

"You want a drink?" Jack asked me as he poured himself a stiff one. He was a tequila drinker—that night it was Patrón Silver in a glass rimmed with lime.

"No, thank you," I said. I often drank with him during our late-night meetings, but given the seriousness of what just transpired, it didn't feel appropriate.

"Well I need one," he said, then sank into the deep leather chair across from me. He was not a large man, and the oversize chair made him look almost childlike. At fifty, he was still incredibly fit. He wore his shirts a size too small to show off well-defined biceps and pecs. Sometimes he was so scheduled we would do our meetings in the wee hours of the morning, while he was working out in his private gym. I would sit awkwardly on a bench, tablet in hand, breathing in the pungent smell of eucalyptus swirled with rubber. But that night we were in his private sitting room, letting cozy Italian leather provide comfort we didn't deserve.

"Where are we with everything?" he asked.

"I spoke to the woman today," I began. I explained how we had caught a bit of a break that the teenager inserted herself in the process, as she seemed to have a more flexible moral compass than her mother. I hinted that summoning the surgeon had been a stroke of genius, because he was expensive, and the daughter wanted her mom to have the best. I didn't tell him how I had lain awake that night hating myself for doing this, because lawyers are supposed to be dispassionate, and my feelings were irrelevant.

"The woman, Holly," I continued, "she pushed back a little, but I think she'll settle into the arrangement."

Jack nodded, then peered down into his glass for a long, mournful beat. I wondered if he was waiting for me to say something more. When he finally spoke, his voice was somber.

"What was it like at the scene? Y'know, after?"

The fact that I'd made it to the scene before they had loaded Holly into the ambulance was nothing short of a miracle. I don't live anywhere near the valley neighborhood where the collision occurred, but I happened to be in the area at a lunch with a local developer. LA had a terrible housing shortage, and Jack had asked me to look for opportunities to invest in affordable housing because, as he liked to say, *It can't always be about making money.* When I got the urgent call, I had just paid the check and was walking to my car.

I described the scene for Jack the best I could without letting myself get emotional. The man had likely died on impact. The woman was knocked down and rendered unconscious, with a head injury. "I don't imagine she saw much," I said. "And she has a concussion, so even if she did, her memory will likely be unreliable." I tried to sound clinical, detached, unaffected. The performance was not just for him.

He nodded, then asked, "What about witnesses?"

So far, no witnesses had come forward, but I was still holding my breath. "There were fourteen bystanders on the scene when I got there," I told him. "It's unclear if any of them witnessed the collision, but I'll keep an eye on it." I thought about the man with the camera phone but decided not to mention it. The video had not gone viral yet, unlikely it would now.

Jack nodded again. I could tell he was concerned—we both were. But I had a good handle on who was there. I had videoed the crowd on my phone, making sure to document the faces and cars of every onlooker in the vicinity. We were fortunate that there were no banks or government buildings within line of sight that might have had surveillance cameras near the intersection, I'd made sure to check.

"And the dashcam?" he asked somewhat reluctantly. "What's the plan for that?"

The existence of a video was problematic. And the fact that it was in the hands of a teenage girl was more troubling still. I knew how these teenagers are, every damn moment of every damn day winds up on Snapchat or WhatsApp or whatever platform they're using now. If Savannah ever decided to post that dashcam video, things would get ugly real fast.

"The girl gave me the camera and the original data card, but—" Jack stopped me with his hand. We both knew she was smarter than that. In the digital age, if there was one copy, there were a thousand. Savannah probably already had it saved on multiple devices and a cloud or two. There was only one way to keep that video from seeing the light of day, and that was to keep Savannah happy.

"Yeah, I know," Jack said. "It was a stupid question." Jack ran his hands through his graying hair. It was still thick, and his hairline mercifully hadn't budged. He tamed it with pomade that smelled like oranges. I noticed how he spiked it in the front to give the illusion of height. It was still standing tall—unlike the man who'd styled it.

We were doing a bad thing, but Jack wasn't a bad man. In fact, he could be quite generous. If his wife identified a worthy cause—home for battered wives, local boys' clubs, school drama program—he gave generously and anonymously. He had worked hard to build a good life for himself and his family, he was not going to let it be destroyed by one unfortunate accident. Shit happens, and people make mistakes. The world was not going to come tumbling down—he had me to make sure of that.

"The woman," Jack started, "she's OK with, y'know . . . burying the video?"

"It was the teenager who nabbed the dashcam," I said, sidestepping the question. "And it's a damn good thing she did," I added to remind him how much worse things would be if she hadn't.

There was of course another way this could leak. But I didn't dare mention it. Jack already knew about this other potential loose end, and I had to assume he had it handled.

Jack looked up at me with weary eyes, then said something that surprised me. "Do you think we're doing the right thing?"

I didn't answer right away. What we were doing was morally and criminally wrong, we both knew that. *So what is he really asking me?*

I was careful with my answer. "I think what happened is a terrible tragedy, and that we are doing the best we can under difficult circumstances," I said. "Taking aggressive steps to control the damage is in everyone's best interests," I added.

And then he looked at his hands and said, "As long as we don't get caught."

If I believed in God, I might have said, *God willing.* Luckily, I don't. Because if I did, I'd have to accept that we were probably both going to hell.

CHAPTER 8

I scooped up the paperwork and tucked it in my briefcase. All the i's were dotted and the t's crossed, but in the end, it really didn't matter. Our contract was only a Band-Aid on a deep and fragile wound that would have to be tended to carefully and indefinitely. The statute of limitations on vehicular manslaughter was only six years in California, but the unearthing of this crime could create problems way beyond that. Yes, it was a crime, I had to call it what it was. Not the hitting—that was an accident—but the running. There were layers to this incident that went beyond Jack and me, things that could unravel whole lives. I understood Jack's reasons for trying to cover it up. But that didn't mean I agreed with them.

I phoned Jack to tell him the deal was closed. He was pleased but not wholly relieved. I reminded him that, at this point, Holly and Savannah were as guilty in the cover-up as we were. For better or worse, we were in this together. To come forward after signing the NDA would cost them literally everything they had. That, of course, was the whole point in doing it.

Driving home, I thought about how it came to be that I, a nice kid from New Hampshire who played lacrosse and graduated summa cum laude from Yale, came to be a fixer. I had a job my former classmates could understand—personal lawyer—but if they knew what I actually did, they would be appalled.

In my defense, I didn't fully understand the job when I took it. I knew I didn't want to work at a big firm, riding the same elevator to a top floor office every day, competing with other associates to bill a shit ton of hours. Or clerk for a stuffy judge, like some of my classmates were doing. I was young, and craved a lifestyle. After a lifetime of long winters, I loved the idea of California. I told myself it would be temporary—a break from the cold, an adventure in La La Land. With my mother gone, and my brother wrapped up in his kids and his God, I was already adrift—why not float in an ocean of beautiful people under perpetually sunny skies? In the beginning, I wasn't exclusive to Jack and sometimes serviced other clients—moguls merging companies, partners unpartnering, a real estate tycoon or two—but Jack's needs slowly took over my whole life. I hadn't even had a serious girlfriend since the party nail gal, that's how busy he kept me. I barely even had time to be lonely.

Jack had been involved with minor scandals before—alleged inappropriate contact with a personal assistant, an alliance with a corrupt politician, a shady real estate deal—but this was by far the worst. It was my job to fix, not to judge—today's world had enough judges. A highly visible person like Jack lived under a microscope. His every move, his words, even his outfits were scrutinized and shit upon. I had compassion for him. If I didn't, I couldn't do my job.

Technically, the Holly Kendrick ordeal was over. We made a deal, she pledged her silence in exchange for riches beyond her wildest dreams. We should have all breathed a big sigh of relief. But we didn't. Because deep down we all knew this was just the beginning.

ANDY

Three months ago

"He said he was really sorry," Laura said when I finally called her back. I didn't want to be pissy when I talked to my agent, so I had waited a day, until my bad mood wore off. "He still wants to meet with you," she insisted. "In fact, in the end this might be a good thing, he might feel like he owes you one."

I was dubious that one of the most powerful people in Hollywood would ever feel like he owed me anything, but I kept that to myself. "Right. OK," was all I could muster. I wondered why I was getting a second chance. *Maybe the someone better didn't work out?*

"He's going to be on location most of the summer, but we're rescheduling for right when he gets back, in early September," Laura said, and I tried to sound pleased.

"Great." Great that he was rescheduling. Not great that my potential payday was pushed another three months. My marriage was already strained. Our credit card debt was massive and compounding. I honestly didn't know if we would survive the whole summer. Visions of making doll furniture and selling it out of my garage flashed through my mind. Though my marriage probably wouldn't survive that either.

As I clicked off the phone, I felt simultaneously relieved—*He's still interested!*—and ashamed, like an addict chasing one last fix. I was a junkie, and the business was my drug. I chased it to the detriment of my health, my home, my relationships. I got a knot in my stomach every time the mail came. As stressful as it was facing those envelopes rimmed with red with "past due" stamped across their contents, I was not ready to live my life as a raisin in the sun. I wanted to be a screenwriter. The desire was existential. Even my articles read like movies. I set the scene ("Misery wafted through the office like acrid smoke"), described my subjects like characters in a Greek tragedy ("Mr. X had a winning smile that belied his recent failures"). I never judged my subjects, but rather let their behaviors—a "nervous knee," a "too-loud laugh," a "pinched smile"—speak for themselves. When Clooney optioned my Sunday *Times* article on the WikiLeaks whistleblower, he said the piece already read like a movie script. When he paid me to adapt it, I was sure I'd stepped into my destiny. I worked on that script for five glorious years. It never occurred to me that they wouldn't make the movie. Or that my career would grind to a halt.

I rationalized the heartbreaking setback as a test of my resolve. I couldn't quit. I had built a home, moved a wife out from back East. Libby had given up everything—a promising career, a vast community of friends, weekend rituals she'd enjoyed her whole life—her generosity was boundless. I owed it to her to succeed, and succeed big.

I had to sell a script. After three bone-dry years, I finally had a meeting with someone who could pay big and get my movie made. I'd simply have to write something so compelling, so absolutely perfect for him, that he couldn't say no.

I vowed not to let anything distract me. I would prepare for this meeting like my life depended on it.

Because at this fragile point in my career and my marriage, it did.

CHAPTER 9

I just wanted to know how he died. I wasn't planning to go down some deep rabbit hole or anything. The word "suddenly" intrigued me, simple as that.

When people die "suddenly," it can mean any number of things: a heart attack, an aneurism, a plane crash, a car crash, a boating accident. He could have committed suicide (often the case) or been murdered (very rare). Or maybe he was just really old? Holly was good-looking enough to be a trophy wife. A million possibilities ran through my head, I just wanted to know.

First, I had to find out his name. That should be easy enough. Just google the wife. I knew her last name was Kendrick because I saw it on a moving box. Perhaps that was a strange thing to notice, but after ten years working as an investigative reporter, my mind just took in details like that.

I entered "Holly Kendrick" in the search bar and surveyed the results. She didn't have a social media presence, but her name came up in an obituary in the *Bakersfield Californian*. Kevin Michael McCallum is survived by his parents, Elaine and Martin McCallum, and sister, Holly McCallum Kendrick. She had a brother who died. On any other day, I would have been curious about that, but I was on a mission. I skimmed the obit. No mention of the husband, but at least now I had a maiden name.

I did another Google search, using the maiden name this time, and got a hit. A wedding announcement from sixteen years ago. Holly

McCallum wed her high school sweetheart, Gabriel Kendrick, in a simple ceremony. Blah blah blah . . .

I typed the dead husband's name in the search bar. Too many Gabriel Kendricks to count. I added the name of their high school, Bakersfield High, but they didn't keep up on him. I typed their names as a couple. They never owned property, together or separately *(strange?)* or did anything notable together *(not so strange)*. He wasn't on LinkedIn or Facebook or any social media. I smiled to myself, because I knew who would be on social media: *Savannah.*

I found her account almost immediately, and started scrolling backward—one month, two months, three months . . . then there it was—a picture of a young man in military blues, with a heartbreaking caption: Daddy, you may be gone but you'll always be in my heart. The comments section was a treasure trove of sorrow—hearts and flowers and sad-face emojis. I don't know why I was surprised. *Did I not believe Savannah's dad was really dead?* My background had taught me to question everything, even uncontrollable sobs, I guess.

I clocked the date of Savannah's post—May 20—then started scrolling through the comments: OMG I just heard the news . . . My heart is breaking for you . . . Sending hugs . . . Are you OK? Here if you need anything . . . The outpouring was touching but frustratingly short on details. But at least I had an approximate date—on or slightly before May 20. Holly's husband had died a little over three months ago. No wonder she broke down, it was still really fresh.

"What are you looking at?" Libby asked me, peering over my shoulder. She was flushed from Pilates, with matching crescents of sweat under each breast. I hadn't heard her come in. And it suddenly occurred to me that maybe she wanted it that way.

It wasn't a good look for me. Unemployed husband, barely dressed, scrolling through a sixteen-year-old girl's Instagram. I was supposed to be writing—*needed* to be writing—not surfing accounts of underage girls. I could only imagine the thoughts that were pulsing through my wife's mind. *My husband's a pervert, he likes teenage girls, Jesus how could I not have known?* We hadn't had sex in over a month, now she knew why I hadn't been more insistent.

As a journalist, I looked up all sorts of crazy shit. When I was working on an article about a marine who joined ISIS, I had to become an expert on Islamic extremism, the caves of Afghanistan, how to make a dirty bomb. That had surely landed me on the FBI watchlist. But my wife's scornful eye was way more frightening.

"Holly's a widow," I said simply, turning the laptop so she could see Savannah's post. Scrolling revealed more photos—a father-daughter dance, a sweaty track meet hug, one with the three of them, Holly in the middle.

"Jesus," Libby gasped, leaning in close. "How long ago was that?"

"About three months," I said, pointing to the date. I told her about the bench, and Holly's tearful confession, making a point not to describe her heaving breasts as she sobbed. "I just wanted to see what I could learn about his death, it felt disrespectful to ask."

"Yes, of course," Libby reassured me, and I felt relieved, and I imagined she did, too.

"Wait," Libby said. "Then who's Evan?" *Someone who's helping Savannah and me,* Holly had said. I remember thinking that was an odd way to describe him. But I just shrugged. "She didn't say."

"New boyfriend?" Libby postulated, and I shook my head.

"I didn't get that, talking to her. I think she would have told me."

Now it was Libby who shook her head. "Her husband's only been dead for three months. She's probably self-conscious about it. Maybe they were even a thing before the husband died?"

That was not my instinct, but I supposed it was possible. "Yeah, maybe . . ."

"I mean, look at her. She's kind of a bombshell," Libby said, and I took that as my warning—*Don't get too close.* "I would totally believe she could snag a rich boyfriend," she added, and though it was a backhanded compliment, I had to agree.

"I'm sure the truth will come out in time," I said as I closed the computer, indicating that I was not going to do any more digging. I had other things to focus on. My *(rescheduled!)* big meeting was coming up, and I needed to finish the spec script I was writing and get my pitches in order in case he wanted something different.

I looked at Libby. Her gaze was distant, and I could almost hear the wheels turning in her head. *Is she threatened? Jealous?* I'd never known her to be either, but perhaps this was a first.

We both sensed there was something untoward about Holly and Evan's relationship. I didn't think they were lovers, their body language was closed bordering on antagonistic—chairs far apart, arms crossed across their chests, rarely meeting each other's gaze. But Holly didn't consider him a friend, either—she had made that abundantly clear.

I had a hunch she was hiding something. And events would prove me right.

But I also thought whatever they were up to had nothing to do with us. It was none of our business, and we had no reason to be concerned.

And that's where events would prove me wrong.

PART 2

SAVANNAH

Three months ago

A police officer came to my school.

Sadly, this was not unusual. I wouldn't call it a weekly occurrence, but seeing a cop strutting through the quad in his collared pajamas and shiny black strap-on barely got my attention anymore. Usually it was because of some sort of divorce-related brouhaha. *So-and-so does not have custody anymore. Today's not so-and-so's day. So-and-so has a restraining order against him and is not allowed to be here.* We never made a big deal about it. Whoever the kid was, we figured he had already been through enough, we didn't have to make it worse by staring. It wasn't his fault his parents were psycho. Plus, who knew which one of us was going to be next?

Occasionally cops came for some other reason. One time a kid brought a switchblade to school and was waving it around like Luke Skywalker with his trusty light saber. Sometimes it was drugs. The teachers didn't care if kids were using—they knew most of them were. But they would call the police if they saw someone dealing. So yeah, they weren't there every week, but often enough.

On this particular day, the cop du jour was standing on the edge of the quad with our cowboy-hippie principal, Mr. Price, watching us as we scurried to our classes. Passing period was only six minutes—barely time to stop at your locker and change your books. I had geometry next, and I needed my calculator, so was huffing it down one of the crisscrossing concrete walkways that connected our classrooms. No policeman ever paid attention to me, and I happily returned the favor.

As I was rummaging through my locker, the kids around me suddenly scattered, like fish at the sight of a shark. I thought that was weird, so I turned to look. Cowboy Price was standing five feet from me, eyes cast down like he was looking for his belly button. The cop stood a few steps behind him, looking similarly glum.

Driving around with my mom and dad, if one of them saw a police car, they'd say something like, *Careful! There's a cop ahead!* Like he was some kind of dangerous animal. And yeah, some cops are animals. But I never felt nervous around them. Until the day one showed up at my locker.

"Hi, Savannah," Mr. Price said, hands clasped in front of his fly like an altar boy at church. "Could you come with me to my office?" he said kindly.

"I'm going to be late to second period," I warned, as if he didn't know.

"That's OK," he said. I didn't like the way the cop was looking at me, so I asked, "Did I do something wrong?"

Principal Price pressed his lips together, like I had asked him a really difficult question. It was the cop who answered it. "No, Miss. You didn't do anything wrong." *Then why do they want to talk to me?* I suddenly felt the urge to run, but where would I go? Our campus was enclosed by gates with spikes on top, no way in and no way out.

"It's about your parents," Principal Price said softly, and the butterflies in my stomach turned to boulders.

"What about my parents?" I asked.

He pressed his lips together again. Then the policeman took off his hat. And I knew that the worst thing that could ever happen to a girl was happening to me.

My calculator clacked to the ground as my knees buckled.

I lurched forward, like I'd been walloped from behind.

Two sets of hands caught me as I fell.

Principal Price knelt down beside me, and then held me as I screamed.

CHAPTER 10

I've never had much luck with boys. It's pretty obvious why. I didn't get the kind of body that nabs their attention. My mom hit the genetic jackpot with her double-D's and twenty-four-inch waist, but me? At sixteen I looked like Slender Man—tall with Barbie-doll arms, no hips, and ice cream scoops for boobs. Yes, Slender Man was a legend in his own time, but no one in their right mind would want to date him.

There was another reason why I never dated. The boys at my old school were lame. Most of them were high all the time. The ones who wanted to be in school—*needed* to be in school—went straight home, where they spoke Korean or Armenian with their families, and were likely forbidden to so much as talk to me.

So imagine my surprise when a super cute boy on his gap year between high school and going to Harvard (yes, *the* Harvard) hit me up for my Instagram username after track tryouts. I was a hurdler. I kind of fell into it because of my long legs and freakish flexibility. I started out as a dancer, but my parents couldn't afford to keep me in ballet lessons, and they didn't have dance at my old school. So I joined the track team. And to everyone's surprise—including mine—I kind of became a star.

Calabasas High had a good track team. In gymnastics and dance, if you want to win competitions, you have to do private lessons with bitchy prima ballerinas who poke at your belly *(Ribs in!)* and stretch your feet until you cry. That costs money. And we never had much of that. But you don't need pretty feet to win races—you just need to be fast. And speed is free. Sure, you can get stronger legs by doing extra reps in the gym, but we all had access to the gym, and you don't need Svetlana-who-danced-with-the-Bolshoi to teach you how to power squat. Living on the fourth floor of a building with no elevator gave me daily opportunities to develop my quads, and being perpetually late meant I often took the stairs two or three at a time. Rich girls don't have to run for the bus. Which once again meant, *advantage: me.*

I felt pretty good about my tryout. I wasn't in my best shape, and had lost some strength over the summer, but I still did the 100 m in less than fifteen seconds and the 300 m in under fifty, which is pretty good for an incoming junior. I could tell the coach was impressed with my competitiveness, which—unlike my weight—wasn't affected by a month of crying and crowding into my mom's hospital bed.

"You're fast for a white girl," the cute boy said, checking out my legs as I shook them out.

"Oh, gee, that's not racist," I shot back, pretending not to be impressed by the shock of black hair that lilted gently over eyes so blue it was like looking at the sky.

"What's your name?" he asked, and I paused to check him out.

"Why, you want to join my fan club?" I asked. I may not have had any dates, but I'd rehearsed how to get one many times.

"Definitely," he said, like he meant it. So I told him.

"Savannah Kendrick." I spoke my name like I was important. "And yes, I'm new around here, if that was your next question."

"Hello, Savannah. I'm Logan. And I'm new around here, too," he said, offering his hand. Then he asked, "You a junior?"

I nodded, then asked him, "What about you?"

"Graduated last spring," he replied, "but not from here."

I narrowed my eyes at him. "So what, you're some sort of stalker?"

He tilted his head back when he laughed, revealing flawless, straight white teeth. "Couldn't be president of your fan club if I didn't stalk you," he joked. "I'm taking a year off before I start college. I was the captain of my track team. I'm going to be your assistant coach. But only on a volunteer basis. So I can't get fired for wanting to go out with you."

The flirtation was so direct it caught me off guard. I was sure I blushed. And I was sure he saw.

"Is this you, Savannah Kendrick?" he asked, showing me his phone where he had found my Instagram account.

"Yeah," I said, suddenly self-conscious about this hot guy seeing my stupid posts. I cursed myself and hoped he wouldn't scroll through them until after I had weeded out the embarrassing ones.

"OK," he said as he clicked, "I'm now officially stalking you." And he flashed a smile that made me blush all the way to the backs of my ears.

"Lucky me," I sassed him back. I hoped I sounded sarcastic. Even though that's not how I felt at all.

LIBBY

Three months ago

The bathroom faucet broke off in my hand.

Fortunately, it happened when I was trying to turn the water on, not off, so I didn't get drenched. Unfortunately, I urgently needed running water, because my face was plastered with a sea-salt-and-avocado exfoliating and firming mask, which was already dry and pulling my mouth apart like a sad iguana.

I went to the powder room, turned on the faucet (carefully), and rinsed off the mask. As I blotted my cheeks, I noticed the shiny foil wallpaper was starting to curl up just above the baseboard. We had intended to change that wallpaper right after we moved in. But we were too busy. And then we were too broke.

I tried not to bitch about never having enough money—my husband was depressed enough. He was spending every waking minute in his woodshop–man cave, which meant he didn't want to face his feelings or me. He said no one told him why that meeting that was supposed to "change our lives" got canceled—not that it mattered, he wouldn't have believed them anyway. *They don't tell you the truth about anything,* he had said. *They just say whatever makes them not look like assholes.*

I imagined it was hard going from being a reporter whose job was to hunt down facts, to an aspiring screenwriter denied even the most basic ones. But something about this business had him hooked. He had been so hyped about his meeting, practicing his pitches in the mirror, in the shower, in the car on our way to game night. He even dressed up for the meeting—which he never does—in the flat-front trousers I had bought him at Banana Republic and one of his few shirts that doesn't have an '80s rock band on it. I hadn't seen him that excited since the day Clooney wrote him the check that became the down payment to this house. As evidenced by the state of our bathrooms, that was a long time ago.

I flicked at the wallpaper, then contemplated tamping it down with a glue stick. I suddenly laughed out loud at what my life had become. I had a PhD in psychology from Columbia, and was once a well-paid professional. A move cross-country and two kids later, my job was now keeping house, maintaining my rapidly deteriorating looks, and supporting my husband's dream of becoming a Hollywood hotshot.

I had a complicated relationship with my life. I loved California and this neighborhood, but to look like I belonged here took a massive amount of effort. I did what I could at home, with DIY face masks and drugstore waxing kits, but some professional help was still required to fend off the assault of Father Time. And we couldn't afford it.

I found a glue stick in Tatum's room. I glued the wallpaper down and rolled it smooth with the tube. *If only fixing the wrinkles on my face were so easy,* I thought. *Just dab some sticky goo on them and roll them out. If I could invent such a thing, I'd be a millionaire!* At that point it seemed as likely a path to wealth as my husband selling another screenplay.

I put the glue stick back and made Tatum's bed. She hadn't slept in it—she'd slept with me the previous night. Tatum's bed was unmade because her dad had slept there. He was going to be "up late," he'd announced, "preparing for his big meeting" and "didn't want to wake me." Tatum was thrilled like she always is when Daddy "stays up working." Which was a lot. Truth be told, he rarely slept in our bed anymore, and Tatum had the spot next to me pretty much whenever she wanted. We just didn't always tell her so.

I wanted to help my husband succeed in his chosen career, but we couldn't go on like this forever. At some point I would have to confront him, demand he get an actual paying job. But that day I had to fix a faucet.

So I put my failing marriage on hold, and hoped it wouldn't grow as sorry as my sagging face and crumbling house.

CHAPTER 11

I saw her in the supermarket parking lot. She was loading groceries into the brand-new version of my Lexus. I noticed she got the highest trim—low-profile chrome wheels, and mahogany paneling to contrast the buttery-smooth camel interior. We always went for black on black because it doesn't show wear.

Food shopping at ten o'clock on a weekday morning meant, like me, my new neighbor probably didn't have a job. It was unemployed housewives' hour. We shared the parking lot with a handful of nannies and the kids in their charge.

"Holly, hi!" I said, with a wave and a smile. She nearly dropped her watermelon. "Sorry! Didn't mean to startle you." *Why does this woman always look like she just got caught with her fork in someone else's dessert?* She didn't say anything, so I reintroduced myself. "Libby. I live across the street from you."

"Right," she said, nodding. "Sorry, I didn't expect to see you here." *Ummm . . . it's the supermarket a mile from our houses, but OK.*

"How are you liking the house?" I asked her, trying not to sound too envious. Andy and I had wandered in there when it was for sale. The previous owner had "lovingly restored" it, our friendly neighborhood Realtor had told us, and for once he wasn't exaggerating.

"We like it very much," Holly replied somewhat robotically. I wondered if she had a pole up her ass, or was just not a good conversationalist. I couldn't help but notice she'd had her roots touched up and her hair cut in flattering waves around her face. I hadn't had a haircut in two months and had resorted to covering my newly sprouted grays with hair dye I bought off the internet.

"We loved it when we saw it," I gushed, hoping to flatter her into opening up to me. "That kitchen is to die for! Do you like to cook?" My eyes wandered over to her groceries—kettle chips with a Diet Coke chaser—and I immediately regretted the question.

"I like baking better," she said, "but I don't mind it."

"I insist on having you all over for dinner," I blurted. *What is wrong with me?* I was in no position to host a dinner party, my girls were in bed by seven o'clock. And compared to hers, my kitchen, with its parquet floor and yellowing appliances, looked like a junkyard. But I was crazy curious about her shiny new car, her shiny new locks, and the man I suspected was her shiny new boyfriend. And I couldn't very well invite myself over to her house.

"I'm not with Evan," she insisted, and I pretended I believed her. "Maybe your husband didn't tell you . . . ?" She picked at her manicure, and I cursed my own nails, which I had chewed down to tiny nubs. I hated going to the nail salon. It embarrassed me to have my hands and feet massaged by hardworking immigrants who surely needed a massage more than I did. I didn't think they were talking about me in whatever Southeast Asian dialect they were speaking, but their constant clucking made me and my white privilege feel like a pampered, spoiled brat. I don't know when colorful, perfectly sculpted nails became part of the uniform worn by the respectable modern woman, but after keeping up with the trends—round nails, square nails, french, black, coffin—I was over it.

"Yes, I'm sorry for your loss," I said, well aware why she couldn't reveal Evan as her boyfriend a mere three months after her husband's death. But seriously, who did she think she was fooling? He was sitting at her kitchen table at nine o'clock at night! Maybe he hadn't moved in yet, but he clearly had bought that house, and the Louis Vuitton bag slung over her shoulder to go with it. "I'll send you some possible dates for a proper getting-to-know-one-another dinner," I said, then suggested, "Shall we exchange numbers?"

I took out my phone. But as I readied my fingers to type in her number, she said the unthinkable.

"I don't mean to be rude," she started, "but we're just not ready to make new friends. I'm not ready," she said. Then punctuated her snub with the slam of her trunk.

My mouth dropped open so wide a bird could have flown into it. Maybe one did, because for several seconds I couldn't speak or swallow. I finally managed a "Right, of course." She thanked me for understanding and then drove off, leaving me standing in that parking lot like a discarded piece of trash.

Never in my life had I met someone as rude and condescending as my new neighbor Holly Kendrick. *What kind of person rejects an offer of friendship? A person who is hiding something, that's who.*

And I was determined to find out what it was.

JACK

My wife was in a playful mood that night.

When I walked into the bedroom, she put music on—"Sailing" by Christopher Cross, an '80s soft rock classic—grabbed my hand, and swirled into me like yarn to a spool. I was not in the mood to dance, but I couldn't refuse her, never could.

I met Kate when I spilled coffee on her at an airport Starbucks. I was so charmed by her laugh—and that her reaction to being doused with hot coffee was to laugh—that I moved my seat twenty rows back to sit next to her. Twelve months later we were married. In his speech at our wedding, my new father-in-law referred to the incident as "the definition of a happy accident." Everybody laughed.

Of course, most accidents aren't happy. I've been lucky not to have too many of the unhappy kind. I fell and broke my hand skiing, I hit a golf ball through a window, I gave a kid who's allergic to nuts a cookie that could have killed him. At the time, these accidents were devastating. Breaking my hand ruined my vacation, fixing that window cost a full two weeks' pay, and there is nothing more horrifying than watching a child go into anaphylactic shock because you forgot to ask, *Are you OK with nuts?* But my hand healed, my bank account rebounded, and that kid lived to eat another cookie. Those were the worst accidents of my life. Until this one.

"Sailing . . . la-la-la-la . . . ," Kate sang, her head tilted up toward the sky. She was a terrible singer, and any other day I would have laughed. But that day her unabashed joy broke my heart. Because I knew that if she found out what had happened, and what I'd done to cover it up, she would never feel this happy again.

I love it when baseball announcers say, *I betcha Joe Batter wishes he could have that pitch back!* Even if you never played baseball, you know what they mean. We've all had those *if only* moments. *If only* I'd swung at that pitch. *If only* I hadn't. I could have been the hero. I could have saved the day.

As my wife pressed her face to my chest and rocked me slowly left and right, I had a thousand *if onlys* churning through my mind—*if only* the sun wasn't so blinding, *if only* that truck had moved out of the way, *if only* that couple had exited the car sooner, or later, or not at all. I could have played that game for days.

The tragic thing about *if onlys*, if you're wishing for them, it's too late. Once a pitch is thrown, you can't get it back.

I would have traded all my life's *if onlys* to get that day back, but of course, just like that missed perfect pitch, it was too late.

So I danced with my wife, knowing full well it might be the last time, and because my heart didn't have room for any more regrets.

CHAPTER 12

I *literally* lived in the house of my dreams. When I looked around, I could hardly believe it was really all mine.

I did not grow up wealthy—far from it—but I still dared to dream what my perfect house would be like. I dreamed of a long driveway that wound up a gentle hill. I dreamed of that driveway ending at a majestic gate hugged by flowering, vibrant-pink bougainvillea. I dreamed of that gate opening to a gently bubbling fountain that lured colorful birds and the occasional deer.

I dreamed of a front door so wide and welcoming that people would approach with as much excitement as Charlie at the chocolate factory. Once inside, I dreamed of a grand staircase right out of *Gone with the Wind* that flared into banistered overlooks on either side. I dreamed the house would have a room for every purpose—a chef's kitchen for preparing gourmet meals, a lush lanai to entertain, a gym, a screening room, a master bedroom so luxurious it felt like a suite at the Ritz. All of this was at stake now. If we couldn't keep the lid on this, I could lose it all.

Evan and I met in my private study that night. I had it decorated more like a hunting lodge than an office, with deep leather chairs and a plush bearskin rug. The walls were lined with my favorite books, which ranged from Deepak Chopra and Eckhart Tolle to vintage Robert Ludlum and Tom Clancy. No one went in there but me, and Evan on the rare occasion we discussed business at my house.

"Am I going to go to jail for this?" I asked my lawyer as I examined the signatures of Holly and Savannah Kendrick. It felt strange having a legal document for an illegal act, but I trusted Evan had reasons for wanting it.

He seemed prepared for my absurd question. "No one has anything to gain by exposing your connection to this," he replied. It was true, of course, but that was no guarantee that they wouldn't. Our devil's bargain was rancid, but just because we all swallowed it, didn't mean we could all keep it down. Guilty feelings can be boxed up, but life has a way of jostling them free. For some they leak out slowly, seeping into the deep crevices of your conscience, haunting your dreams until you die. For others, they build up like steam in a pressure cooker, threatening to blow you wide open. This was not going to go away. The only unknown was who was going to slow rot, and who was going to explode.

"Think of your family," Evan said, as if I needed to be reminded. This was, of course, all about my family.

My greatest sadness was that I only had one child. I had wanted more children. But pregnancy was hard for my wife. She had what they call hyperemesis gravidarum, which is Latin for *I can't stop vomiting, please kill me now.* It was horribly, violently, heartbreakingly awful. Even high doses of Zofran, the medicine they give to cancer patients undergoing chemotherapy, couldn't quell her fits of nausea. For nearly nine months, Kate lived on the bathroom floor with her head by the toilet. There were days she literally wanted to die. Watching her suffer was like being handcuffed to a fire truck while your house burned down. It was the worst kind of torture. At one point she begged her doctor to put her in a medically induced coma and keep her there until the baby was born. When the doctor said no, they didn't do that, I didn't know whether to feel relieved or disappointed.

Most women with hyperemesis gravidarum start to feel better in their third trimester, but Kate was sick well into her ninth month. She desperately wanted to have a vaginal birth, but when the vomiting continued into her thirty-seventh week, I convinced her to have a C-section. I was going out of town for work, I didn't want to leave with her sick like that, and—selfishly—I wanted to witness the birth of our child, especially since I suspected there might not be another one. She didn't want to have a scheduled C-section, but she did it for me.

We were warned that babies who didn't get the opportunity to travel through the birth canal could be born with fluid in their lungs, but we still panicked when our baby couldn't breathe. Kate barely got to hold him before he was wrestled from her arms and tethered to a ventilator. He was in the NICU for thirteen days. Kate never left his side. When she wasn't permitted to hold him, she'd sneak her fingers through the tiny window in the incubator, just to touch his foot with a desperate pinky finger. Taken too soon from her womb, he was still part of her, and she wouldn't—*couldn't*—let go.

Kate's pregnancy was impossibly hard, but those two weeks after her baby was taken from her nearly broke her. There was no place to lie down in the neonatal intensive care unit, so she didn't sleep. There was no food allowed, so she didn't eat. She pumped every two hours to keep her milk up, enduring the prying eyes of whoever was in the NICU that day, because she refused to leave. And I abandoned her during the worst of it, because I was contractually obligated to go do a movie, and Hollywood couldn't wait, not even for me.

Leaving her like that was hell. I vowed to never, ever, let anything hurt her again. This settlement, cover-up, bribe—whatever you wanted to call it—I wasn't doing it for me. I could have handled the fallout. I was doing it for her. Because unbeknownst to her, she had a role in this, too.

I slid the contract back in the envelope. "Take it with you," I instructed, handing it to Evan. I had asked my lawyer to handle sensitive situations in the past, but none as fraught as this. I was a highly visible person in a highly visible industry. If the details of this incident got out, my life would be decimated. Because as bad as things seemed, the truth was even worse. And Evan knew I would risk everything to keep it hidden.

"What now?" I asked as he snugged the envelope into his briefcase.

"We move on," he said simply.

I didn't know whether to laugh or cry. Because of course we should move on, but in my heart, I knew I never could.

SAVANNAH

Three months ago

I'd never been in a police car before.

The seats were super uncomfortable, you had to sit straight up like you were in church. It smelled like unwashed armpits and barf, and I wondered how many people had thrown up back here. A few months back, a girl at school drank a fifth of whiskey as a dare, but she left in an ambulance, so it must have been someone else's bad day I was smelling.

There was a cage between the driver and me that reminded me of our fire escape at home, with its tic-tac-toe metalwork and holes barely large enough to stick a finger through. Our fire escape was the closest thing we'd ever had to a balcony. I liked to sit out there at night and watch the cars go by, squinting at them to blur their lights into a psychedelic swirl of color. But I wasn't on my fire escape. I was in the back of a police car on my way to the hospital, to hold the hand of my one remaining parent.

"You OK back there?" the cop asked me, craning his neck to look for himself.

"Yes," I said, though I really wasn't. I don't know how long I'd sobbed at my locker before Mr. Price peeled me off him, but by the time he'd slid me into the police car, I had cried myself dry.

I replayed Mr. Price's pronouncement in my head. "Your parents were in an accident." He paused, then said something completely nonsensical. "Unfortunately your dad didn't make it." For a few seconds I genuinely didn't understand. What Mr. Price was saying was impossible. My dad couldn't be dead. I'd seen him just that morning, drinking his coffee out of the #1 Dad! mug I had bought for half price the day after Father's Day. Dad was a big coffee drinker. He brewed a whole pot every morning and drank it black and crazy hot. They didn't have cream and sugar at his outpost in Afghanistan's Korengal Valley, where he'd had his first cup, and I guess he came to like it that way. As for why he drank it so hot, I really couldn't tell you.

"We need to talk about your birthday," he had said when I sat down at the kitchen table for breakfast that morning. "It's your sweet sixteen, we need to do something special."

"I know something special we can do," I'd responded, and he shut me up with a look.

"We're not buying you a car," he'd admonished, and I probably rolled my eyes, like I always did when I didn't get my way. And then that was it. I left for school. I'm not even sure I said goodbye.

And now Mr. Price was saying he was dead? How was that possible? We hadn't even finished our conversation. I never expected Dad to buy me a new car, but it didn't stop me from pestering him. He had already hinted I would be getting the Cherokee, and Mom would get something new and cute, like a MINI Cooper or a cabriolet. I had learned to drive in that Jeep. I even made it my own with a few well-placed dings on the bumper *(Bumpers are for bumping!)*. After I scraped the dumpster behind our building for the third time *(It was wider than it looked!)*, Dad installed a dashcam so he could analyze my every mistake. It wasn't enough that I had to listen to him in the car beside me *(Signal **before** you turn! Stop **behind** the line!)*, he wanted to scrutinize my driving in our living room, too.

We put the dashcam app on my phone. Dad said it was because my phone was newer and had more memory than his, but I think he just wanted an excuse to peek in on my social life—see who I was texting, at what time and why. We had, in fact, never looked at the dashcam stream, I wasn't even sure it worked.

"I'll go in with you when we get to the hospital," the cop said, "to make sure they take you straight to your mom, OK?" I nodded. I was sure I could have found her myself, but I wasn't about to say no to a cop.

"She's going to be OK," he said. "The driver nicked her pretty good, but from what I saw, her injuries aren't life-threatening."

Nicked her? I supposed it was possible for a speeding car to nick a person, in the way a tractor might nick a blade of grass. I knew he was trying to make me feel better, but the more he talked, the more it made me want to cry. I wished he would just shut up.

"She's a victim, but she's also our star witness," he rambled on. "We need her better so she can help us catch the guy!"

He found my eyes in the rearview, so I mustered a nod. I had never thought of my mom as a victim before. Or a star witness. Or a widow. But I guess she was all of those things now.

In front of us, a car was stopped. The chatty cop flipped a switch, and his siren chirped a warning—*get out of the way!* I knew he was just showing off, but I wanted out of that smelly squad car, so I was grateful for anything that would make that happen faster.

I looked down at my phone. The dashcam app was at the bottom right corner of my screen. I remembered my dad asking me what I wanted the password to be. I don't know what I told him, if I told him anything at all. I panicked a little—*what if the cops ask me and I can't remember it?*

"We're here," the cop said as he turned into the driveway. I had never entered a hospital through the ambulance entrance before. Aggressive red letters screamed "Emergency" like a bloodstain against the cold concrete wall. I thought it would be busier, with paramedics rushing around like on all those medical shows on TV. But the only person there was a security guard, sitting in a plastic chair, staring at his phone. He didn't even look up at us.

The car lurched as we pulled up to the curb. I didn't bother trying to open my door—it didn't even have a handle on the inside. "One second, honey," the cop said as he clicked off his seat belt. As he rounded the back of the car to let me out, I tucked my phone away. There would be time to tell him about the dashcam later, I didn't want to get into it while my mom was lying alone in a hospital bed.

He opened the door for me, and I made sure to thank him as I got out. I glanced at his shiny brass name tag—KELLOGG. *Like the cereal,* I thought. His beer belly pushed against the bottom buttons of his shirt, stretching the fabric, revealing two tiny patches of bare skin. It was a sweltering day, and I remember thinking how it must suck to have to wear a polyester suit, especially one that was two sizes too small.

"I don't want you to worry," Kellogg said. "We're going to find the guy who did this."

Once I figured out how to log in to the app I would tell him about the camera. By the way he was talking about Mom being their "star witness," I gathered no one knew about it, at least not yet. It would blow the case wide open. Whoever discovered that video would be a hero, maybe even get promoted. Kellogg looked like a guy who could use a promotion and the new uniform that came with it.

But I didn't mention it.

And that turned out to be both a stroke of genius, and a catastrophic mistake.

CHAPTER 13

"You need a ride?" a raspy, cool-guy voice called to me as I walked off the practice field.

I looked over to see Logan, my ridiculously hot assistant track coach, leaning against his shiny black SUV, hands in his pockets, eyes fixed on me. It was a nice car for a kid just out of high school. I noticed a Devils sticker on the back bumper—his former school team, perhaps? He'd stuck it on upside down and drawn a vertical line through the letter *V* so it looked like it spelled Slimed.

I tried to play it cool, hoping whatever color might be spreading across my cheeks would be mistaken for postworkout flush. "My mom's coming," I said, "but thanks." I don't know why he wanted to give me a ride—I looked disgusting. My straight hair was in a low ponytail, and I could feel the sticky strands crisscrossing my sweaty back like a blonde spiderweb. *Ugh. Why couldn't I be one of those girls with cute, puffy hair that I could swirl atop my head like cotton candy?*

"Call her off," he demanded. "Tell her one of the coaches needs to talk to you about your form." *My form?* I didn't know whether to laugh or cringe. But then he smiled, and I knew he was kidding. "Ha ha sorry, that was cheesy, even for me." His laugh was like the whoosh of a waterslide, smooth and exhilarating, and hearing it felt like riding a wave.

"She's already on her way," I told him. I had texted her as soon as practice was over. And I would never bail on her. We didn't do that to each other, not now, not ever, not even for a boy.

"Tomorrow, then," he said. "I'll buy you a taco, best one you've ever had." He looked at me expectantly, and I suddenly got afraid. *Holy shit, is he asking me out?* I had never been asked out in my life, so I wasn't sure if that's what was happening.

"Yeah, maybe," I said, unsure how to respond. He was a coach. *Is going out with a coach even allowed?*

My mom's car pulled up. She'd had that perky Lexus for almost a month, but it still surprised me to see her driving it. We had some work to do before she looked like she belonged behind the wheel. The haircut helped. But she still wore too much makeup. And those cheap faux Ray-Bans really had to go.

I waved to her *(coming!)* so she wouldn't honk. "I gotta go."

"Is that your mom?" Logan said, glancing at her, and I knew what he was thinking. Even those cheap sunglasses couldn't hide that my mom was a Betty, blessed with full, pouty lips and perfect skin. People loved to say how we "didn't look anything alike." I knew what they were implying, but it happened so often I stopped getting offended.

"No, but I'll get in her car anyway," I snarked.

"A risk taker, I like it," he said, and I felt my neck redden.

"See you tomorrow," he called after me as I walked toward Mom's Lexus. "For tacos!" he reminded, as if I possibly could have forgotten his invitation from thirty seconds ago.

"We'll see," I shouted back, then climbed in the car.

"Who's that boy?" Mom asked as I clicked on my seat belt.

I felt my cheeks redden. *Is it too soon for me to be talking up a boy? Or is Mom worried because she saw me crushing on someone out of my league?*

"He used to run track, he's helping manage the team," I said, careful not to use the word "coach." Or reveal that he already graduated, and from another school. I didn't want to add "improper" to my growing wall of shame.

"He's cute," my mom remarked, and I quickly changed the subject.

"What's for dinner?"

My mom cooked dinner every night. Usually it was something simple—pasta with homemade sauce, turkey meatloaf, some sort of stir fry. She wasn't a bad cook, as long as you didn't mind eating the same eight recipes on endless repeat.

"I thought we'd go out," she said. "Someplace nice. To celebrate you making the track team." She glanced over at me. I must have been looking at her like she had three heads, because she added, "Unless you don't want to?"

We never went out to dinner. Not even since the accident. *Especially* since the accident. "Like where?" I asked cautiously, not knowing what "someplace nice" meant in the new version of our life.

"I found a nice sushi place near us?" she said, her voice going up like it was a question. "Not a little hole-in-the-wall like the one in our old neighborhood, an actual sit-down place."

She seemed like she was trying to sell me on it, so I nodded. "That sounds great!"

For most people, going out for sushi was probably no big deal. But for my mom, in this moment, it was huge. She drove the car they gave her, and moved into her new Louis Vuitton bag, but other than that, she still lived like we had to watch every penny. I had to drag her to get a haircut, and she only agreed to go to a "by appointment only" salon because she found a Groupon. Her closet at home was mostly empty, and she still only bought "special" foods like macadamia nuts and Italian coffee if they were on sale.

"I just need to shower," I said brightly to show her I was into it. "I'll be quick!" I had felt guilty about spending my dad's killer's money at first, too. The first time I tapped my new debit card was at a McDonald's for fries and an apple pie. As soon as I did it, I felt so sick to my stomach I ran outside and puked behind a tree. But after crying until my eyes burned, I got mad. That money was ours. We earned it with our blood, sweat, and a shit ton of tears. After two months of hating myself, I decided I was not going to let those murderers make me feel like the criminal here. And that meant spending that money. At the mention of sit-down sushi, I stupidly thought my mom might finally be coming around, too.

We pulled into our garage, which was empty except for the handful of unmarked boxes against the back wall that neither one of us wanted to touch. My dad probably had some cool T-shirts I could crop or tie in the back, but I didn't look. I wasn't ready to see his stuff, smell his smell, ugly cry until my eyes swelled, just for a few lousy T-shirts.

I hopped out of the car, glancing at my mom as I reached for my backpack. She still had her hands on the wheel. She'd had her nails done pale pink, and her diamond solitaire drooped to one side. She didn't wear the wedding band anymore, just the diamond, because it was pretty and she didn't have many pretty things. She had a faraway look in her eyes that made me feel nervous, but I wasn't sure why.

"This is our life now, Mom," I said gently. I almost added, *Dad would want us to enjoy it,* but I didn't. I knew she didn't believe that. And to be honest, I wasn't sure I believed it either. So I said, "We have to learn to enjoy it," instead.

"I am enjoying it," she insisted. "I'm just hungry!" She smiled, and I knew it was a lie. Both the hunger and the smile. There were so many lies between us now, there was no point in calling her on it. Besides, I told just as many.

"Ten minutes," I promised, then shut the door. I felt a ping of excitement that Mom and I were going out. Setting the table for two after a whole life of being a three felt sad and weird. But maybe we could find some new rituals now? Like getting our nails done together, or going to movies or concerts or even on trips. I liked baking bread and shopping at thrift stores with Mom back in the day, she always made it fun by playing kooky playlists in the car and singing along with the windows open. But we could do so much more now. And then maybe, once we learned to have fun again, all the lying would stop.

As I turned on the shower, I was smiling, because I thought that sushi was a sign that things were looking up. Thinking back, it's kind of incredible how very wrong I was.

LIBBY

Three months ago

"Cool watch," the Goth salesgirl said as I set my garbage bag full of clothes on the counter. The trendy Studio City thrift store was only a few towns over, but felt like another planet.

"Thanks," I said curtly, meeting her heavily lined eyes, making sure to convey that—unlike the items in the trash bag—the watch wasn't for sale. I had to hold on to one vestige of my former life, or risk losing it entirely.

She opened the bag and took out the first item—a pair of dark-wash, boot-cut 7 For All Mankind jeans that still fit but weren't in style anymore. I tried to look indifferent as she inspected them. I felt a little rush as she put them in the "yes" pile. *I can surprise the girls with sushi tonight!* My daughters didn't eat raw fish, but they loved the rolls—avocado, vegetable, sweet and creamy California—and we hadn't had them for a while.

I tried not to think about all the other things we hadn't had for a while, or how lean the coming months would be. My fortieth birthday was coming up. I was terrified to bring up the subject with Andy. Six months ago, I dared to fantasize about having a big blowout bash, but now even a small party was out of the question. We had near six-figure credit card debt. We could barely afford a picnic for two in the backyard. And I was selling my $200 designer jeans for twenty bucks at a thrift shop.

"Is this Hermès?" the Goth gal asked, and I nodded. The scarf was a gift from my mother, but I never liked it and was relieved to have an excuse to part with it.

Things had become strained between my mother and me, especially since I told her we couldn't afford to visit this summer, and if she wanted to see her granddaughters, she'd have to fly us out. *You have a degree,* she'd said when I complained about being broke. *Go out and get a job!*

But it wasn't that easy at my age, with one kid in preschool and the other in second grade. I didn't want to hire someone to do what I enjoyed doing myself—hearing about their day on the ride home from school, taking them to the park, to swimming lessons or an art class. And without hiring a thirty-dollar-an-hour nanny (with a car and impeccable driving record), I wasn't really available to work. Was I supposed to tell my potential employer, *I'd like to work for you, but I have to leave by two thirty, except on Tuesdays, when I have to be out by one o'clock. Also I volunteer in the classroom Friday mornings, so I can't come in until after ten o'clock. Also I'm not willing to miss school plays, concerts, and won't come in if my kids are sick, so you can depend on me but not really, because when you have kids, sick days happen.* Sick days do happen. They happen a lot.

Tell Andy to help with the kids, my mother would say. And he would help when he could. But his schedule was volatile. Plus he was supposed to be writing, which is tough enough when you're not chasing kids around.

Ruby Gloom fished a dress coat out of the bag and put it in the "no" pile without even looking at it.

"That's Betsey Johnson," I admonished her. That coat had cost $300, and I had only worn it once.

"Out of season," she shot back. And that was it for Betsey.

I had thought about telling my husband I wanted to go back to work, but even if Andy were to agree to be Mr. Mom, I had another impediment to getting a job. I didn't know anyone here. Referrals were everything in a psychology practice. Back in New York, I was part of a robust network. I had built a brand, established my specialty (family and systems development), and, after three years of hosting free seminars, I was just starting to get paying customers. There were probably teaching jobs here that I was qualified for, but I would never get them. I could explain to someone who knew me personally why I took eight years off to birth and raise babies, but I couldn't expect someone I cold called to make sense of it. After nearly a decade on the sidelines, professionally I was irrelevant now. I'd have to start over. At forty. The prospect was terrifying. Because it wasn't a viable prospect at all.

No, I couldn't talk to Andy about my birthday. I couldn't really talk to him about anything these days. We barely even saw each other. He stayed up late to write. I got up early to get the kids to school. Since having kids, we had diverged into two completely different universes. He lived in his imagination. I lived in the kitchen. I loved being a mom, but good lord I had no idea how much of my day would be consumed by food. Shop for food, prepare food, serve food, clean up food, pack food to go—it was never ending. The stay-at-home mom had not evolved much beyond a wild animal—*hunt, feed, rest, repeat.* I was the busy lioness, in constant search of our next meal, while my male lion husband lounged in his cave.

"There's a Goodwill across the street if you want to donate the rest of these," the salesgirl said, putting the nos back in the trash bag and sliding it toward me.

"Great, thanks," I said, implying I might just do that, even though I could have used a little goodwill myself.

"Would you like cash or store credit?" the salesgirl asked.

"Cash."

As she counted out the money—*a whole $140!*—I felt relieved that, at least for one night, I would have a little cash in my pocket. It would be gone after one trip to the grocery store, of course. But my girls would have sushi, and some lucky stranger would wear Hermès meant for me.

CHAPTER 14

Too much free time is a dangerous thing.

With the girls still in school, the lasagna already prepped, and my workout, shower, and hair done, I had nothing better to do than rage about being snubbed by my new neighbor Holly Kendrick.

"What if she murdered him?" I asked Andy when he emerged from his writing to forage for some lunch. "Maybe that's why she wouldn't talk about it, because she had him, y'know . . ." I made a gun with my hand, pulled the trigger with my finger. "Poof. Disappear."

"That's plausible," he said flatly. "When's the lasagna going to be done?"

"The lasagna's for dinner, have a sandwich," I told him. "But seriously. Three months after her husband dying, she has a new boyfriend and a two-million-dollar house? How does that happen?"

"We don't know Evan's her boyfriend," Andy countered as he pulled some bread from the freezer. "Is this all the bread we have?" he said, fondling a frozen Ezekiel loaf. He was curious by nature, but he never made assumptions. He knew from his past career how a wrong assumption could send an investigation completely off the rails. He was analytical to an extreme. But that didn't mean I couldn't prod him.

"There's rye in the breadbasket," I said, pointing. I could have made him a sandwich. I knew where all the condiments he liked were—pickles in the door, red onion in the bottom drawer. But I had been cooking all morning—that damn lasagna took forever—and I had just cleaned the kitchen and didn't feel like messing it up again.

"If Evan's not her boyfriend, then who is he?" I pressed. I knew he wouldn't commit to a theory, but I wanted him to consider mine.

"I don't know," he began. "Could be a lawyer, real estate agent, her insurance adjuster, a family friend, her therapist, her sober companion—"

"All right, all right," I interrupted. "You made your point. But what do you think is most likely?" He was looking through the refrigerator. "I'll make your sandwich if you tell me I'm probably right," I bargained.

"Right about what?" he asked. "Her being a murderer?"

"Well what's your theory?" I said, nudging him out of the way and extracting the red onion from the crisper. "How does a newly widowed woman with no job and no class land the nicest house on the block?" I asked, knowing the "no class" remark was a low blow, but not inaccurate given how she had treated me.

"It is mysterious," he said, probably because I was making his sandwich and he wanted to stay in my good graces, at least until I'd finished.

"I think she and Evan are a thing and have been for a while," I said boldly. "He's there at all hours, and reeks of money. Did you see his car?" I knew he had. My husband noticed everything, filing even the most minute details away in his brain until they fit together to tell the story. His analytical mind was one of the qualities I admired most about him, and I wanted him to put it to work.

"She's got a brand-new car, too," I added.

"Maybe they are a thing," he conceded as I handed him his sandwich. "Thanks," he said, and took a bite.

"She's obviously hiding something," I pointed out. "She ran away from me like I was holding a grenade."

Just then the doorbell rang. Andy was eating his sandwich, so I went to answer it. I figured it was the gardener. We hadn't paid him in two months, no doubt he wanted to collect. I loved living in the hills, but the upkeep was massive. If we didn't trim our trees and clear away the dead branches, the fire department would do it for us and then charge us a fortune. I had taken over the upkeep of the flower beds, trimming my roses every week and planting the annuals, but we still needed our gardener to clear the hillside, so I had to give him something. I grabbed my checkbook off my desk in the hall, then opened the door, an apology on my lips.

But it wasn't our gardener. "Hi, Libby," my neighbor Holly Kendrick said as she handed me a snow-white orchid in an onyx china pot. "Here. This is for you."

Shame rose up from the pit of my stomach. "Wow. Thank you," I mustered, tucking the checkbook in my waistband and taking the flower from her. It was from Gelson's down the street—I could tell by how it was wrapped, in premium-grade cellophane and a ribbon made of hemp. I liked to linger in their flower shop, but even the smallest arrangements were expensive, and I never indulged. Holly had bought the biggest one, two feet tall with over a dozen budding flowers. I knew it cost almost $100. I loved having orchids in the house, but I silently wondered if I could return it to pay my gardener.

"I felt terrible after what I said to you the other day," she began. "I didn't mean to be rude. I'm just a little overwhelmed these days."

"Yes, I'm sure," I said. The plant felt heavy in my hands. Almost as heavy as the shame weighing down my chest.

"I'd love to have you over for coffee," she offered. "I have scones in the oven, they will be ready in about twenty minutes?" She said it like a question, and it took me a second to understand.

"Oh! You mean right now?" I confirmed.

"Or we could do it some other time," she said quickly.

"A scone sounds wonderful. I just have to finish something in the kitchen," I said, which was true. Andy never cleaned up after himself, and I hated coming back to dirty plates and counters. "Five minutes?"

"Perfect." She smiled and turned to go. As she started down my front path, I noticed she walked with a limp, as if her left knee couldn't bend all the way. The shame in my chest hung so low I nearly tripped over it.

I closed the door. Andy immediately popped his head out of the kitchen. He was smiling. And not just because of the sandwich.

"Don't," I started, and he laughed.

"If you're not back in an hour, I'll call the SWAT team," he teased.

"Maybe she's not a murderer," I conceded. "But I still bet her new boyfriend is the one buying me flowers."

His smile turned sad. "Sorry it's not me," he said. And I could tell by his rueful expression that he meant it.

"I'll fill you in after," I assured him, ignoring his apology.

"I'm sure you will," he said with a sly smile. And I was grateful that we'd have something to talk about that would not end in a fight.

JACK

Three months ago

The first order of business was to hide the car.

I had a four-car garage, so it was no problem just to stash the SUV in one of the spaces until we figured out our next move. Evan said the next forty-eight hours would be critical in terms of witnesses coming forward or the police finding evidence. The victims, he said, would be "dealt with," then reminded me there were things we couldn't control. So we would just have to sit tight.

Once safely inside the garage, I inspected the vehicle. Of all the cars I had bought in my lifetime, this one was by far the biggest—an oversize SUV with a full third row and enough horsepower to pull a boat. Not that I had a boat. I wasn't really a boat person, but I liked having the ability to pull one if I needed to. My day-to-day car was a Porsche 911 convertible coupe, which was so compact it probably would have fit inside the SUV in its entirety. I shuddered to think what the collision would have been like had it happened in the convertible instead.

I walked to the front of the SUV to inspect the point of impact. The behemoth's front bumper had taken the Cherokee's door clean off, yet surprisingly barely had a mark. The headlights were both still intact, and there was no visible damage to the hood or passenger-side tire well. As far as I could see, there were no remnants of red paint anywhere on the car that could link the two vehicles together. Of course I wasn't in the business of investigating, or covering up, crimes. A trained eye might very well have noticed something I didn't.

If no witnesses came forward to identify the car, it was still possible there was forensic evidence at the scene. I looked closely to see if anything might have fallen off—the hood ornament, a side view mirror, a strip of trim. They would likely find something. All I could do was hope it wouldn't be enough to positively ID the vehicle and trace it back to me. Because then they'd figure out what I was really hiding, that I was guilty of something else entirely.

I wondered how long and hard the police would look for the perpetrator. Murder investigations sometimes take years. Cases go cold, then suddenly warm back to life with an unexpected recollection or new piece of evidence. How determined would the cops be to solve the case? And how foolish was I to think this would eventually just go away?

I remember hearing a case about a prominent real estate developer who was murdered in his home in White Plains. Detectives interviewed the dead guy's neighbors. One of them recalled seeing an unfamiliar car parked across the street that morning—a white Camry. His security camera had a picture. I guess there were a lot of white Camrys in the state of New York, because two years later they still hadn't found it. So they put the case on ice.

I don't know what compelled the detective to reopen the file after those two long years—pressure from the family? A spell of boredom? But he did, and this time he found something—a tiny detail he'd originally overlooked. The Camry had a transponder in it—a flat, white box glued to the windshield that allowed the car to cruise through tolls and be charged automatically. With that one distinguishing element, using security cameras across the tristate area, the detective was able to track that Camry all the way from the crime scene to a rental car outfit over three hundred miles away. It took six more months, but they caught the guy, and two years later he was convicted. When I read the story, the murderer was awaiting the death penalty in a maximum-security prison. All because of that little white box.

I didn't know what was going to give us away, but I had no doubt there was something out there that could. It was just a matter of if someone found it.

CHAPTER 15

"Your ten o'clock is here," my assistant said, poking her head into my office. "He's early," she added, to make sure I knew I didn't have to rush. I looked at my watch. It was only 9:40. I was already impressed.

"You can bring him back," I said, eager to get the day started.

I didn't have to come to the office every day—I could read scripts at home—but I liked being on the lot. I had been in the movie business for almost thirty years, but I was still enamored with the process. A movie set was like the human body, with all its organs—costumes, sets, props, lights—working in harmony to create something bigger than the sum of its parts. Making movies was nothing short of magic—we literally created whole worlds—and I loved seeing them come to life.

I had a studio deal, which meant I got an office and a staff, and a budget to buy and develop scripts. The funny thing about having a studio deal is, if you don't spend the money the studio gives you, they take it away. It is counter-productive to be frugal. You have to go after the fanciest writers, the most expensive books, the biggest stars, because if at the end of the year you're under budget, your budget for next year will be that much less.

Unlike some producers, my deal was richer than it was when I was lured into it six years ago. I'd had box office success as an actor, director, and producer, and the studio rewarded me handsomely. But it was September, and I'd hardly bought anything this year. To keep the money flowing, I needed to spend.

Being away all summer on someone else's movie didn't help matters. My development team had been reading books and scripts and hearing pitches, but nothing really happens when I'm away. And I was a little busy before I left trying to cover up a murder.

I had to make up for lost time. I needed projects, and all the writers I knew were working, so I had to branch out. I was excited about the guy coming in this morning. He had been an investigative reporter, and his portfolio of articles was as eclectic as it was deep. I'd read one of his scripts, as well as a handful of articles he'd written for the *New York Times*, and knew his writing to be colorful and sharp. I was hopeful he'd have a movie idea for me—a true story I could option, or a new script that hadn't yet made the rounds. The studio's money was burning a hole in my pocket, and I needed a project to keep my mind from going to dark places, which—since the horrific events of the spring—it was prone to do.

The walls of my office were glass, and I could see my assistant escorting my meeting through the bullpen. I had blinds for privacy, but I rarely used them. I liked looking out at my staff. They were hard workers, and their studiousness made me feel lucky to be in a position to reward them. But I also wanted them to feel they could always come talk to me, that I wasn't some king holed away in a castle, that I served them, as they served me.

I met my assistant's eyes through the glass door, and she understood that meant to come on in. As she reached for the door handle, the man opened it for her, and I liked him immediately.

"Andrew, this is Jack," she said as he followed her in. I rose from my desk to shake his hand. His grip was confident. He was taller than I was—no surprise there, most people were—and in good shape. He had a runner's body, lean with narrow shoulders. His blue eyes were rimmed with intelligence, and his wavy hair had just enough gray to make me trust him.

"Good to meet you, Andrew," I said. "Thanks for coming in."

"Please, call me Andy," he replied. "Only my parole officer calls me Andrew."

I laughed at the joke, and offered him a seat. "Please, sit down."

He sat across from me, and as he crossed his feet, I noticed his shiny Chuck Taylors. "I like your sneakers," I said. "Can you believe I used to play tennis in those?"

"Wish I'd worn them last time," he said. And I was confused. Because this was our first meeting. *Wasn't it?*

"Have you been in before?" I asked, and he suddenly looked a little panicked.

"No! Sorry. I . . . there was a mix-up. We had the wrong day, I had the wrong day."

And now I remembered. We were scheduled to meet on *that* day. I had no idea what my staff had told him. Had they mentioned an accident? My pulse quickened. He was an investigative journalist—detail-oriented, groomed to be curious. I tried to sound jocular when I spoke.

"I canceled on you last-minute, didn't I?"

"No, I'm sure you didn't," he said quickly. "I'm just lousy at checking messages." He was trying to cover for me. But I had treated him badly. He had not forgotten.

"Well, better late than never," I said, eyeing the fat folder in his hand. "Let's see what you've got there."

I made a point to sound enthusiastic. It's a good thing that I'm an actor, because I was anything but. The last thing I wanted was to be reminded of that day, by a guy resourceful enough to put the pieces together. Was I being paranoid? Probably. But I couldn't afford to take any chances.

I settled in to hear about the new spec he was going to leave behind, and his handful of pitches, but there was no way I was going into business with him, no matter how good his stuff was.

I'd politely hear him out, as I'd promised his agent I would.

And then never, ever, see him again.

SAVANNAH

Three months ago

The nurse offered to escort me to my mom's bedside, but I said no thanks. I didn't want anyone around me when I lost my shit. She told me she was "going to be OK," that she was "resting comfortably," but once she buzzed me in I still damn near sprinted to see for myself.

But when I got to her stall, I froze. Because there was a strange man hovering over her bed.

I knew he wasn't a doctor. A doctor wouldn't wear a shiny, expensive suit to work, where patients could bleed and throw up on it. He might have one, but he'd be smart enough to leave it at home.

He didn't have the signature clipboard of an administrator, or wear a badge, so it was unlikely he worked there. I thought for a second he might be a chaplain. But a chaplain would be praying, not hovering over my mom like a hungry vulture.

So who is he, and what does he want with my mom? I took a step closer. That's when I noticed he had something under his arm. *Is it a purse? Yes, holy shit, it's my mom's purse. What the hell is he doing with my mom's purse? If he's stealing it, why is he just standing there? Wouldn't he be running for the door?*

I thought about going to get Kellogg, the cop who had just dropped me off. Judging by that belly, he was probably still on the premises, trying to charm himself a cup of coffee and a muffin from the nurses' station.

But I didn't want to leave my mom alone with this creep, not even for a minute.

He reached under his arm and set the purse at Mom's feet. *OK, so not stealing it, putting it back. But why did he have it in the first place? And why is he staring at her like he wants to eat her for lunch?*

"Can I help you?" I asked, and not in a nice way.

He spun to face me. "You must be Savannah," he said. He tried to sound confident, but I heard uncertainty in his voice. *Let him wonder,* I thought.

"Who are you, and what do you want?" I glanced at my mom. She was sleeping. I wanted to go to her, *needed* to go to her, but the suit was standing in my way.

"I want to help you," he said, and I knew immediately what he was. I almost kicked him in the nuts. I didn't need help from some sleazeball ambulance chaser. Once the cops had the video, this case would be open and shut.

I waved my phone and told him to fuck off. "Dashcam, dickhead," I said. "I have video. So you can leave now, we don't need your help." I didn't actually have the video yet, it wouldn't upload to my phone until I got the camera and synced them. But he didn't have to know that.

I saw a flicker of surprise in his eyes. He had taken me for a helpless little girl, and I'd ruined his plan for an easy score. I thought for sure he would leave then, but he didn't. So I pushed him harder. "We're not hiring a lawyer who tailed us to the hospital," I told him. "You're wasting your time here."

And then he said something I didn't expect.

"How much do you want for it?" He must have seen from my reaction that I didn't understand, so he added, "I'll buy it from you."

And then I realized I had gotten it wrong. Mr. Expensive Suit wasn't a personal injury lawyer. He was a crook. There was only one reason someone would want to buy that video—they didn't want anyone else to see it. The vulture didn't want to profit off our tragedy, he wanted to cover it up.

My dad joined the marines on his eighteenth birthday. He loved to tell the story about how the recruiters came to his high school, on *that* day—the very first day he was eligible to enlist. He understood it to be "God's will" that he sign up, and serving his country was his proudest accomplishment. Dad spent a lifetime fighting for what was right—in Afghanistan, then after he came home as a "big brother" to like a dozen messed up kids. He was so straight and narrow he wouldn't even let me sneak soda into my water cup at McDonald's, because "stealing was stealing," and we didn't do that. My dad was maniacal about doing the right thing. And look where that got him. Dead in the morgue, with barely an extra month's rent in the bank.

I loved and respected my dad, but I didn't want to end up like him. And he was not here to stop me.

I looked at my mom. She was resting, but with tubes jammed in her hand and one leg dangling from a sling, she looked anything but peaceful. My fear turned to rage. I wanted to punch him in his fat, smug face.

If there was a way to take this creep and his fancy Italian suit for everything he had, I would do it.

Which meant I had to get my hands on that dashcam.

Before Kellogg and his LAPD buddies did.

CHAPTER 16

His kiss took me completely by surprise.

I was gazing down at the tacos. He'd ordered one of each—six in total—including a vegan one that was just peppers and onions and not really a taco at all. There were two kinds of beef—carne asada and some type of steak. I had thought carne asada *was* steak, but apparently they are different. Then there was chicken cut in little cubes, shredded pork carnitas, and some fried, breaded nuggets they claimed were fish.

Logan had reminded me of our "date" the moment I walked out on the field. "We on for tacos?" he'd asked as I picked a spot to stretch. He was wearing a tight, black wicking shirt that hugged a chest so perfectly puffed out and firm it looked like two partially submerged volleyballs. I remember wondering if it was hairy. A little chest hair is sexy. But if it crept its way onto his back, that would be gross. I wanted to go out with a boy, not a primate.

I had told my mom "some of the girls on the team" were going out for tacos after workout, which was potentially true when I told her—I didn't know for certain Logan hadn't invited anyone else. And we *were* having tacos. I felt a little bad, abandoning her for dinner. I didn't like to think of her eating alone. But she moved me to Calabasas so I would have a life, so I figured I should try to have one.

The taco joint turned out to be just a truck with some picnic tables around it. Most of the customers were Mexican. There was only one other gringo there, some guy with a guitar slung over his shoulder, who took his tacos to go. Logan ordered in Spanish, probably to try to impress me. I didn't let on that I spoke it better than he did. I'd gotten pretty fluent talking to my old neighbors, and then of course took it freshman and sophomore years just to have easy A's.

We chose a table in the shade, under a tree with purple flowers on it. It was late afternoon—after five o'clock—but still sunny and hot, and my bare arms and legs were sticky with sweat. I was staring down at the steak taco, garnished simply with chopped onion and a burst of cilantro, when he lifted my chin with his finger and kissed me square on the lips.

It wasn't my first kiss. But it was by far the best. He tasted like lime, and I remembered him sucking on one while we waited for our order. He had offered me one, too, and I waved it away—*too sour!* But on his lips, it was sweet as candy.

It was a soft, open-mouth kiss. His tongue flicked gently under my upper lip, but not in an aggressive way. I'm pretty sure I kissed him back, at least enough so that he would know I didn't mind. As he pulled away, he let his nose press against mine, lingering a few seconds like we were Lady and the Tramp. I had a good nose, strong and straight, same as my dad, and I often thanked him for passing that one perfect feature on to me.

"I wanted to do that since the first moment I saw you," Logan said. It was a clichéd line, but I fell for it, because I'd felt the same way. "Thought I'd better do it before we both had taco breath." I tried not to think about Dad in that moment—how he'd tell me to be careful, take it slow, don't give too much away. I'd always rolled my eyes when he talked to me about boys, but I'd have given anything to hear another one of his dumb dad-talks, that day or any day.

Logan held up the plate to offer me a taco. I picked the steak— ombré pink-to-brown strips hugged by a misshapen corn tortilla. And, for reasons not related to the taste, it was the best taco I'd ever had.

Later, when he was driving me home, he reached for my hand and didn't let go for the whole twenty minutes it took to get to my house.

His hand was big and warm, and for the first time since Dad was gone I felt safe, like someone had my back again. When we pulled up to my house, we kissed again, taco breath and all.

"I'd better go," I said when I came up for air. He made a frowny face, and I laughed. "Unlike you, I still have homework."

"When can I see you again?" he asked, placing his hand softly on my thigh.

"Um . . . tomorrow at track practice?" I said. *Duh!*

"No, I mean . . . like this." He skimmed my thigh with the back of his hand, and I got goose bumps all over.

"Whenever you want," I said.

He kissed me again. "How about now?" he said, his mouth exploring the nape of my neck.

"Except for now," I said, playfully squirming out of the reach of his lips.

"I want us to be a thing," he said. "I'm really into you." I didn't say it, but I was really into him, too. But I was on the track team, and he was a coach. I was already lying about so many things, I didn't want to have to lie about this, too.

"What about Coach Cooper?" I asked. "I don't think he'd approve." I loved being on the track team. It made me feel special, like I was part of something. Plus when I was counting steps, I didn't have room to think about Dad, how he was gone forever, or how disappointed he'd be in me for what I'd done. I wanted to hang out with Logan, but not if it meant getting kicked off the team.

"I'll quit coaching," he said. I must have looked alarmed, because he added, "It's not like they're paying me. I just did it because my dad wanted me to take a gap year, and I had nothing else to do." I couldn't tell if he was serious. We'd had one date. Hardly enough to know if it would become anything more.

"Why'd he want you to take a gap year?" I asked. I'd heard of kids taking a year off to sock some money away, but Logan didn't look and act like a guy who couldn't afford to go to college. For one thing, he had a nice car—a newish Ford Expedition with all the bells and whistles. Plus he spent his afternoons volunteering. If he needed money, he'd be working at a real job. "You in AA or something?" I joked, then suddenly wished I hadn't. *Oh my God, what if he is?*

But he didn't take offense. "I skipped a grade," he said, pointing to his noggin. Then in a forced, low-octave voice he added, "He wants me to mature a little. I'm only seventeen."

This was startling to me. "You're only seventeen?" I said, making no attempt to hide my shock.

"You're only sixteen!" he shot back, then laughed. Maybe it should have struck me as weird that he knew how old I was, or that he was volunteer-coaching high school track instead of going to Harvard, but I wasn't in a suspicious mood. Most juniors were sixteen, and plenty of kids volunteered in their gap year, especially if they didn't need a paying job.

"I just thought you were older," I offered, and it was true. I had thought he was a full two years older than I was, eighteen at the least.

"You won't once you get to know me," he replied, then flicked his eyes up to peer over my shoulder. "Your mom's waving at us."

I turned to look. My mom had just flipped on the front light and was standing on the stoop, hand waving in the air like a contestant in a beauty pageant.

"Shit. I'll see you tomorrow." I opened the car door. I wasn't ready for my mom to meet him and ask a bunch of questions. But it was too late. She was already walking down the path. My heart broke a little as I saw her try to keep from limping.

"Hi there," she said through the open passenger-side door. "I'm Holly, Savannah's mom." She smiled at him, then glared at me for not making the introduction.

"Hi, I'm Logan," Logan said with a little wave from behind the wheel.

"Thanks for driving her home," Mom said, and my heart raced in my chest. *What if she asks about the other girls?* I hadn't told Logan I'd lied to her about our date.

"It was my absolute pleasure," Logan said, then flashed that killer smile. "You have a lovely home," he added, gazing up at our house, and I wondered if he was trying to butter her up.

"Thank you. Are you a classmate of Savannah's?" Mom asked, no doubt wondering what a boy was doing at a girls' track team dinner. I braced myself for her reaction when he told her he was a coach.

But he didn't tell her he was a coach. He said something utterly mind-blowing.

"No, I'm her boyfriend."

My mom looked at me, and I shrugged a little. I could feel the rush of blood burning across my cheeks. I could have contradicted him. But I didn't.

And just like that, I had a boyfriend.

LIBBY

"Where did you get this diamond?" the jeweler asked as he examined the 2.5 carat rock through his 10x loop.

"It was my grandmother's," I said. "She gave it to me right before she died." I had intended to make myself a ring for my fortieth to honor her memory, but we needed a roof over our heads more than I needed a new diamond ring. And we'd eaten through my haul from the thrift store in exactly one day.

He slid it under a microscope and examined it from every angle. "It's almost too perfect to be real," he said a little aggressively. Grandma's diamond was dazzlingly rare, and indisputably real. Only the most discerning jeweler would appreciate its value, and I was hoping he was one of them.

"She was from Belgium," I said by way of explanation. Antwerp was well known to have the best diamond cutters in the world. "It's a VVS1," I added, sliding the certificate of authenticity across the counter, waiting to retract my hand until I was sure he saw my Rolex—a 1940s chronograph that would signal I was credible as the owner of such a rare and precious gem. "Only one microscopic inclusion."

"A clear bubble near the point," he said quickly to show off that he had seen it.

"That's right," I confirmed. That bubble was the only thing preventing the stone from earning an IF, or "internally flawless," rating—nearly impossible for a stone of that size. As he set the diamond on a scale with fine-point tweezers, I remembered the day Grandma gave it to me. We were visiting her in her Chappaqua home, and she called me up to her bedroom. I was eighteen. She died not long after that, during the summer before I went to college.

Your grandpa bought this for me, she had said as she held up a small, black velvet pouch. Her advanced Parkinson's made her hands shake in a way that scared me, but I knew something important was about to happen, so I didn't dare look away. She made me open the pouch, because she "didn't trust" her hands, and I thought the contents must be something delicate, like a prissy antique brooch or dangly earrings I would never wear.

I tipped the pouch, and the perfectly round diamond rolled out into my palm. Even in the dim evening light its brilliance was cartoonish. She flipped on her desk lamp, and a thousand tiny rainbows danced across my hand. *Don't tell your mom,* she'd said with a twitchy wink, and I suddenly knew what she was giving me was extremely valuable. Now, twenty years later, I held my breath as I waited for the snooty jeweler to tell me just how much it was worth.

"It's as close to colorless as I've ever seen," the jeweler said, not really to me. The certificate of authenticity said it was a D, which is the highest color grade. It appeared Mr. Snooty Jeweler Man agreed.

"Why would you part with this?" he asked incredulously. He seemed a little offended that I wanted to sell it. Perfectly clear, round stones were not only expensive, they were hard to find. Even if I had the money, I would probably never be able to replace it.

"Can you sell it?" I asked, ignoring his question. Of course I still wanted it. But I had two daughters, and they needed to eat.

"Without question," he replied. I knew his answer should have made me happy, but instead I felt the sudden urge to cry. I hoped there was no such thing as ghosts, because if there were, Grandma's was surely going to be pissed.

"How long?" I asked, then took a slow, deep breath to hold back my tears.

"I have a couple of clients who I think might be interested," he said. "Give me a week."

And then I choked out the question I was terrified to ask. "How much?" I had a number in my head. If he couldn't hit it, I would have to go elsewhere. I had identified two other jewelers who peddled high-end stones, and their addresses were already programmed into my nav.

He scooted sideways on his stool and typed a quick search into his computer, then swiveled the screen so I could see. I almost gasped. It was worth more than I thought. A year's worth of mortgage payments, with enough left over to keep my kids in dance lessons, pay down our credit cards, and finally get my hair done.

"Yes, that would work," I said simply. Andy's meeting with mega mogul Jack Kimball, our supposed savior, was on the books for the first week in September. But we still had to make it through the summer. And I had no more clothes left to sell.

I said a silent apology to Grandma as I signed the consignment contract. If she didn't want me to sell it, maybe she could gather some of her supernatural friends and make something happen for my husband.

I slid the contract back across the counter, then retracted my shaking hands.

That diamond had been my safety net.

And now I had none.

CHAPTER 17

I wanted to hate her.

But when I was sitting across from her in her Martha Stewart–perfect kitchen, eating scones fresh from her gleaming Bosch oven, and drinking espresso pressed from her top-line Breville, it suddenly became impossible. Because I realized, if my husband were working, I would buy those things, too. *Perhaps we have more in common than I'd thought?*

"I'm really jealous of your house," I blurted, because keeping it in was harder than just saying it. "It's absolutely perfect." I meant it as a compliment, but when I said it, she looked kind of stressed out.

"It's too much," she said. "What do I need with a table for twelve?" she added, indicating the textured, hand-carved, reclaimed barnwood table with matching high-back chairs. Her disdain for her Provençal-perfect dining set confused me. I would have died for a dining room like hers. *Maybe she isn't much like me after all?*

"I'm guessing you moved from a smaller place?" I probed. The Connecticut brick Colonial I grew up in had a table that could seat sixteen. We rarely used it, but my sisters and I still had to dust the chandelier and polish the silver at least twice a year.

She quickly pivoted. "Sorry. I'm just not used to it," she said, avoiding the question. "Savannah loves it here, I did it for her. So she could go to a good school." *Aha!* She had not only moved from a smaller place, but also a lesser neighborhood. I suddenly felt like my husband, collecting facts to find the story. My theory of the rich boyfriend scooping her out of poverty was gaining traction. *How else could she possibly have gone from rags to riches in a few short months?*

"We moved here for the schools, too," I said to show some solidarity. "Where was she before?" I asked, being careful to make it about Savannah so she didn't feel like I was prying into her past.

"Her dad worked at the courthouse in Van Nuys, so we lived near there," she said. I tried to imagine what a residence in Van Nuys might look like. All I knew was that they had a lot of car dealerships there. I had gone to one when we were shopping for my Lexus. "She was at the local high school," Holly added. "It was not ideal."

Her face flickered with sadness, and for a moment I thought she might cry. I suddenly felt terrible. My new neighbor invited me over for homemade scones, and I was grilling her like a two-bit detective. *What kind of heartless bitch have I become?* I was only picking her life apart because I was unhappy with mine. So she got a new boyfriend who swept her out of poverty to live in a pretty house. Lucky her!

I quickly changed gears. "We should have a dinner party!" I said brightly. "Put that table to good use. I'll make a big pot of spaghetti, you make the dessert, we can celebrate your beautiful new home." She seemed unsure so I added, "I'd love for my girls to meet Savannah. Having a babysitter across the street would be a godsend." I didn't have much use for a babysitter, since Andy and I never went out. But it was a nice idea in theory.

"You want to do a party here?" Holly asked, and I suddenly realized inviting my whole family over to her house was terribly presumptuous.

I quickly backtracked. "Or we'd be happy to have you both over, that's probably easier."

"No," she said, "I think having a party here would be nice." And she smiled a little, which made me smile, too.

"We'll do it together! You don't have to make everything!" I assured her. I imagined us cooking together in her glorious kitchen. Everything looked so sparklingly new.

111

As I played the fantasy in my mind, she said something that surprised me. "I've never had a friend like you, Libby." I suddenly felt self-conscious. *Was I too pushy?* As I wondered what she meant by that, she added, "My old neighbors just kind of kept to themselves, y'know? I figured it would be even more like that here, but you're like the nicest person I've ever met."

I felt a flash of shame. Just a few short minutes ago I was trying to convince my husband she was a murderer, and here she was calling me nice? I was the opposite of nice, but in that moment, I vowed to rise to her opinion of me.

"You're the one hosting!" I countered. "But I'll make my husband do the dishes," I assured her, then tried to lighten the mood with a joke. "You don't want him cooking anything, trust me. The hardest recipe he can handle is microwave popcorn, and he still burns half the kernels." She laughed, and a little snowflake of scone popped out of her mouth.

"Oh! I just spit on you!" she exclaimed, covering her mouth. I waved my hand in the air to assure her I barely noticed.

"I have a four-year-old, I'm used to getting spit on," I joked. I took a bite of my scone, then relaxed back in my chair.

I had never had a friend like Holly Kendrick either.

And I was intrigued by where our budding friendship might go.

JACK

Three months ago

"My mother wants us to come for Thanksgiving," Kate said as she rubbed oil on her face. She complained about how she was "drying up" since turning fifty, but I barely noticed the tiny lines around her eyes and mouth—to me she was more beautiful than ever.

"That's fine," I said from my side of the bed, silently hoping no one would be in jail by then.

I didn't like to keep secrets from Kate. In our twenty years of marriage, I'd never had any secrets to hide. I'd never been tempted to have an affair. I didn't gamble, get drunk, or do drugs—not even pot. Every dollar I made went through Kate. She was so good at managing our money that I made her the CFO of my production company. As a board member, she not only knew exactly how much money we had coming in, she also knew where I was, and who I was with, at all times. As the saying goes, she knew where all the bodies were buried. And I used to like it that way. But now it was a problem.

I had friends who were serial liars. They had affairs, and hid money in cash—which they blew at the track, the craps table, the occasional back alley. Big portions of their lives were walled off from their wives, and they were masters at keeping their debauchery secret. "Compartmentalizing," they called it. *What she doesn't know,* they would say, *can't hurt her.*

Did the wives know about the gambling and affairs? Some did. Some also didn't care. I had a co-star who slept with multiple women who weren't his wife during our film shoot. When I asked him about it—*Does your wife know you run around?*—he said simply, *She likes having a ski house.* I took that to mean yes, she knew, but considered a ski-in, ski-out in Aspen fair compensation for her husband's indiscretions.

"OK, I'll get the tickets," Kate said, then closed the bathroom door for privacy. I'd held her hand as she'd had a baby taken out of her abdomen, but she still wouldn't pee in front of me.

I had convinced myself that I was protecting Kate by not telling her about the accident. A man was dead. My role in it was so much worse than anything she could ever imagine. If I told her what really happened, it would ruin everything we'd built together, destroy everything she'd held dear. My end game was to protect Kate from pain, as she'd already experienced more than enough.

So I had to do something I had never done—keep a secret from my wife. To transfer money to Holly without Kate knowing, I would have to find an asset in our portfolio that my wife wasn't tracking. Then, quickly and quietly, I would have to liquidate it. Then I would have to act like nothing out of the ordinary was going on—by getting up, going to work, talking about my day just like I always did. Evan advised me to get rid of the SUV, or at least keep it off the road for a while, but Kate would find that odd and ask me about it. And I would have to lie to her face. Lying by omission was one thing, but making up a bullshit excuse why we spent a fortune on a new car just to have it sit in the garage was something else entirely. I rationalized that moving the car was just as risky as driving it—as I said to Evan, *Wouldn't it be better just to keep it on the road, like we had nothing to hide?* He said *No, it wouldn't,* but I overruled him—that's how afraid I was of having to lie to my wife.

The first part—figuring out how to do the payoff—turned out to be relatively easy. Evan had an idea where to pull the money from, and I gave him the go-ahead to make the transfer. Twenty-four hours later, it was done.

The other part—keeping this from my wife for eternity—that's what would keep me up at night. I had nightmares about that video popping up on Twitter, then going viral for the world to see. Clouds got hacked, people cracked. Our lives were on thin ice now.

I was worried about physical evidence, mental mistakes, that damn video—but I was also worried about myself. Pretending everything was fine was going to be the hardest acting job of my life. And I would have to play the part until I died.

CHAPTER 18

Everybody on my staff loved the script.

I didn't want to read it. Because I had already decided I wasn't going to hire the squirrely investigative journalist who had spent his summer writing it. I did not want a *New York Times* reporter anywhere near me, especially one who was wondering where the hell I was on the day of the accident. And who could unearth that one critical piece of this horror show I needed to stay buried.

It had been almost four months, but panic still surged through my body every time I got an unexpected knock on my door. I had played the scene out in my mind a thousand times. *There's a detective here to see you,* my assistant would say. And she would let him in. And I would lie. *No, Officer, I don't know anything about an accident.* And he would ask me if anyone on my staff could vouch for my whereabouts at 11:55 a.m. on May 17. And then my staff would have to tell them, *Yes, come to think of it he was acting strange . . .*

Maybe I was being paranoid, but I did not want a reporter who was capable of connecting dots hanging around my office. But I couldn't pass on a script everyone on my staff loved without a reason. It was just a matter of finding one. After twenty-plus years in the business, I had become an expert in passing on scripts. We did it 99 percent of the time. If practice makes perfect, then I was a master at saying the word "no."

It was nine o'clock. My first meeting wasn't until eleven, and the reporter's script was the only one in the recommend pile. It was a tight 102 pages, but I only intended to read the first ten. Most people read scripts on their iPads or computers now, but I still liked them printed, on three-hole paper, secured by shiny brass brads. I liked the reminder that a movie script was different, *special*. It was not just a story told by words on a page, it was a blueprint for an immersive experience—one that would be shaped by camera moves, light, editorial trickery, music, and songs. A script on its own was just a suggestion. A producer's job— *my* job as the producer of films that I sometimes also starred in—was to interpret it, then find the best people to bring it to life. A script wasn't like an embryo with every feature predetermined by its DNA. It was a lump of clay requiring an army of artists to shape and color and bake life into it.

That's not to say that a good script is not important. Having a good blueprint, with an exciting premise, memorable characters, and great dialogue, is critical to the end product being worth anything. Producers search tirelessly for great scripts, they are as rare as a snowstorm in September. I hadn't read one for a long, long time. No one on my staff had, either, and I knew they were getting antsy to find something for me. Even if this script was a little better than the others in my pile, it would be easy to find a reason to reject it. No script was perfect—they always needed work. And I didn't want to work on this one—*period.*

I opened the script and began to read. The writing style was crisp and engaging, and the lead character was as intriguing as any I had ever met. The conflict was expertly set up, and I decided to read a little past page ten just to be sure the writer wouldn't be able to sustain it. A lot of scripts start strong, then go nowhere. I fully expected this one to peter out by the end of the first act, like most of them do. Then I could validate my staff for liking it *(great premise!)* but ultimately dismiss it for falling apart.

I continued reading. By the time I looked to see what page I was on, I was well into act two—page 53. My heart was pounding. I couldn't put it down.

I realized I was quite possibly in the middle of that rare September snowstorm. If I knew it, others would, too. I was told I had the script exclusively through the weekend, which meant I had until Monday to make an uncontested offer.

I recalled Al Pacino's brilliant line from *The Godfather* about keeping your friends close, but your enemies closer. If this writer's potential to discover the truth made him my enemy, did that mean I'd be wise to keep him close? Or was I just grasping for a reason to buy this script?

I wanted this scary reporter out of my life, but I was competitive, and we needed scripts. I could probably get it for a song—the guy was not exactly a known quantity, and unlikely the agent knew how good it was, big agents very rarely read. I could secure it with a lowball option, then never look at it again. Producers bought and buried scripts all the time just so no one else could have them. But if I bought it and sat on it, that might piss this potential enemy off, give him a reason to want to hurt me. And that was the last thing I wanted.

I closed the script. I wouldn't finish it.

Because I already knew what I was going to do.

I looked at the pile of other scripts to "consider." And I settled in to read.

PART 3

HOLLY

Three months ago

Savannah stood behind me as I cried my way up the stairs.

Our apartment was on the fourth floor. We didn't have an elevator, so there was no other way to get to it except one agonizing step at a time.

My left knee was bound in a rigid, full-leg splint that was cinched so tight the flesh above it bulged out like bread dough. Any sudden movement sent a shockwave through the incision site so intense it was like getting hit in the eye with a hammer. So I leaned on the rail, took deep breaths, and exhaled my way up.

I reached the first landing, and Savannah handed me my crutches. "You're doing great, Mom," she encouraged. "Just two more flights to go." I hated crying in front of her, but there was no point trying to hold it in. Savannah understood it was all I could do just to stay upright.

I gave Savannah the crutches back as I braced to mount the second flight. Pain was tearing through my leg like a siren, so piercing and relentless it trampled out the possibility of any thought other than *How long until I can rest?* Deep down, I was grateful for the pain. Because on the other side of the physical pain was heartbreak that hurt an order of magnitude worse.

"We've got to get that leg elevated, Mom," Savannah said sternly. I looked down at my foot. It had swelled to the size of a cantaloupe. I nodded and steeled myself to keep going.

After twenty grueling minutes we finally reached the front door to my apartment. I was sobbing so hard I couldn't see. Savannah opened the door and helped me inside. She directed me toward the couch, then ran to the kitchen to get an ice pack.

She propped my leg up on pillows and snugged the ice around my ankle. Then she held up two bottles. "Tylenol or Vicodin?" she asked. I saw she had been crying, too. I took her hand and squeezed it.

"Ice cream?" I responded, and she smiled through her tears. She went to the kitchen and came back with two spoons and a pint of Häagen-Dazs vanilla—the only ice cream worth eating. We always ate ice cream when one of us was down, and a double dose was certainly called for.

"I can't go up and down those stairs again," I warned. "You're going to have to do everything."

"I know," she said. "I don't mind." She took a bite of ice cream, then passed me the pint. I scraped some off the top, then flipped the spoon upside down to let it melt across my tongue. I felt guilty asking my daughter to take care of me, but I couldn't accept help from anyone else. Two friends from my old Bakersfield crew had come to see me at the hospital. They'd brought white carnations, a pan of baked ziti, and a whole bunch of questions—*How did it happen? Did they catch the guy who did it? Are you going to be OK for money?* I guess my mom told their moms what had happened, and they were sent to get details and report back. It was nice to see them, but I couldn't eat their casseroles with one side of my mouth and lie to them out of the other. *I'll be OK,* I told them. *I just need to rest. The police are on top of it. Go home.*

"Thanks for all the goodies," I said to my daughter, who'd already stocked the fridge with all my favorite foods. She was still sucking ice cream off her spoon, so I took another bite. As the sweet cream slid down the back of my throat, I added, "We need to be careful about money. Even more than we used to be."

"We're going to be OK, Mom," Savannah assured me as she took the pint out of my outstretched hand. "He gave me a debit card."

Savannah's words hit me like a slap in the face. I should have been relieved to have a sugar daddy. We certainly needed one. And it's not like I didn't know we had accepted his offer. But eating food that he paid for here in my apartment made the whole arrangement feel frighteningly real.

"Savannah," I said, trying to keep my voice from shaking, "I think we've done a really bad thing." As soon as I said it, I knew it came out wrong. "*I've* done a really bad thing." This was on me. I was the adult. I shamed our family, corrupted my daughter, sinned beyond redemption.

"What he did was worse," she replied flatly, and I didn't know if I should be horrified or relieved. She had found a way to justify it. It felt cruel to take that away from her after everything she'd been through. Plus I couldn't support us. And what kind of a mother would let her own child drop out of school to pay her bills?

Savannah took a bite of ice cream, then offered me the carton. I waved it away.

There was no food I loved more than Häagen-Dazs vanilla. But I suddenly had lost my appetite.

CHAPTER 19

"I like your plates!" Libby exclaimed as she removed them from the buffet. I hadn't asked her to set the table, but she was clearly a take-charge kind of person. I learned that when she invited herself and her entire family over for dinner at my house. "Where did you get them?" she asked as she set them on the table.

"Pottery Barn," I replied. I decided not to tell her I had bought them special that very morning. The plain white CorningWare plates we'd brought with us were flimsy, and I was embarrassed to put them out.

"Oh, I love Pottery Barn!" Libby said in her upbeat, cheerleader voice. I wondered if she was always this enthusiastic, or just really liked dinner parties.

"The place mats are from there, too," I told her, even though she hadn't asked. I had bought the thick burgundy mats that morning, too, along with a dozen cloth napkins and three scented candles. It was a strange experience, shopping at Pottery Barn. I had never been in one before, as I knew it to be two price points higher than we could ever afford. But when Savannah and I moved in, the china cabinet was empty, and I needed dishes worthy of this house and my new friends.

What struck me while plate shopping was how empty the store was. It was enormous—two stories with an escalator up the middle—but I was practically the only one there. I remember wondering how a place like that stayed in business. When it was time to check out, a saleswoman appeared out of nowhere and opened a register just for me. As she was ringing up my purchase, a second saleswoman swooped in and wrapped my plates one by one in thick oatmeal-colored paper. I wanted to tell her just to wrap them in the place mats instead of wasting all that paper, but I didn't want to seem tacky or ungrateful.

"I'd like to go there and get new everything," Libby sighed, and I wondered why she couldn't. I had always thought people in rich neighborhoods could buy whatever they wanted. She had a Rolex—surely she could afford new dishes.

"I think everything's ready," I said. "Shall we call everybody?"

As promised, Libby had brought over a big pot of sauce, and we cooked two boxes of spaghetti in the big lobster pot I'd brought from the apartment. I had never used it for lobster, but it was great for making soup and the occasional pot roast, which Gabe liked to recycle into sandwiches and take to work. I didn't cook in big quantities anymore, now that it was just Savannah and me. The only reason I still had the pot was because it was too big to fit in the trash.

I watched with a tiny puff of pride as Libby surveyed my selection of wooden spoons. I hadn't picked them, but they were still mine, and it made me feel good to be able to share them. My kitchen at our old apartment was so small you couldn't open the fridge and the oven at the same time—the doors would bump—so the experience of making a meal with a friend was all new to me. It was fun having someone to taste test and talk with as I chopped and stirred, and for those glorious few moments I let myself forget how I'd come to have such an impressive array of wooden spoons. When I'd accepted Libby's invitation to get our families together, I thought I was doing it for Savannah—to show her I was trying, inject a seed of optimism in a landscape that had grown cold and barren. It hadn't occurred to me that I might actually enjoy it. As I watched Libby stir the spaghetti with my long-handled bamboo spaghetti server, I was suddenly super glad I'd kept that big pot.

"They're on their way!" Libby announced as she hung up her phone. Savannah was upstairs with her new boyfriend. We had developed the habit of texting each other in the house, and not just because the stairs hurt my knee. Her dad would have never allowed her to be alone with a boy in her room, but I was grateful she'd found someone to adore her. She deserved that and so much more.

"Savannah's coming down now, too," I announced, and Libby raised a conspiratorial eyebrow.

"How do you like the new boyfriend?" she asked in a gossipy tone, and I just shrugged.

"We'll see if he sticks," I replied. I was actually a little surprised that Savannah had said "sure" when I suggested she invite Logan to our dinner party, given that their budding romance was so fresh. I had thought she'd be more private about her new boyfriend—her *first* boyfriend! But if she was ready to share him with me, I had no choice but to share her with him, too. I'd had her largely to myself up until the accident, for movie nights and ping-pong and late-night bake-offs. And of course for these last three months, too, minus the revelry. It was a little bittersweet to see my daughter stepping into new relationships, what every mother wants and fears in equal measure.

The doorbell rang. As Libby went to open the door for her husband and kids, I looked at my table. I had never hosted dinner for seven, so this was yet another first in a week full of new things—new dishes, new boyfriend, new friends, new traditions. I felt a flicker of an emotion I hadn't felt for a long time—I wasn't sure, but I thought it might be hope. Growing up in Bakersfield, I was never particularly proud of the creaky prefab we called home, but I did love how neighbors would stop by with extra tomatoes from their gardens or lemons from their yards. And how it often turned into an impromptu picnic—a pasta salad with whatever ingredients we had on hand, on lawn chairs in the front yard with kids and dogs running amok. For a moment I let myself slip into a daydream of Calabasas being my new, improved Bakersfield. It was foolish, of course. But I didn't know that yet.

"Hi, beauties," Libby sang as she opened the door for her husband and daughters. "Can you say hello to Miss Holly?"

"Hello, Miss Holly," the little one said robotically as the older one waved.

I waved back, and Andy nudged them across the threshold. "Thanks for having us," he said.

"Thanks for coming," I replied, trying to sound like having neighbors over for dinner was perfectly normal.

"Let's take off those shoes so we don't get Miss Holly's beautiful house all muddy," Libby instructed, and the girls plopped down on the floor to remove their shoes.

"Can I help with anything?" Andy asked, and I shook my head.

"Just need to take the garlic bread out of the oven, everything else is on the table." I'd made the bread from scratch. It takes a whole day to make a loaf of bread, plus an overnight for the dough to rise, but I enjoyed it. *And what else do I have to do?* The days were long without a job. Not that I missed staring at a spreadsheet all day. Work was boring. I sat under the same fluorescent light, having the same conversations with the same coworkers, patients, and insurance people for eight hours every day. No, I didn't miss work. What I missed was being useful. That perfect balance of needing a job and the job needing me. Now that I was a kept woman, going back to work was pointless. And so I baked.

"I'll get the bread," Savannah called out as she descended the stairs. Her boyfriend appeared on the landing a moment later, and I tried not to think about what they were doing up in her room. We'd of course had "the talk." She was sixteen—I assumed they were fooling around. I figured she might as well do it here, where she'd feel the most in control of how far they went.

"Why don't we all sit down?" I suggested. Tatum and Margaux looked up at their mom, and she shooed them into the dining room. I had asked her to set all the places the same, so there were no "kid" seats—Libby's daughters would drink from glasses and eat with adult-size forks just like the rest of us. Gabe had always insisted Savannah feel like an equal at the dinner table, not be babied like he had been by his grandparents. *Kids get bossed around all day,* he once told me. *Raise your hand, wait your turn, say thank you. Let mealtime be a break from that.* We had a few spilled glasses of milk along the way, but we got a confident, independent kid out of it. If it wasn't for all those empowering family dinners, the last three months might have gone very differently. I tried not to wonder whether Savannah's boldness would have filled her dad with pride or regret.

"You have such a nice house," Logan said as he reached the bottom of the stairs. "Thank you for inviting me to join tonight." I smiled at him, then introduced him to Libby, Andy, and the girls. As he shook Andy's hand, Libby leaned over and whispered in my ear. "His sneakers cost eight hundred dollars."

I glanced down at them. I had no reason to doubt her, but they just looked like normal sneakers to me. I watched how he pulled out the chair for Savannah, then waited for her to sit. *A nice boy from a nice family,* my mother would have said, even without knowing how much his sneakers cost.

My mother never forgave me for marrying Gabriel. *You're pretty enough to marry up,* she'd said. *Don't marry a marine, marry a millionaire!* But I had no idea how to meet a millionaire. I know it sounds shallow, but part of the reason I wanted to move to Calabasas was so Savannah would meet kids from families with means. Not just so she could marry one, but so she could be one herself. Sure, we had money now. But I had no idea how this would end. I had suppressed evidence of a crime, accepted a bribe, lied to the police. I did it to help Savannah have a better life than I did, but she would only be helped if I didn't get caught. If I wound up in jail where I belonged, she'd need the kind of friends who could afford $800 sneakers.

"This garlic bread is amazing," Logan raved as he helped himself to a second piece, making sure to offer the basket to Savannah before he set it back down. We ate family-style, passing bowls back and forth and all helping ourselves. Libby asked Logan a million questions—*Are you still living at home? What will you study at Harvard? What inspired you to take a gap year?* She even got away with the dreaded *So how did you two meet?* without eliciting an eye roll. She was a skilled conversationalist, peppering her questions with anecdotes about her own schooling, why she chose William & Mary for undergrad and Columbia for her PhD. Andy chimed in as well, describing how he dumped his premed track for an economics degree once he realized what a "bitch" organic chem *(whatever that is?)* turned out to be.

I enjoyed hearing their stories, but I had absolutely nothing to add. As they chatted about favorite professors and books, I tried to make myself as small as possible, praying the conversation would not turn to me. I never went to college. Me and my rudimentary math skills took a job as a bookkeeper right out of high school. I had no idea who William or Mary was, or what you might learn from going to school with them, and I didn't want to make a fool out of myself for asking. Libby was kind enough to only look at me when the conversation turned to simpler things, like my salad—*Were the croutons homemade?*— or what restaurants we'd been to—*If you haven't tried Delmonico's, you must!*—or if I thought *this heat wave will ever break?*

Everything about the evening confirmed what I already knew.

I was a complete and total fraud. I didn't belong in this house or this neighborhood. And I was not going to be friends with Libby.

I was both an outsider and a prisoner in my own home.

They could never know what I'd done, where I came from, who I really was.

I could never be close to anyone. I could never again be myself.

This was the life I'd chosen with my lies and my crimes. The only question that remained was if it was worth living.

EVAN

Three months ago

The changes I was making to Jack's legal documents had to be notarized, which meant letting one other person in on our sin.

I decided not to use my regular notary public, or one that would come to my house, choosing a high-volume UPS Store instead. I dressed down so I wouldn't be memorable and showed up for my appointment early so as not to risk pissing anyone off.

As was the case with most rich people, Jack's money was all spread out. He had business accounts, investment accounts, real estate holdings, a personal savings account, a flow-through S corporation, a joint checking account with Kate, an equity line of credit, and—just in case all hell broke loose—a safe full of hundreds in his closet.

Jack's cash flow was an intricate matrix of wire transfers taking money in through one entity and paying it out through another. Money was deposited into Jack's business account from the studio. The business account paid him a salary through his S corp. If he produced a movie, we set up a production account just for that picture, and he got an additional salary, or salaries—depending on how many jobs he was doing—that flowed through his S corp to whatever account he specified.

Jack had a business manager and a CPA, but all transactions were monitored by Jack's wife, Kate. In her job as CFO of Jack's company, she authorized every transaction and audited the books every month for accuracy. She personally approved the movement of every dollar in and out of their accounts. In normal times, this was a huge weight off Jack's shoulders. But now it was a problem. Because Jack needed money. More money than was in that safe. And he couldn't tell his wife.

There was one account the Mrs. didn't monitor. She didn't monitor it because she understood that it was not to be touched. It was the trust fund Jack had set up for their son. Money was put into this account but was never taken out.

Jack started depositing money into his only son's trust fund the day he was born. Now, after many movies and many years, it had grown to over $5 million. Jack and Kate went to extreme measures to keep this money safe. No couple plans to get divorced, but in the event they ever had to divide their estate, Jack and Kate wanted to make sure their son's money could not be touched, even by the two of them. So they made me the trustee. I had total control over it until their son turned eighteen. I never imagined I would do anything but gift it to him.

But Jack told me I would no longer be giving this money to his son. Instead, I was to give it to Holly. Every last cent. I was to change the terms of the trust without telling anyone, including Kate.

"Sign here," the gray-haired notary instructed without so much as looking at me. I was grateful for her indifference, and I complied in silence. There were so many ways this could end badly. It wouldn't take much for our circle of trust to collapse, so I tried not to think about the obvious weak link, and how this financial juggling act might break our fragile pact wide open.

I rolled my thumb on the inkpad and stamped my fingerprint in her ledger.

This bribery plot suddenly—*literally*—had my fingerprints all over it.

If one person cracked, we were all going down.

CHAPTER 20

I woke up in a cold sweat.

It wasn't the first time I'd had a nightmare about the accident, but this dream was particularly gruesome.

I was back at the scene of the crash, walking toward the wreckage, just as I had done in real life. As I peered down at Holly's husband's dead body, his mangled limbs suddenly came alive like Medusa's head of snakes, snapping at me with foaming white fangs. The snakes' eyes flashed with rage as they strained against their tether, desperate to bite me but unable to reach. The dead man's bloody brain matter was oozing out of his skull like hamburger meat through a grinder. I tried to run, but as so often happens in dreams, I couldn't move my legs. My feet were cemented to the pavement as Medusa's snakes engulfed my feet, my legs, my torso. I cried out as I braced myself to drown in a rising sea of blood and guts.

It was a little after five a.m. when I gasped myself awake. I was too shaken to go back to sleep, so I got up, showered, and opened my laptop at my kitchen table. As the coffee brewed, I clicked on my email. I saw that Jack had found a script he liked and was considering making an offer on it. He had production legal handle those deals, so there was nothing for me to do, but he copied me so I would know what he was up to. I glanced at the subject line—"possible new business"—then archived it in the appropriate folder.

Holly's credit card statement had also arrived. I had to keep track of what she was spending to make sure the $5 million we had allotted wasn't in danger of running out. We'd paid cash for the house and the car, which meant she had a little under $3 million left to fund her new life. I had the money in index funds with projected annual interest of about 6 percent. If she didn't spend more than $180,000 per year, that $3 million would last her forever. With no mortgage or car payment to make, I thought it more than enough.

I moved the credit card statement to the encrypted server where I kept all the documents related to the accident. Then I opened it. It was my job to know how she was spending my client's money. And to be honest, I was curious.

We had given her two credit cards, one for her and one for Savannah, so I knew which one of them was buying what. I tried not to panic when I saw Savannah's statement. She'd been to the Apple Store, Sephora, Victoria's Secret, Lady Foot Locker, and Louis Vuitton, all in one billing cycle. It wasn't a total surprise, I knew she would splurge. What I didn't know was if her spending would slow down or accelerate. What if she was testing the arrangement? Setting the stage for more demands? Would I dare say no to her if she asked? That video evidence was damning, and she was too smart not to have made a copy. Which meant we had no choice but to keep paying. The situation was as stable as a grenade. And Savannah had her finger on the pin.

Holly, on the other hand, had barely bought anything. She spent a modest amount at a hair salon, $135 at Pottery Barn, a couple hundred bucks on gas. The rest of her charges were at the grocery store. She went almost every day. They were mostly small amounts—under twenty dollars. Except for one charge at a sushi place, all her meals were made in her kitchen with food she bought at Gelson's.

I tried to imagine what kinds of things she bought on those twenty-some-odd trips to the grocery store. I figured a lot of fresh produce, because why else would she have to go every day? Before I showed her the house, I outfitted the kitchen with everything I could think of—German knives, a stand mixer, an electric kettle, a full complement of measuring cups and spoons. Jack insisted that I do everything myself, he didn't want to risk anyone else knowing what we had done. I had never stocked a proper kitchen, but luckily the saleswoman at Bloomingdale's had, and was all too happy to help.

I thought about my own credit card statement, how different it was. I hadn't been to the grocery store once. Most of my charges were from restaurants—lunches with colleagues, dinner dates with women I'd never see again, or, on the nights I didn't want to chase or be chased, with myself alone at the bar.

My brother used to rib me about being an "incurable bachelor." And it's true, I had been a bit of a playboy. I had a lot of disposable income, and plenty of choices of what and whom to spend it on. Jack gave me access to all the hottest restaurants, clubs, and yes, even women, but after a while it started to feel like I was reliving the same date over and over again. My fancy suits attracted women who wanted to be dazzled, and I suppose I wore them because I feared if I didn't dazzle, I might disappear.

But Holly was different. She wasn't chasing anyone or anything. She knew what it was like to grow up with nothing, feel that toxic mixture of longing and shame that comes from watching other people be handed what you had to suffer for. She knew what it was like to find yourself with riches you weren't sure you deserved, and how being surrounded by things you always thought were meant for other people—a new car, a shoe shine, a proper haircut—made you feel like an imposter in your own life. And, like me, she lived with the kind of ferocious grief that came with losing someone who fought to give you a comfortable, carefree life, but died before they could share it with you.

Holly and I were close to the same age—she was thirty-seven, I was thirty-eight. I wondered if we had met under different circumstances, without the stench of the accident between us, if maybe she might have liked me? I never talked about myself to her, of course, so she had no idea how much we had in common. Or how deeply I was drawn to her for her stoic integrity and gentle beauty. I was ready for a different kind of woman, a different kind of life—one that was not all about where to be, but *how* to be. Holly made me realize that. And now there was no going back.

I could never tell her how I felt, that would be wildly inappropriate. But that didn't stop me from wishing I could.

ANDY

Three months ago

When the courier arrived with an express letter, I knew it was bad news.

We were late on our mortgage, and I had at least a dozen unpaid bills. Tatum's trip to urgent care after she fell off the swing and her arm swelled up like a football cost us over $400, and I hadn't paid a nickel of it. The fall didn't break her wrist, but it did cause serious injury to our pocketbook. We literally had nothing left.

I wondered why Libby hadn't divorced me. Then I realized—we couldn't afford to get divorced. Because that involves paying lawyers, and you need money for that. You also need a hell of a lot more money to maintain two residences instead of one. If we got divorced, Libby would be living in a shitty one-room apartment, and I'd be in a refrigerator box.

I signed for the letter, then looked at the return address. It didn't have the word "collections" in it, creditors were too smart for that. They didn't want to tip the delinquent recipient off before he signed for it and risk it coming back unopened.

I didn't recognize the name as someone we owed money to, but that was no surprise. At this point my debts probably extended well into the sphere of strangers. I was about to open it when I saw it wasn't addressed to me. This certified letter that I had just signed for was for Libby.

I got nervous for a whole new host of reasons. *Maybe she had called a divorce lawyer after all?* Her parents never offered to give us money, but they would certainly help her get out of a shitty marriage. Once divorced, she'd probably want to move back home to New York. I couldn't afford a long custody battle, so if I wanted to see my kids, I'd have to go, too. A divorce would effectively end my career. The thought filled me with equal parts disappointment and relief.

"Is that for me?" Libby asked as she appeared out of nowhere. The woman was like a cat, I never heard her coming. Or maybe the torrent of my tormented thoughts was so loud it drowned out the sound of her approaching footsteps.

"It is," I said matter-of-factly, then offered her the envelope. But she didn't take it from me. Her hazelnut-brown eyes flicked up to meet mine. It would break my heart to give up my career, but it would smash it to pieces to lose her.

"You can open it," she said. I tried to read her expression. Normally I was pretty good at reading body language. She had her hands on her hips, which usually signaled confidence, but could also indicate impatience or boredom. Her lips were pinched in a tight smile. People often smiled like that when they pitied you or felt bad about something that happened or was about to happen. All bad signs for me in that moment.

I must have hesitated or looked uncertain, because she egged me on. "Go ahead. It's not going to bite you."

She shifted her weight. If hands on hips meant impatience, it was growing.

I slid my thumb under the flap. The envelope was creamy and thick—the kind high-end law firms use—and I tried not to look nervous as I eased out the contents. It was two pages stapled together. The first page was a letter.

"Dear Mrs. Berenson," I read aloud. "We are pleased to inform you that the 2.5 carat loose round diamond you placed with us on consignment has sold." I stopped reading and looked up at Libby. Her smile had flipped. Her eyes were shiny.

"Oh, Lib . . . ," I said, letting the letter droop toward the floor. A tear leaked out and rolled down her cheek. I pulled her toward me and

Susan Walter

encircled her in a hug. The second page was a check—high five figures, enough to give us room to breathe again.

"I'm not giving up on you," she said into my chest.

Tears stung my eyes as I held her tight. We both knew she didn't have to do this. She could have insisted we pack up and leave.

But she didn't. Because she was gloriously stubborn and fiercely loyal and the best wife a man could ever hope for.

I kissed her hair, and in that moment, vowed to get us back on track—by working my ass off and writing a script the great Jack Kimball couldn't turn down.

CHAPTER 21

It was Monday afternoon, and we still hadn't heard from Jack.

He'd had the script exclusively for a week, and today was the deadline.

I waited until after lunch, then called Laura, my agent. She hadn't heard anything, and her attempt to cheer me up only made me feel worse. "If he doesn't want it, there are plenty of other buyers," she encouraged. But I knew how this would go. Laura would have to huddle with her colleagues and make a list of who else might "respond" to the material. That would take a week. Then she would have to call all the potential interested parties to tease that something big was coming. That would take another week, possibly more, depending on how many companies she was targeting. Then, in a coordinated attack, she would send the script to the five, ten, or however many potential buyers she had lined up. Then we would wait for them to read it.

It would take another two weeks minimum for responses to start coming in. Whoever Laura sent the script to would either pass or send it up the line to their boss or bosses. That's where most spec sales fizzled out. It only took one person at a given company to say no for a project to die. And there was always one.

I had written this script specifically for Jack. The protagonist—a scrappy CIA agent in a strained marriage (which I wrote vividly from personal experience)—was engineered to showcase Jack's particular brand of stoic charisma. It was an expensive movie to make, with its exotic European locations and big action scenes, and so wouldn't move forward without a star. Hollywood didn't make many stars. If Jack didn't want to play the lead, our odds of landing another actor with his star power were slimmer than a lame horse winning the Kentucky Derby.

Libby had taken control of our finances so I could spend the summer writing. It made sense, given that she and her diamond were the breadwinners this year, and I was all too happy to have the chore of juggling bills off my plate. I knew there were things she had gone without for many months, and she certainly deserved them, but with no guarantees I was ever going to work again, I knew she wouldn't indulge. She didn't complain, but I could tell she wasn't happy. I can't say I wished she hadn't sold her rock, because I don't know how we would have stayed afloat if she hadn't. But her patience was growing thin. We had burned through over half of our windfall in three short months. Watching our bank balance drop every month put us both on edge. And if this spec didn't sell, things were going to get a whole lot worse.

I holed up in the garage to wait for news, checking my phone every fifteen minutes to make sure I hadn't missed an email or call. I had run out of things to build, so was organizing my tools. I was hungry, but I didn't dare venture back into the house. Libby was probably in the kitchen making dinner. It was almost five o'clock—we sat down as a family between five thirty and six. Libby was an excellent cook, and for that I was truly grateful. It would have been a really long year if she wasn't.

Another two cycles of phone checking went by, then Margaux appeared in the doorway to collect me for dinner. Libby had made chicken Kiev, a favorite of the kids. She served the creamy stuffed chicken with a crisp garden salad. I knew from my memory that it was delicious, but all I could taste that night was disappointment.

The girls were chatty, but I was so lost in self-loathing I didn't hear a word they said. I didn't know how I would face the day tomorrow. Until tonight I had dared to hope.

Now I didn't even have that.

HOLLY

Three months ago

The morgue called, asking what I wanted to do with my husband's dead body.

It had been ten days, and they couldn't keep it anymore, the morgue lady said as sweetly as a person can when they're telling you your dead relative has overstayed his welcome. I tried to imagine what it was like for her, having to call people to tell them to come get their corpses. Who would want that job? In my job as a dentist's bookkeeper, I occasionally had to call patients about an overdue bill, and I thought that was hard. I suddenly realized I'd had it easy.

I had been "home" for two days. It was the same apartment I'd lived in since Savannah was a baby, but without Gabe it didn't feel like home at all. I was still in bed when the phone rang, with my leg propped up on pillows—Gabe's pillows. Gabe always slept with two—one under his head, and one under his knees, so his back didn't hurt when he woke up.

Gabe wasn't the cuddliest bedmate, we didn't spoon or anything, but not having him in bed was as jarring as losing a tooth—the hole next to me was gaping and bottomless and stung like salt on an open wound. Gabe didn't snore, but he did sleep with his mouth open, and I had come to rely on the gentle *haaaaaaa* of him breathing to lull me to sleep. With him gone, I had to open the window to let in some traffic noise, because otherwise the silence made my ears ring.

I slid my leg off the pillow tower so I could sit up. "I'm sorry," I told the morgue lady, easing my butt back to lean against the headboard. "But I'm not sure what to do about that?"

I rearranged the pillows, but I couldn't get comfortable. I always liked our mattress, but without Gabe's 165 compact pounds gently tilting it toward the center, it felt stiff and cold. It would have made more sense for me to sleep on his side now—it was closer to the door, and less steps on my aching knee to get to the bathroom. But I couldn't bring myself to do it. So I stayed on "my" side, and when I woke up in the night to pee, I took the long way around the foot of the bed, avoiding the empty space I held for no one.

It wasn't just the nights that were hard. I knew how to work the coffee maker, of course, but I had grown accustomed to waking to a full pot. I broke down in tears when I couldn't find the coffee filters. Savannah had to peel me away from the counter and make the coffee for me. I wondered if she'd made it before she went for her morning run today, because I couldn't face making it myself and I really needed a cup.

"You should have gotten some forms in the mail," Morgue Lady said. Savannah had collected the mail while I was in the hospital, and it was piled on the coffee table. Gabe always opened the mail. If there was anything for me, he would put it on the little secretary I used as my writing desk. I didn't know what to do with his mail, so I just left it all sitting in a heap.

"Sorry," I said again. "I'll look for it," I promised. I dreaded getting out of bed, because that meant facing a whole new set of unfamiliar circumstances. We had a rhythm to our mornings. Gabe would shower first, so the bathroom would be warm and steamy for me when it was my turn. He always hung his wet towel over the curtain rod because he thought the towels would get smelly if we didn't spread them out to dry. The bristles on the electric toothbrush we shared would be damp when I reached for it, and he pretty much always left the cap off the toothpaste. But now the toothbrush was dry, the curtain rod was barren, and the bathroom felt chilly and hollow and strange.

"I can recommend a funeral home if you'd like," the morgue woman said as I cried silently on my side of the call. "Do you live in the area?"

"Not far," I managed.

She rattled off the names of a couple of local funeral homes, but I didn't write them down. Then she explained the procedure for releasing the body, and told me that once I decided on a funeral home, I would have to sign some more forms. "How many death certificates do you want?" she asked. "They cost fifteen dollars each."

Fifteen dollars seemed like a lot for a piece of paper, plus couldn't I just copy it if I needed more? "Just one, I guess?" I said, not understanding why anyone would want more than that.

"You'll need originals to collect any life insurance, social security, or military pension," she warned. "Or close out any bank accounts not held jointly." I didn't think Gabe had bought life insurance or had secret bank accounts. It was possible he had military benefits, but I had no idea how to track those down. Or how social security worked.

"I see. I guess two, then?" I said.

"You can always order more," she said quickly, and I tried not to panic that I would not know how to do this. "Just have the funeral home call me," she said kindly. "I'll coordinate all the paperwork with them." And then she hung up.

I looked over at my husband's dresser. There was still a cup of coffee on it, in the stout #1 DAD! mug Savannah had bought him last Father's Day. I picked it up and peered inside. The coffee had evaporated, leaving a thick layer of sludge on the bottom. There was a crescent-shaped stain where his mouth had been. I could still see the tiny vertical imprints of his lips.

I slid my hand under the handle as I had seen him do a thousand times. As I cradled the mug in my palm, I imagined his hand on top of mine, pressing it into the cup's gentle curve. I closed my eyes and imagined him holding me steady, like he always did.

"Don't let go," a voice called out, and it took me a few seconds to realize it was mine. *Who am I talking to?* There was no one there but me. Those hands that had held me, steered me, loved me, were rotting in the morgue, along with the shoulders I used to lean on and the eyes that always saw beauty in me, even on my ugly days.

I gripped the mug with both hands and pulled the cold ceramic shell to my chest. "Don't let go," I repeated, then realized maybe the command was meant for me? My husband wasn't hanging on to this life anymore, the morgue lady made that crystal clear. But just because he had slipped away, didn't mean he was out of my reach. We were soul mates, I knew it from the moment we met. The soul was eternal—my Sunday school teacher taught me that. Gabe was not gone, he had just moved on. I couldn't bring him back, but I could follow him where he went.

I opened my eyes. I'd lived in this apartment for fifteen years, but suddenly nothing about it was familiar to me.

I didn't belong here anymore, that was clear.

The only question was how far I would have to go to find home again.

CHAPTER 22

I had taken three of the Vicodin they had prescribed me, which meant I should have seventeen left.

Savannah was at a track meet. Normally I would have gone, but when I thought about trying to navigate slippery metal bleachers with a leg that could barely bend, I lost my nerve. I had a temporary handicap placard, but sometimes they just parked you in an open field. Everybody had a reason for "needing" to park close—*I have stuff to unload, I have my dog in the car, I need to be somewhere right after.* I couldn't expect special privileges, even with the placard. And I wasn't good on uneven surfaces, I'd found that out the hard way.

"Take one every four to six hours as needed for pain," the label said. I popped off the top, then poured the pills out onto a plate—one of my old CorningWare ones, not one of the fancy ones from Pottery Barn, though this arguably was a special occasion. The pills were chalky and white, and left a powdery residue on my fingers. My brother had died from an overdose. One might conclude it ran in the family.

I gazed out the front window, into the yard. I never did find out what kind of flowers those were. I might have enjoyed doing some gardening when my knee was better. I had a good instinct for plants. Back at our old place we sometimes grew tomatoes on the fire escape. We always had the best ones. They were so sweet we ate them like apples, right off the vine.

I thought about Savannah, about how easy it was for her to settle into this new life. Logan was the center of her universe now. They spent every waking minute together, I rarely saw her without him. If Gabe were alive, he'd insist on meeting the parents to be sure they were kind and decent people. It's not that I didn't care, I just knew there was nothing I could do if they weren't. Savannah would find a way to hang out with Logan whether I liked his parents or not. Plus there was no way Logan's mom and dad could be more despicable than me. I was a worthless, limping, lying gold digger. They were certainly a step up, if not a whole staircase higher than I was.

I missed my alone time with Savannah, but I was grateful she had found a boy to love and hoped it would last. I started dating Gabe when we were sixteen. People think you don't know what love is at that age, but I'm living proof that some people do. We were together for two years, then apart for the next four. He was more appealing in the letters he wrote me than any man I met while he was deployed, and I married him the moment he got back. We were twenty-two. Savannah was born that very same year.

I knew their relationship was barely three weeks old, but I could tell by how she looked at him that Savannah was head over heels. He made her happy down to her bones—a good antidote for being with me. I felt relieved when she texted to say she wouldn't be home for dinner or until late, because then she wouldn't have to see me crying, which I did almost daily. I also didn't have to worry about infecting her with my pathetic self-pity. She deserved to be happy. She deserved to be free.

I knew that she loved me, but with Evan paying for everything, she didn't really need me anymore. I certainly wasn't providing for her, quite the opposite. If anything, I had become a burden. Her future was bright. Mine was an abyss.

I hadn't heard from Libby since our dinner party last week, and I knew why—I was a complete and total bore. We were probably close in age, but she had way more in common with Logan, who knew about politics and faraway places and what to say at dinner parties. Libby and I struggled to find anything to talk about beyond our favorite recipes and the weather. Any hope I had of us being friends was gone by dessert. I couldn't relate to her stories about heading off to college and starting a career. And I had nothing to offer her but lies.

I counted out the Vicodin, then lined them up like little soldiers on the plate. There were eighteen, not seventeen. They must have given me one extra by mistake. I figured nine or ten would do the trick, but I'd take as many as I could get down.

I didn't write a note, what was there to say? The only person on this earth I cared about would know why I was doing this. Between Logan and Evan, she would build a life not weighed down by me.

I took the pills one at a time.

Then went upstairs to my bed to wait for death.

EVAN

Three months ago

I didn't know the first thing about buying a house.

I knew how it worked, of course. Find one that's available, make an offer, put down a deposit, go into escrow, have an inspection. I knew how to do all of that. I just didn't know how to *choose* a house, especially one that wasn't for me.

I lived in a beachfront condo. When you grow up in New England surrounded by woods, the idea of seeing the ocean every day is irresistible. I had underground parking, a doorman, twenty-four-hour concierge service—it was more like a hotel than a home. But it worked for me, and was low maintenance. I didn't have to worry about cutting the grass or who was going to get my mail when I had business out of town, the HOA took care of everything. I didn't pick it to impress potential girlfriends, but on the rare occasion I brought one home it did the trick.

But I wasn't shopping for a cool pad with curb appeal this time. I was shopping for a home. It had to be someplace a family would live—warm and inviting, a place to create memories and feel safe.

I thought about my childhood house. It was barely more than a mobile home, with its leaky aluminum windows and slick vinyl floors. But my mom did her best to make it feel cozy. She sewed curtains from retired bedspreads and disguised our cheap living room furniture with afghans she crocheted herself. But the thing that really made it feel like a home was the food. There was always something cooking on the stove.

When I came home from school, I went straight to the kitchen. Most of our "How was your day?" conversations happened when I was burrowing in the refrigerator and Mom was standing over a pot of soup.

My condo was vastly superior to the creaky tract home of my childhood, but it always just felt like a place to live. It had a gourmet kitchen, but I rarely used it. My built-in Sub-Zero was stocked with beer and bottled water. I had a Thermador six-burner range, but I didn't cook, and nobody had cooked for me since I was in high school. A home-cooked meal is an expression of love, and twenty years is a long time to go without one.

I started my house search on a real estate site to get a sense of what was available in the neighborhood Holly liked, and what it would cost. I had intended to just skim through the listings, but house hunting—even for someone else—was unexpectedly addicting. As I scrolled through pictures of lush yards, sparkling pools, and expansive master suites, I slipped into fantasies of living there myself. Of course it was absurd—it was just me, what did I need with a four-bedroom house? I barely used the extra bedroom in my condo. Occasionally I had friends in from out of town, but mostly I used the neatly made four-poster bed as a staging area for contracts when I was working on a complicated case.

Holly said she only needed two bedrooms, but even the smallest houses in the neighborhood she liked had three or four, with at least as many bathrooms. I didn't want her to have to deal with aging plumbing or outdated air-conditioning, so I limited my search to new construction or recently remodeled. She wouldn't have the wherewithal to replace a leaky roof, so whatever I got needed to have a new one.

I knew the house the moment I saw it. It was elegant but romantic, with beguiling gables and swirls of flowers hugging the front walk. It wasn't new, but the previous owners had completely gutted it, installing new everything—floors, windows, light fixtures, appliances. It was a "smart home," which meant it was wired with sensors that would alert the alarm company, and ultimately me, if she left the garage door open or if a smoke alarm went off. I had no intention of spying on Holly, but we were paying for the house—if someone was climbing through an open window, or the sprinklers stayed on for hours on end, I needed to know about it.

But what sealed the deal for me was the kitchen. When I'd asked Holly what kind of house she wanted, she'd mentioned two things: Calabasas neighborhood and a cook's kitchen. She wanted a kitchen she could make dinner in, she'd told me, because she cooked every night. The oven needed to be "decent," she'd said, because she also liked to bake. This kitchen had two ovens, both brand-new and top-of-the-line.

I called the agent and arranged for a tour. It cost more than I had intended to spend, but I didn't want a house with problems. If something's a bargain there's usually a reason, and I couldn't afford to run back and forth fixing things. Plus I wanted her to have something nice. I thought she'd earned that. That I liked the house was irrelevant. Because she would never invite me over. Once I handed her the keys, I would likely never go inside it again.

I took the tour, then immediately made a cash offer.

I don't know why I was excited when they accepted it, I wasn't going to live there.

I had a perfectly nice place to live, but I suddenly realized I wanted more. Not just a home. But also someone to come home to.

But it wasn't my time to dream. I would give Holly the home she deserved. Then go back to my HOA and Sub-Zero full of beer.

CHAPTER 23

I was on the freeway when the alarm company called.

"Sorry to bother you," the dispatcher said, "but we got a flood alert at your Calabasas home."

"What's a flood alert?" I asked. It wasn't raining, so what could be flooding?

"Sensors indicate water is pooling inside the house," she said. "An appliance might be leaking, or the washing machine could be overflowing, I'm sorry I don't know, I can't see inside."

I thanked her, then hung up the phone to call Holly. It went straight to voice mail.

I thought about water pooling somewhere in the house. If it didn't get mopped up soon, it would warp the floorboards, seep into the walls. If not dried out properly, mold could grow, and suddenly we'd have a costly repair and a bunch of insurance adjusters asking a lot of questions.

I canceled my plans and headed to the house. Most likely it was nothing—a sensor malfunction or false alarm. Or maybe something had spilled but had already been cleaned up, and the sensors needed to be reset. I hadn't walked Holly through all the functions of her smart house. It was probably time I did, to avoid these false alarms in the future.

I parked across the street, jogged up to the front door, and rang the bell. No one answered, so I knocked—gently at first, then more aggressively. "Holly!" I said to the closed door. "It's Evan."

No answer.

I didn't have a key, but I could open the garage with my phone and enter through there. I felt uncomfortable just barging in, but I had canceled my day, I wasn't leaving until I was sure nothing was wrong.

I walked the curved stone path toward the driveway, which was shaded by trees bursting with vibrant purple flowers. The colorful front yard was one of my favorite things about this house, I loved how in California you could have flowers all year long.

I opened the garage. Holly's car was there, and I felt a flutter of nervousness, and not just because I was barging in on her unexpectedly. *It's my fault,* I planned to tell her, *I should have told you how your smart features worked.* And then hopefully we'd have a laugh.

"Holly!" I called out as I entered the house. "It's Evan." I started down the hall, making as much noise as I could so as not to startle her. "Hello??"

I made my way toward the kitchen. The dispatcher said it was likely a leaky appliance, so I'd check the dishwasher, and the washing machine after that.

I stepped into the breakfast nook. The kitchen was spotless, and nothing was running. I peeked in the cabinet under the double kitchen sink. It was bone dry. I was just about to head into the laundry room when I saw the pill bottle, open and on its side. Next to it was a CorningWare dinner plate. Six pills formed a perfect line across the center of it.

I picked up the bottle. It was Vicodin. And it was empty.

"Holly!" I said loudly. I raced through the dining room, living room, office, and den. Like the kitchen they were all spotless.

I charged the staircase, taking the steps two at a time. By the time I reached the top, my pulse was as hard and fast as a drumroll.

"HOLLY!"

I didn't hear the water running until I was halfway down the hall. The shower was on in the master bathroom. I sprinted toward it.

The bathroom door was open. What I saw shattered my heart like a hammer on glass.

Holly was lying facedown in the shower. Water rained down on her lifeless body, soaking her hair, spattering violently against her water-logged jeans. She was barefoot but otherwise dressed. The one eye that was visible was closed. Her face was ashen pale.

"No, no, no . . ."

I bolted over to her and put two fingers to her neck. The icy-cold water pummeled me as I searched and prayed for a pulse.

And there it was, faint and uneven under my fingertips.

"Holly, stay with me," I pleaded as I kicked off the water and dialed 911.

"C'mon, c'mon, c'mon," I barked at the phone. We were both soaking wet now. I fumbled for a towel and patted her face.

"Hey, I'm going to get you out of here, OK?" Her head rolled lifelessly to one side. Her lips were blue. Panic rose up the back of my neck. I couldn't wait for paramedics. She needed medical attention now.

"I'm going to lift you up, OK?"

I squatted down beside her and wedged my arms under her body. Her arms and legs drooped toward the floor as I hoisted her up and out of the shower.

Adrenaline pulsed through my body as I galloped down the hall. By the time the 911 operator picked up, I was already halfway down the stairs.

"911, what's your emergency?"

The phone was in my back pocket. I couldn't reach it, so I shouted. "I need an ambulance!"

Somehow I'd reached the bottom of the stairs. Holly's wet jeans were slippery, and I struggled to hold on as I beelined for the door.

"You've dialed 911, what's your emergency?" the voice repeated.

"Forget it, I'll take her myself!" I yelled to the dispatcher who couldn't hear me as I balanced Holly on my raised knee to unlock the front door.

A moment later I was out in the searing hot sunshine, charging across the lawn toward my car. As I wondered how the hell I was going to get her in the back seat, a figure came running out of the house across the street. It was the woman who had brought us cookies. This time I was glad to see her.

"Oh my God, what happened?" she said, hurrying over to me. Holly was blue-lipped and soaking wet. I didn't answer, and she didn't ask again.

"Open the car door!" I ordered, and she hurried over to my side. The car was locked, but the smart key in my pants pocket chirped it unlocked when she pulled on the door handle.

"I'll go around and grab her feet," the neighbor said, and in a flash she had the other door open and was easing Holly's legs across the seat.

We clicked a seat belt around Holly's torso and slammed the doors closed.

"What else can I do?" she asked as I jumped behind the wheel.

"Find her daughter, Savannah," I said. "Tell her to meet me at the hospital."

Then I put the car in gear and floored it.

ANDY

Three months ago

We got ready for bed in silence.

Letting go of that diamond felt like someone had died. Not a human being with skin and bones and blood in her veins, but a complex persona that had been meticulously crafted and shaped for almost forty years.

Libby came from money, and had a specific vision for her life—*our* life—that included a showpiece home, luxury cars, first-class travel. These were things she'd always known and assumed she would always have. Having money for ski trips and beach houses and fine jewelry was part of her identity. These things shaped not just how other people saw her, but how she saw herself.

It's not that she was a snob or bought stuff to make her feel superior. She simply had always been surrounded by nice things, so she didn't recognize herself without them. She came to the marriage with a rich portfolio: family heirlooms to furnish our apartment on the Upper West Side, a brand-new Land Rover for weekend getaways, generous wedding gifts from family friends. My income from the *Times* was enough to sustain us in the historic, one-bedroom walk-up her dad secured for us at below-market rent, and her network of friends provided enough dinner parties to satisfy our cravings for nightlife. Our future was secure—bright, even.

But I had this crazy dream, and loving me made her passionate for me to pursue it. I knew her to have an adventurous streak, but I also knew she relished the chance to break out of her cocoon, silence her stuffy aunts and "concerned" mother who warned her that marrying a writer was a recipe for heartbreak. And so we left our yuppie-chic New York life for a chance at fame, fortune, and a self-congratulatory "I told you so."

It may not be very liberated of me, but I wanted to take care of Libby in every way—emotionally, physically, and financially. Part of what made me fall in love with her was that she "just knew" I was destined for greatness. She built me up. She made me feel invincible. Even when things started to go south, she never lost faith. She was like a champion athlete who assumes she can't lose because she never has. Failure was never part of her lexicon, so it didn't seem possible to her. And so it became impossible to me.

But today, the impossible became possible. Parting with a cherished family heirloom was like opening the door to failure, pulling out a chair for him, and inviting him to stay. Yesterday's Libby would never have done that. Today's Libby was someone else entirely.

I watched Libby as she slid her White + Warren featherweight cashmere sweater over her head. Before folding it and putting it away, she inspected it for pills, removing a couple that had formed under the armpits and flicking them into the trash. Yes, she was accustomed to nice things, but she never took them for granted. You rooted for her to have designer threads because she appreciated and took care of them. And took care of herself to look good in them. I understood the temptation to see her as materialistic or shallow, but the possessions she had accumulated over the years were more than things to her. They were intrinsic to who she was—to who she'd always been. Until that day.

I thought back to our first date in New York. I took her to a falafel house, where everything on the menu was less than four dollars. The three two-top tables and all the seats at the counter were taken, so we ate on a park bench between a crying baby and a homeless man who smelled like soup. I thought I'd never see her again. But two days after our ill-conceived date, I got a card in my mailbox thanking me for the "delicious adventure." I was stunned. Not that she'd enjoyed the date—the food and conversation were quite good—but by the overt optimism of the gesture. She didn't have to say *I hope to see you again*, because the prompt delivery of her handwritten note said it for her. She was grace personified, even while sandwiched between a malodorous nomad and a crying baby.

She had her back to me as she slipped out of her bra and into her satin pajamas. She was no less graceful, but the sheen of optimism she once so effortlessly radiated had been worn away. It sounds hyperbolic, and she would never, ever say it, but part of her died that day.

I only hoped I could bring her back to life.

CHAPTER 24

"I think we should move back to New York," Libby said when I got back from my impromptu meeting with my agent.

Since the deadline had passed and Jack hadn't called, I didn't want to waste even a minute finding a new potential buyer for my script. So I hauled my ass down to Beverly Hills to talk to Laura in person.

Everyone who works at a Hollywood talent agency, from the top dog down to the guy who sorts the mail, wears a suit, so I dressed up a little, in flat-front trousers and a button-down shirt. Agents don't expect clients to dress as well as they do, but I always felt self-conscious standing among them if I looked like a schlub. They had parking in the building, so I wore my dress shoes, too.

Normally it takes my agent a week to put a list of potential buyers together for a pitch or a script, but I made her do it while I waited. She was not optimistic about the script's prospects—*this guy doesn't do big-budget action, that guy already overspent this year*—but by the end of the meeting she had a slim list and promised to try.

I stopped for coffee and a sandwich on the way home. I didn't want to be hungry and frazzled when I saw Libby, it would be hard enough to feign optimism even with a full stomach and fully caffeinated.

But it wouldn't have mattered if I came home whistling Dixie, she had made up her mind. She wanted to leave LA. She had given up on me.

I do this silly thing when I have to make a tough decision. I flip a coin. Not to make the decision for me, but to see how I really feel.

Heads, we stay in California and keep grinding. Tails, we cut our losses and go back to our families and lives we once knew. I flipped a coin in my mind and pretended it came up tails—leave California. I should have felt relief. My career was agonizing. And I had no real prospects. But I didn't feel relieved. I felt despair. I was an addict, and I didn't want to give up my drug, even if it would heal my finances and my marriage. But it wasn't only up to me. As a screenwriter, I was also a salesman. I pumped myself up to make one last pitch.

"I had a good meeting with Laura today," I said a little too brightly. "She's sending out the spec, there's still a chance it could sell." I tried not to sound like a desperate Willy Loman, but acting was never my forte, and she wasn't convinced.

"It's not just that," she started. "Something happened while you were gone." Her lip started to quiver. Libby was not easily rattled. I suddenly got scared.

"What happened?" I asked. She sucked in her cheeks, like she was trying not to cry. "Lib, what is it?" I coaxed. Her hands were shaking. I pulled out a chair for her, but she waved it off.

"I think Holly tried to kill herself," she finally blurted, and then she started to cry.

She told me about seeing Evan carrying Holly's limp body out of the house, and how she ran outside to help him. She described how she'd taken hold of Holly's cold, pruney feet, and how she pulled on them to get her into Evan's back seat. "She had us all over to dinner, and I didn't even say thank you!" She was sobbing hard now. I reached for her and pulled her close.

"OK, first of all, we all said thank you, and her pain has nothing to do with you, so don't go there," I said into her hair. I realized I had no "second of all," so I just held her and let her cry.

"It's just not working out how I thought," she finally said, and I knew her despair was not just about Holly. "I think we'd have a better life back in New York."

I thought about going back to a cramped apartment in the city, and to a job that forced me to live out of suitcases for months at a time. I thought about trading my car for a MetroCard and cramming into the subway when I couldn't get a cab. But mostly, I thought about having to tell all my family and friends that the grand California adventure was a failure. That I was a failure. That I had failed my wife.

I was about to try to put this conversation off, say something like *Let's talk about it when you're not so upset*, when my phone rang in my pocket. I looked at her for the OK to answer it. She nodded, *Go ahead.*

I pulled out my phone and looked at the caller ID. It was my agency. I got a little dopamine rush like I always do as I answered. "This is Andy."

An assistant told me, "I have Laura for you," and a moment later my agent clicked on. Her words were like a dam breaking. I had to lean against the wall to keep from being toppled by the tidal wave of emotions that slammed through my chest—shock and disbelief, followed by a blast of pure euphoria.

I turned to look at Libby. Her brows were frozen in perplexed anticipation.

"Jack Kimball wants to buy my script," I said.

Her hand flew over her mouth. She looked unsure so I assured her.

"I sold a movie," I said. "The offer came in five minutes ago."

We looked at each other in stunned silence. And then we did something we hadn't done for a very long time.

We held each other, and we laughed.

HOLLY

Three months ago

I couldn't sleep, so I got up and ran a bath.

The hot water wasn't good for my inflamed knee, but neither was insomnia, and I thought soaking in the tub might quiet my mind.

As scalding water poured out of the tap, I let my tears mingle with the steamy air to camouflage my grief. But it didn't work. Because grief isn't like sadness.

Sadness is thick, like a heavy fog that clouds your vision so you can't see any of the good things around you.

But grief is something else. It's not fog, it's a storm. It rages inside you, tearing at your organs, pulling at your heart, lungs, skin, until they feel like they are going to rip wide open, exposing the most delicate parts of you, leaving them bloody and raw.

Grief is savage, like love. I think maybe it's the same thing as love? It's love that is trapped inside you, a bird that can't spread its wings so it flaps violently in protest until it's exhausted and broken and utterly without hope.

No, grief is not sadness. It's love that is desperately, urgently lost, an intense longing that pools in your lungs and balls up in your throat, so that when you try to talk it just pours out of you like sludge.

I understood now why grieving people turned to God. I didn't go to church anymore, but I read enough of the Bible to know God's capacity to receive love is limitless. He could absorb all that grief-stricken love and bounce it back at you, filling you up, making you whole again.

When I was a kid growing up in the desert of Bakersfield, I used to daydream of living in the woods, surrounded by streams and pine trees that stretched halfway to heaven. I never loved the white-hot heat of the West. If God gave me a second chance, I hoped it would be far away from here, in that emerald forest of my dreams.

Of course I didn't deserve a second chance. I was a lying, criming, worthless whore. I had just lost the only person who would have understood why I did what I'd done. And the only person good and kind enough to forgive me.

I was all alone now. No one could help me. I couldn't share myself with anyone, because no one could know what I really was.

And so I sank down into the bath, and I prayed.

CHAPTER 25

I suddenly realized I didn't want to die.

The timing of this realization was rather unfortunate, because I had just taken twelve Vicodin and I'd likely be dead within the hour.

I was already starting to feel the effect. I was lying on my bed—a beautiful California king with a tufted headboard and sheets from Ralph Lauren—but couldn't feel any part of my body touching it. My arms, legs, head, and torso all felt like they were floating. It was a very pleasant feeling, how you might feel if you were made entirely out of whipped cream.

I almost laughed at my predicament. Because until fifteen minutes ago, when I swallowed all those pills, I could have easily gone on living without doing anything at all. But now, in order not to die, I was going to have to work very hard to stay alive.

Savannah once asked me what irony was. I remember struggling to explain it. Irony is one of those concepts that is hard to define, except by giving an example of it, and at the time, I couldn't for the life of me think of one. Discovering I wanted to live right when I was about to die, now there's irony for you! I made a mental note, in the unlikely event I ever saw Savannah again, to offer this moment as an example.

I don't know if being so close to death was what made me want to live, or if it was something else entirely. Maybe I suddenly wanted to live because, for the first time in over three months, every cell in my body didn't hurt like hell. Vicodin will do that for you. Turns out that when you're not in the choke hold of debilitating pain, being alive doesn't completely suck. I'd kind of forgotten that. The Vicodin-induced full-body numbness had the unexpected side effect of refreshing my memory.

Riding my opioid raft toward death gave me a brash new perspective on things. I felt a surge of pride. I had been hit by a car and survived. I'd had my kneecap removed with a straw and learned to walk again. I lived in a house nice enough to be in a magazine. I had a luxury SUV, a great new haircut, and an oven that produced the most perfectly crumbly blueberry scones you've ever tasted. I had a beautiful, caring daughter who made me proud every day. *Why on earth would I want to die?* I had a great life. Now all I had to do was figure out how to save it.

In order to not die, I was going to need some medical help. Which meant getting to a hospital. If I'd had my phone, I could've called 911. But I'd left it downstairs, because I had planned on being dead—and you don't need a phone when you don't have a pulse.

I felt myself start to nod off. I knew if I fell asleep it was game over, so I forced my eyes open. I told myself I had to get up. My legs were numb, but I managed to swing them off the side of the bed. I couldn't feel my feet, but I could see with my eyes that they had made contact with the floor. *Progress!*

I tried to stand but wound up in a crumpled heap. *OK, so walking is out of the question, but maybe I can crawl?*

I maneuvered myself onto hands and knees. I had never seen my carpet so close up, it was really pretty! The vanilla-colored Berber with pebbles of brown looked like pralines and cream. I imagined licking it. *Not now, maybe later.*

I realized if I was going to go in search of medical help, I needed to wake up a bit. A little cold water on my face might do the trick. And great news! The bathroom was within crawling distance!

Hand, hand, foot, foot—I bear crawled toward the bathroom. My eyesight was getting a little blurry, but I knew I'd reached the bathroom when cool tile replaced scratchy wool under my palms. I didn't think I could crawl into the tub, but the shower was an option, and that was even closer!

My legs were getting really heavy now, but I was a badass widow and the baker of the world's best scones, what did I need with legs? I could G. I. Joe crawl my way to the shower! And that's exactly what I did.

On my knees I was tall enough to reach the faucet handle. I turned it all the way cold, then yanked it as hard as I could.

Water tumbled down on me. I couldn't really feel it, but I could see it, and I lay back under the spray. It was glorious. But it didn't wake me up.

I felt my head separate from my body. For several seconds I was hovering above myself. Then I was in a field, with tall grass in every direction. The sky was every color—white, green, blue, yellow. I was riding a rainbow across a sparkly, starry sky. It was absolutely glorious.

I thought for a moment this might be heaven.

In my mind's eye, I was smiling.

Because wherever I was, I was in God's hands. He would take all that love that was bottled up inside me.

And he would set me free.

EVAN

Three months ago

I went to Holly's apartment to tell her I'd found a house.

We never talked on the phone. I didn't want there to be a trail of phone records linking us together, so all our conversations were in person. This probably seems extreme, but so were the circumstances. I had to take every possible precaution.

I thought about bringing flowers, but then thought better of it. She wasn't my friend. I would be well advised to keep our relationship as transactional as possible.

Holly's apartment was in an older building called Le Chateau. It amused me when these low-end apartments had fancy names. *Who do they think they are fooling?*

I was a little bit shocked to discover her building didn't have an elevator. My heart pinged with shame as I imagined her hauling her bum leg up three flights of stairs. I made a mental note to find a physical therapist who would come to her.

I dressed down for the visit, in track pants and a sweatshirt. I didn't want to call attention to myself. I left the Yale hat at home, opting for a Dodger-blue one instead.

I knocked on the door with no idea what I would do if she wasn't home or still in bed. I hadn't called—*couldn't* call—and I didn't feel like camping out on the stairs all day. But she surprised me by answering almost immediately.

I must have looked surprised, because she said, "I was in the kitchen making breakfast."

She let me in and pointed to the couch—not a couch, actually, but a futon with a blanket draped over it, similar to the one I'd had in my college dorm room. I sat as instructed.

Her apartment was neat and homey and painfully small. Her furniture was cheap but not ratty. Pictures of Savannah crowded the walls—school portraits, Savannah on ice skates, in a dance leotard, on a horse. Sitting there, I recalled the flimsy wood paneling and worn parquet floors of my childhood home. I hadn't realized what a dump it was until I moved out. I wondered if Holly would have the same revelation.

"I made an offer on a home I think you'll like," I began. I had thought she would want to hear about it, but she dismissed the conversation with a wave of her hand.

"I'm sure it's fine, I don't need to see it, not now."

She was agitated. Her mouth was pinched. She was in pain.

"Thank you for trusting me," I said, hoping she would glean the double meaning. I wasn't just talking about the house. She looked at me intently, and I knew she understood.

"Where's my car?" she asked. I told her I'd had it towed, that we would get her a new one whenever she wanted. She shook her head. That's not why she asked.

"What are you doing with it?" she pressed. And I felt some relief. Because I realized she didn't want to get caught any more than we did.

"Dismantling it," I said simply. Since it was operable and parked at the time of the accident, the police had just left it there. So Jack asked a guy who worked on his movies, a Teamster who likely had mob connections, to get rid of it. And for $1,000, he did, no questions asked.

"The police asked me where the car was. I said I didn't know," she said, and I read between the lines—*So don't tell me.*

I nodded. I understood. I kind of wished I didn't know either.

"I have to rest now," she said abruptly. Her head was still bandaged, but the bruising had gone down. I had a sudden urge to hug her, but I didn't, of course.

"I think you'll really like the house," I offered. I don't know why this was so important to me, it clearly wasn't important to her.

"The only thing I care about is Savannah," she said. I nodded. I suddenly wondered what it would be like to have someone to "only care" about. The closest I ever came to putting someone's needs before my own was working for Jack. But he paid me for that. I was loyal to him, because that was my job.

"We're taking every precaution," I assured her.

She opened the door for me. As I took one last glance around the meager apartment, at her dorm room futon and aging TV, I realized just how little she had.

But she had something I didn't. She had someone to "only care" about, something bigger than her pain, her needs, even her loss.

And I envied her for that.

CHAPTER 26

It was a fourteen-minute drive to the hospital, but I did it in eight.

There would probably be a warrant out for my arrest once I got there, after all the red lights I ran, but I didn't think about that. All I could think about was Holly not dying.

The neighbor and I had slid her in on her side so her front was facing out, but when I took the speed bumps in her neighborhood at fifty miles per hour, she bounced onto her back. I knew that was dangerous, that she could choke on her own tongue, but I didn't dare stop, not even to readjust her.

The first two red lights I ran were in residential neighborhoods, so I didn't bother to slow down. The third one was a little scarier. When the cars in front of me stopped at the intersection, I swerved into the left turn lane, leaned on my horn, and barreled past them. I don't know if it was a sound strategy, or I was just lucky, but we came out the other side in one piece. So I did it two more times.

When I finally saw the American flag flying high in front of the hospital, I became a horse running for the barn. The earth could have parted in front of me, and even that would not have stopped me.

I screeched to a stop in front of the "Ambulances Only" entrance and jumped out of the car. I didn't recognize the sound of my own voice when I screamed, "HELP! SOMEBODY HELP ME!"

I tore the car door open and lurched for Holly's seat belt. She had rolled over onto it, and I had to lift her torso with one hand to free the buckle. I hooked my arms under her armpits, and as I dragged her body across the seat, a security guard shouted at me. "Hold on, I'll get a gurney!"

I couldn't wait for a gurney. Holly's face was white as chalk. I flipped her over and hoisted her fireman-style over my shoulder. The double doors swung open as I approached, and I charged through them like a man possessed.

"Lay her down here," an orderly commanded as he wheeled a gurney toward us. I eased her down onto her butt, and he guided her shoulders onto the bed. Her lifeless legs were dangling off the side, so I gently swung them up and laid them straight.

"Did she drown?" the man asked, searching her wrist for a pulse. There was so much adrenaline coursing through my body I had forgotten we were both soaking wet.

"Overdose," I told him. "Found her in the shower." He pressed a button, and another set of doors opened. I followed him as he pushed her through.

A doctor in scrubs jogged over to us. He looked like a frat boy barely out of college, with his shaggy hair and shiny, pink cheeks. He took the stethoscope from around his neck and pressed it to her chest.

"Vicodin," I said helplessly. "I don't know how many." I could feel a lump forming in my chest. This was my fault. The deal we made was my idea. I did this to her. If she died, it would be because I killed her.

"Pulse is 115, breathing is shallow," he said to a nurse who had appeared out of nowhere. He shone a pen light in her eyes. "Let's start with 0.4 milligrams of NARCAN IV push, repeat every ten minutes until she becomes responsive. Get RT to prepare a ventilator in case her respiratory effort doesn't improve. Place a nasogastric tube for gastric lavage. And send a toxicology screen, acetaminophen level, and liver panel to test for hepatotoxicity." The nurse nodded and started wheeling her away. I tried to follow. The doctor stopped me with his hand.

"You the husband?" he asked. And for a second I almost said yes.

"No," I replied, "we're not married." I realized my answer implied that we were together. In a way, we were—bound by something much more permanent than marriage.

"The Narcan should stabilize her," he said matter-of-factly, "but we'll need to do some tests to know the extent of any organ damage once we remove any remaining tablets from her stomach."

I repeated the words in my head. *Should stabilize her . . . do some tests . . .* "What kind of organ damage?" I asked.

"Her pupils were responsive, so brain function looks good," he said robotically, like he was talking about a science experiment, not a human life. "But toxicity in the liver is a concern. She's not out of the woods yet."

I didn't know I was crying until a tear rolled onto my lip.

It was in that moment that I realized, somehow, and completely unexpectedly, Holly had become my somebody to "only care" about.

And I didn't know what the hell I would do if I lost her.

ANDY

Three months ago

The blank page is a wondrous thing.

Many writers fear it. They hate starting a new project. They procrastinate for days, weeks, or even forever.

But I love the blank page. I love being in a state of boundless possibility. I love the reminder that—even as a mere human—I have the ability to create whole worlds. Writing is a superpower. Writers conjure human emotions—horror, sadness, exhilaration, despair—simply by arranging words on a page. Churning up a person's emotions is a great responsibility, and I have never taken it lightly.

When I was just starting out as a writer, I had the audacity to think that what I was creating with my words came from me. I thought the ideas, images, and stories that popped into my head were mine, that my brain had generated them, that I was some sort of wizard.

But now I know that the ability to create is a very different kind of gift. When I write, I am not manufacturing, as one might do in a factory or a lab, I am receiving. My job is not to mine my mind for characters, it's to ask them to visit me, then completely surrender to them. Writing is listening. It's spiritual, in the sense that what I write is not *of* me, but rather flows *through* me. Flipping on my computer and greeting the blank page is an act of surrender—like saying a prayer—then humbly trusting in God's sacred gift.

That's not to say there is no craft involved in writing a book or a script. What I receive is not fully formed. I have to pair the images that flow into my head with words, then shape those words into beautiful sentences, and those sentences into a coherent narrative with a beginning, middle, and end. Creating is a dance with the divine. The blank page is the invitation. The ideas are the invited guests. I use words to wrangle them. It requires skill and faith in equal measure.

Some writing teachers will tell you, if you want to be a writer, you need to write every day. But I don't agree with that. You need life experiences to understand what you are receiving—otherwise you can't authentically transcribe them. You can't create emotional content without experiencing emotions. Original stories are a tangle of what is divinely offered to you, and everything you've learned, felt, observed, experienced. Put more simply, you need to breathe in to breathe out. Living is breathing in. Putting words on the page is breathing out.

I always take a moment when I sit down in front of the blank page to give thanks for what I am about to receive. I make a silent promise to listen and to trust. And then I let it flow.

As I brought my fingers to the keyboard to begin the script that would either keep me in the game or be the end of this grand experiment, I reminded myself to open my heart. Because if I didn't write from my heart, I would have nothing.

I took a big breath in, then one long, glorious breath out.

And my fingers began to type.

CHAPTER 27

The contract arrived in my inbox when Libby was making dinner.

I scrolled through it. It was just a first draft, but I was encouraged that they'd sent it so quickly, because it signaled they were serious about getting to work.

At this stage, there were no guarantees my script would get made into a film, but Laura was going to try to negotiate a penalty if it didn't, which she hoped would increase the chances that it would.

I wasn't getting paid in full yet, but the option fee was fair, and I would get that money right away. I also got a guaranteed writing step, which meant they would pay me to get the script ready for production, giving me a portion up front, and the rest when I finished. The two fees combined amounted to a little over a hundred grand—enough to feed and house us well into next year.

My eventual payday, if Jack moved forward with the movie, was almost seven figures. This was more than "get the girls back in dance lessons" money, it was life changing. It was "pay off the mortgage and get Libby's diamond back" money. And I was going to do everything in my power to get it.

"Guess what I just got from Jack Kimball," I called out to my wife, waving my iPad in the air, open to the contract. It was taco night. Libby was scooping out avocados to make guacamole, and she had a fleck of green mash on her nose.

"Chlamydia?" she guessed, then laughed at her own joke.

"It was only our first date!" I joked back. "I'm not that kind of guy."

"Let's see it!" she demanded as she wiped her hands on a towel. As she went to grab the iPad, I pulled it back out of her reach. She narrowed her eyes.

"I don't have to take the deal," I teased. "We can still go back to New York, it's not too late."

"You know I never really wanted to go back to New York," she said. And I knew she was telling the truth. Because she had an even bigger ego than I did, the last thing she wanted was to give her dad an opportunity to say *I told you so.*

I passed her the iPad. Her hand floated over her mouth. "That's almost . . . ," she started, but then stopped herself, like she was afraid to say the words. So I said them for her.

"A million dollars," I said. "But only if they make the movie." And they very rarely make the movie. The odds were one in a thousand. But I didn't tell her that. I wanted her to enjoy the moment. She'd earned it.

"Of course they're going to make the movie," she insisted, and I just smiled. "It's brilliant! Just like you."

She threw her arms around me. Then grabbed my face and kissed me hard on the mouth. "I'm so proud of you!" she said, her voice cracking with emotion. And then she suddenly frowned. "How'd you get avocado on your nose?"

"From your nose," I told her. She looked at her reflection in a butter knife, and then she laughed.

"Oh dear!" She reached for a towel, wiped my nose and then her own. Her smile made me feel light on my feet. I couldn't remember the last time I felt buoyant like that, and in that moment I realized just how bleak the last twelve months had been.

"Where do we sign?" she asked, eagerly scrolling through the document. Her face was lit with excitement. And I almost cried with happiness. The old Libby was back.

"This is just a draft," I said. "My lawyer has to mark it up, it's going to be a while."

Her face lit up. "So you could get even more!"

I hadn't thought about that. It was unlikely, but I didn't want to burst her bubble. "Yeah, I guess I could."

She got to the end of the document, then suddenly got quiet. Her eyebrows crunched into little caterpillars. Something was wrong.

"What's that face?" I asked. She looked confused, and for a second I worried that maybe it wasn't real, that the meeting, the offer, all of it, had just been one big joke. The thought of moving back to New York with my tail between my legs suddenly reared up like a painful memory, filling me with a dull ache of dread.

She turned the iPad to face me. She had scrolled to the signature page. No one had signed it yet, but this was normal, it was only a draft. *Is that what she is so concerned about? That he hasn't signed it?*

"He'll sign it when it's final," I assured her. "And then I will, too." She shook her head and pointed to the section where Jack was supposed to sign and date.

"What?" I still didn't get it. Her eyebrows arched up like a cat stretching its back.

"Look at the company name," she prodded.

I squinted at the signature line, at the name of the LLC that was hiring me—Jack Kimball's LLC.

"Happy Accident Enterprises," I read aloud.

Again, the cat eyebrows. "Don't you remember?"

I shook my head. I had no idea what she was talking about. She clucked her tongue, closed the contract, and opened the browser. A few clicks later she was on the LA County website. She showed me the public record for the house across the street—Holly's house. She pointed at the name listed as the owner.

"Happy Accident Enterprises," I read again, but this time my tongue stumbled on the words.

Our eyes met. I had a prickly feeling on my arms.

"Does that mean what I think it means?" she asked.

176

I nodded as I spoke aloud what she already knew. "Jack Kimball owns Holly's house."

Her mouth drifted open. "But . . . how? I mean . . . why? What possible connection could Jack Kimball have to Holly?"

I shook my head. I had no idea.

But I had a sudden, pressing urge to find out.

PART 4

SAVANNAH

Three months ago

What is a human life worth?

We learned in tenth grade US history that "all men are created equal," but everyone knows that's complete horseshit. An accomplished life is worth more than a do-nothing life. A healthy life is worth more than a sickly life. Young lives are worth more than tired, old lives. Dad always said we're all equal in the eyes of God, but if that's true, it must be God's best-kept secret, because we sure don't treat each other that way.

I was back in the smelly police cruiser, on my way to the scene of the accident, which also happened to be the street where I lived. When I told Officer Kellogg I left "something important" in my mom's car, I had thought he would say no, he couldn't take me, it was an active crime scene, I'd have to wait. But he must have felt sorry for me, because here I was on my way there.

Other than the occasional crackle of the police radio, we rode in silence. The North Valley neighborhood we were traversing was not LA's finest. As we turned east toward my neighborhood, I peered out at long strings of homeless encampments, dotted with colorful tents, and walled off by shopping carts. As I took in the filth and sadness of my neighbors, I asked myself again: *What is a human life worth?*

I pondered Fancy Suit Man's offer. If I sold him the video and our silence along with it, that meant we could never sue him or the asswipe who sent him. When cases like ours go to trial, in order to decide the amount of an award, a jury has to determine the value of what was lost.

So once again I had to ask: *What is a human life worth?*

Or, more specifically, what was *my dad's* life worth?

Dad never made a lot of money, but he took care of us in every way. He did everything dads do, from servicing the car and keeping the internet on, to cheering me on at my track meets and consoling me with milkshakes when the cheering didn't work. He taught me how to surf, how to play "Jingle Bells" on the guitar, and how to light a campfire without any matches. He bought me dumb gifts like rainbow socks (each toe a different color) and a puzzle with my face on it. And, with the exception of the time he invited a puppy that wasn't housetrained to stay at our apartment for three weeks, he made my mom really happy.

It was not just my dad's life that was part of the calculation here. Fancy Suit Man was protecting someone. If the video was as incriminating as we both assumed, someone worth a whole lot more than my dad would likely be going to jail.

So what was *that guy's* life worth?

This was becoming a very complicated equation.

Mom and I didn't need much. But we definitely needed help. Because Mom couldn't pay the bills from her hospital bed. And we'd need a lot more money than I could make working at the mall.

Of course we would get nothing if the police had already found the camera. Most likely they had—they were detectives, collecting evidence was kind of their job. But if they hadn't, why couldn't I take it? It was mine, after all, Dad bought it for me. You could say it was wrong, but you could also say I had every right.

There were a handful of cop cars and twice as many people standing guard at the crime scene when we pulled up. We parked across the street from my building, and suddenly I couldn't move. I peered out at the street where my dad had taken his last breath. These buildings, trees, sky were the last things he ever saw. How could I ever come here without thinking,

This is where my dad died, this is where my dad died, this is where my dad died, on endless repeat?

My vision blurred as panic attacked like a thousand knives stabbing me at once. I was about to shout, *Forget it, I can't do this, let's just go!* when I heard a man laugh. *Who the fuck is laughing?* I looked out the window to see two cops leaning against their cruiser, smiling and joking like this was some ordinary day. These guys didn't care about my dad. His death was just business as usual for them. In that moment I knew, if I wanted any chance of getting what my dad's life was worth—however much that was—I'd have to go and get it myself.

Kellogg opened the door for me. "You ready, kid?" I answered by sucking up my rage and getting out of the car. If there was evidence to be found, I wanted to find it. If there was a deal to be made, I wanted to be the one making it.

The hot midday sun blasted the asphalt under my feet as I walked toward the Cherokee. I saw dark polyester pit stains under Kellogg's arms as he raised the yellow police tape so I could slip underneath. "It's OK," I heard him say to someone who wasn't me, "she's family."

I shielded my eyes from what I knew lay just beyond the car—shattered glass, a crumpled door, little orange cones to mark the spots where bits of evidence might be—and kept my focus on the Cherokee. *Just look at the car, Savannah, just look at the car.*

The driver's-side door had been removed, so I had a clear line of sight into the car. I glanced at the rearview mirror, where my dad had clipped the golf ball–size camera.

And saw that it was gone.

My heart sank. Mom and I were in the hands of the justice system now—a system that would screw us like it always screwed people like us. I didn't know how many eyes were watching me, but I could feel a lot of them. It would look suspicious if, after making Kellogg drive me all the way across town, I didn't take something.

I looked down at the floor mat. Mom's key chain had fallen beside the brake pedal—a little troll with neon-green hair. It was a stupid thing to take, but I figured it could pass as something with sentimental value, a trinket to remember my dad by.

I crouched down to pick it up. As my fingers closed around the pudgy figurine, something under the seat caught my eye. It was so dark down there I almost didn't see it. The interior of the Jeep was inky black, just like the dashcam—which had fallen off the mirror and was right there for the taking.

As I slipped the little black golf ball that would blow up our lives into my sleeve, I thought about Mom. She would never agree to the man's obscene offer, but she was unconscious, so it was kind of up to me. Hit-and-run was a crime, and Mom would want justice—she'd say Dad deserved it. But justice wouldn't bring my dad back. And sending some rich guy to jail would not solve our problems. But his money would.

As I walked away from the scene with our future up my sleeve, I once again wondered: *What is a human life worth?*

It appeared we were about to find out.

Mom wouldn't like what I did, but I was her only daughter, she would forgive me.

It never occurred to me that she might not forgive herself.

CHAPTER 28

I should have paid more attention to her.

I was so jazzed about having a boyfriend, I completely forgot about my mom. I forgot that her knee hurt every time she took a step. I forgot that her best friend and constant companion had been violently taken from her. I forgot that she was alone all day every day.

I tried not to cry the whole ride to the hospital, but I couldn't stop. Libby hadn't said the word "suicide." She didn't have to. Her face was so puffy when Logan and I pulled up to the house, I knew she'd been crying. She cried again as she described helping Evan load Mom's floppy body into the car. She'd tried to sound hopeful that everything was going to be OK, which was supposed to make me feel better, but only made me feel worse. Because if everything truly is going to be OK, you don't have to say it. And if she'd truly believed it, she wouldn't have been crying so hard.

Libby had offered to drive me to the hospital, but Logan had insisted. I was a blubbering mess, but he didn't say anything. He didn't even look at me. At one point he tried to hold my hand, but I didn't hold his back, so he let go.

I had thought my dad dying was the worst thing that could ever happen to me. But Dad's death was an accident. If Mom died, it would be my fault. I would have killed her with my selfishness. I know kids sometimes think it's their fault when something bad happens to a parent, but in this case, it would be true.

I should have known something was wrong when she didn't show up to the meet. She always came to my meets. She's not one of those moms who pushes her way to the front row and shouts *C'mon, c'mon!* during my races. But she's always there, at the top of the bleachers, watching and silently rooting for me.

But today, for the first time, she hadn't come. And I, for the first time, barely even noticed.

Maybe it was the money that changed me. I used to be a decent human being—caring and respectful. Now I was trash. They say money corrupts. I was a blatant case in point.

I thought back to our old life, the one when we were poor. We couldn't afford designer anything or sit-down sushi restaurants, but my life somehow still felt full. I would have preferred not to have to buy someone else's "previously loved" jeans and sweaters, but thrifting wasn't so bad. Mom turned it into a game: Who can get the biggest haul for fifty bucks? I always won. There wasn't a prize, except the satisfaction of telling Dad I'd out-shopped Mom *again*. We had a lot less, but we had a lot more, too. More time together, more laughs, more just being ourselves. I suddenly realized, money *can't* buy happiness. But it sure as shit can take it away.

I thought Logan would just drop me off, but he parked and came inside with me. Mom had been admitted and was in a private room. We walked there in silence. I was too disgusted with myself to speak. And what do you say to a girl who drove her own mother to try to kill herself? Logan liked me now, but if he knew what a monster I was, he would dump me like rotten milk.

Mom's door was open. She was sleeping. She had a tube up her nose and looked really pale. I wanted to run toward her and run away, both at the same time, and so I just stood there like a dumbass.

I knew from what Libby told us that Evan was the one who found her, so it made sense that he would be there, sitting by the bed. He seemed to be watching her sleep. I couldn't decide if it was sweet or creepy. *But who am I to judge?*

He stood up when he saw me. "Savannah," he said. "I am so sorry . . ." I started to cry. Because I was the one who should be apologizing. He looked like he wanted to hug me, and I wasn't sure how I felt about that. He had saved my mom's leg and now her life. All this time I'd needed him to be the enemy, but what if it turned out he was something very different?

"Hi, I'm Logan," Logan announced, "Savannah's boyfriend." There was a tense beat of silence. Or maybe I was just imagining it, because I knew I didn't deserve a boyfriend, and maybe Evan knew it, too.

"Evan," he said. "I'm a family friend."

Evan took a step back so I could take the place by my mom's bedside. "We'll leave you alone with her," he said kindly, and I saw he was looking at Logan.

"You want to be alone with her, babe?" Logan asked, and I wasn't sure, but I nodded.

I remembered the last time Mom was in the hospital, how I had crawled into bed beside her. I'd stayed all night like that, protecting her as she protected me.

But I had failed her. I didn't deserve her company or her comfort.

I put my face close to hers. "I'm so sorry, Mommy," I said into her cheek, but she didn't stir. I grabbed her hand. "I'm here now."

I was so close to her I could almost hear her heartbeat.

I squeezed my eyes shut in silent prayer. *Please, God, I'll give everything back, please just make her well,* I prayed—not with my words, but with my heart.

I laid my head down beside her and waited for God's answer to my prayer.

LIBBY

Three months ago

"Can I get as many toppings as I want?" Margaux asked, gazing upon the colorful bins of candy at the self-serve frozen yogurt place on the Boulevard. I didn't feel comfortable spending what it would cost to go to the other "happiest place on earth," but the girls were long overdue for a special treat, so fro-yo would have to do. They loved watching the creamy confection ooze out of the machine, and that they could pull the lever themselves. And we all marveled at the exotic list of flavors—German chocolate cake, lemon chiffon, red velvet cheesecake—and made sure to try them all.

"Absolutely," I replied. The assortment of toppings was staggering—gummy worms, Oreos, strawberries, kiwis, chocolate fudge. It was every dentist's worst nightmare. "As many toppings as you want."

"Even if it costs more?"

I heard nervousness in my daughter's voice, and my heart broke a little.

My parents never worried about money. We lived in a nice house with plenty of room for our family of five. My sisters and I never fought over the bathroom because we each had our own. My mom had a study for reading, a music room for practicing her piano, and a dressing room with so many shoes she needed a ladder to reach them all.

When things got old—car, television, living room furniture—we replaced them. My parents sometimes haggled over details—*What color? How big? Leather or velvet?*—but never about how much it cost.

Everything was decided based on what we liked. *Should we rent a ski house in Aspen or Stowe? Should we visit Barbados or Greece? Should we buy a Mercedes or a BMW?* It was never, *Well what's cheaper?* Only, *What do you prefer?*

Most people would probably consider me spoiled. I understand now that it's not normal to always have whatever you want, but I never knew anything different. My sisters and I were not ungracious. We said "thank you" and helped around the house. But we were never denied things we wanted because they were too expensive. I was never afraid of being broke, because having to worry about money was not real to me. Until it was.

Since Andy's career went cold, every choice I made about what to buy was about how much it cost. I chose the spaghetti that cost $0.99 over the one that was $1.79. I bought no-name brands, clipped coupons, and watched for sales. Every purchase was a calculation. If something wasn't a good value, I didn't buy it. This was new for me.

I used to have people to help me around the house, but we couldn't afford that anymore. The first person we let go was our once-a-week housekeeper. I did all the laundry now, mopped the floors, scrubbed the toilets. Not long after we let Rosa go, we reduced our gardener from once a week to once a month. He mowed the lawn and trimmed the trees (I didn't have the tools for that), and I weeded the garden and raked the pine needles and leaves. We stopped going to restaurants and Disneyland. I became the art teacher, and dance lessons were put on hold.

It didn't upset me to have to do these things, yet I felt unhappy. I just didn't know who I was anymore. I didn't recognize the thoughts I was having—*I'll wait for it to go on sale, maybe it's cheaper online?*—or some of the things I said to my daughters—*you can wear that dress again, no we're not buying raspberries.* Who was this person? I wasn't someone who tells her children they can't have raspberries. Or sells her jewelry to pay for food.

But people change.

Sometimes for the better, sometimes not.

"When it comes to ice cream, we get whatever we want," I told my daughter.

Then silently wondered what happened to the me I used to know.

CHAPTER 29

I knew I should bring a gift, but what do you bring a woman who just tried to kill herself?

Obviously not a bottle of wine, that would be macabre. And she was such a good baker, she didn't need my cookies—plus I'd already done that, when I thought there was a man around the house to eat them. Flowers seemed inappropriate—nobody died, thank God. And she had brought me that beautiful orchid, I didn't want to be a copycat.

The old me would have known exactly what to bring. I used to be confident about these things, and about myself. But I had grown to question everything, from what to bring to a sick friend, to what kind of person I had become.

I decided on a fruit basket. Everybody likes fruit—it's sweet and colorful and doesn't make you fat. I packed the basket myself, with apples, pears, kiwis, grapes, and tangerines—best I could do given the season—then wrapped it in plastic and secured it with a cheery yellow ribbon. I waited until late morning, when I knew Savannah would be in school, then walked across the street and rang the bell.

Holly had only been home from the hospital for a few hours, but I didn't want her to be alone that first day back. I wanted her to know she had friends who cared about her, who she could talk to. Yes, I was curious why my husband's A-list employer owned her house, but I would not bring it up. I wanted her to feel supported, not judged. So I would stifle my curiosity and just be her friend.

Holly answered the door wearing baggy USMC sweatpants and a plain white T-shirt. Without makeup she looked so young! If her daughter had looked anything like her, they could have passed for sisters.

"I brought you some fruit," I said, and she smiled a little, like people do when they are too embarrassed to say anything. "I know you probably need to rest, but I didn't want you to be alone today," I added by way of apology, but also so she would know I was not about to let her do this again. Savannah had texted me that the blood work showed no permanent damage, but she would be suffering from what felt like a really bad hangover for at least a couple of days.

"That's so kind of you," Holly said, eyeing the shiny red apples and twirls of green grapes. Then she got suddenly sad. "I can't imagine what you must think of me."

"I can't imagine what you must think of me!" I said, redirecting all shame and regret onto myself. "I knew you were going through a difficult time, and I wasn't there for you, I'm a terrible friend. Forgive me."

She twisted her hair with a nervous finger as she met my gaze. "I just put some coffee on," she started, and I couldn't tell if she wanted to invite me in or get rid of me.

"If you want to be alone, I would of course understand," I said in a tone that suggested leaving her alone was not an option. "But you don't have to be," I continued. "I put my favorite pears in that basket without saving any for myself, they would go great with that coffee you are making!" OK, not very subtle, but I really didn't want her to send me away.

"If you don't mind me looking like this," she said, indicating her makeup-less face. I smiled with relief.

"Are you kidding? You look absolutely radiant!" I countered. "If I had skin like yours, I wouldn't wear a scrap of makeup, ever!"

And now her smile was genuine. She opened the door wider, and I stepped inside.

"I can smell the coffee from here," I said, breathing in the rich caramelly aroma. Her house was immaculate. Or, I should probably say, *Jack Kimball's house was immaculate*, given that I knew he was the one who owned it. I pushed the thought away. This was not the time to reveal I had stumbled upon the identity of Happy Accident Enterprises. I was here as a friend, not a nosy Nancy.

I sliced the pears as she poured me a cup of Peet's best dark roast, and we settled into her sunny breakfast nook. I had intended to keep the conversation light, with talk of my second grader declaring she had a boyfriend, and my befuddlement that the gardenias I planted last spring were all dying. But she wanted to tackle the elephant in the room, so I followed her lead.

"Evan told me you helped him, y'know . . . ," she began, then looked down at her fingernails. I noticed she had let her manicure go, they were chipped and uneven just like mine.

"Right place, right time," I said, trying to defuse the gravity of what had happened. "He would have been just fine without me." I was all too happy to let him be the hero. Truth is, besides steering her waterlogged legs onto his back seat, I didn't really do a thing.

"It's kind of a miracle that he found me," she said, then went on to explain, "I guess he got some sort of flood alert, he thought he was just coming over to reset the alarm." It was clear she still wanted me to think they weren't together. If her suicide attempt was spurred by guilty feelings about the relationship, I didn't want to push. So I let it ride.

"Well, thank goodness for that alarm," I said, then couldn't help myself from adding, "but honestly, I think people have a sixth sense about their loved ones." I told her about an incident Margaux once had in a community pool. A girl who couldn't swim had followed her into the deep end, then started to panic when she realized she was in over her head. My nose was in a book—Margaux was a good swimmer, and there was a lifeguard on duty—but the moment the panicked girl grabbed on to my daughter, I felt an urgent impulse to look up. I was in that water in three seconds flat. "I think we can sense when the people we care about are in trouble," I opined.

"Oh, Evan doesn't care about me," Holly replied. "I know what it probably looks like, but it's not like that," she said. "We barely know each other."

I didn't want to contradict her, but I saw the look in Evan's eyes when he was carrying her out of the house. It was not the look of a man who didn't care. I wondered if her dead husband had seen that look, too, and if it had something to do with his untimely death. I still didn't have any idea how her husband had died. What if he'd found out about his wife's admirer and driven off a cliff? I knew it was dangerous to ask, but my curiosity got the best of me. "So, how do you know Evan?"

Her answer was as surprising as if her head turned into a bird and flew out the window.

"He works for the man who owns this house," she said. And of course I knew who that was. Because my husband worked for him, too.

"Oh! So you're renting!" I said, seizing on the opportunity to change the subject to something less emotionally charged. The fact that Jack Kimball owned her house and employed my husband was a crazy coincidence, but hardly scandalous. Jack Kimball probably owned many houses. He was a mogul, and moguls own properties—that's why they're moguls.

"Do you know who owns your house?" I asked, eager to share the coincidence. If she didn't already know, surely she'd get a kick out of learning *the* Jack Kimball was her landlord. And that my husband also had a connection to him.

"No," she said. "Evan found it, we only deal with him."

I thought about the house being owned by an LLC, and how it was entirely possible she didn't know who owned it, just as I hadn't until a few days ago—and probably never would have, if it weren't for Andy's contract.

"And you never asked him?" I said, setting up my big reveal. I couldn't wait to tell her she had a celebrity landlord. If I sensed she was uncomfortable that I was snooping around, I would just explain that I looked up the public record to see how much it sold for to know what my house was worth. People do that all the time.

"I'm not allowed to know," she said, and my excitement mounted. It made perfect sense that Jack Kimball would want to preserve his privacy. But I figured we could keep it our little secret.

"Because the man who owns this house . . . ," she began, then looked down into her cup.

"What about the man who owns this house?" I asked, thinking maybe she did know after all, and was just baiting me.

She put down her coffee and looked me square in the eye. "The man who owns this house killed my husband."

I nearly fell out of my chair. I must have looked incredulous because she explained, "He lets us live here for free. So we don't try to find out who he is and press charges."

I was too flabbergasted to speak. If what she was saying was true, Jack Kimball—the man who single-handedly was about to pull us out of poverty—was a killer.

And nobody knew it but me.

JACK

I wish I had been the one behind the wheel. I would have turned myself in right then and there. I would have faced the consequences, apologized, endured my punishment.

Yes, it would have been the end of my career, but I've had a good run. I've had success beyond my wildest dreams, provided well for my family, and lived my fifty years on earth to the fullest.

I thought about saying that I did it, but it was too risky. Not because I feared going to jail—I wasn't worried about that, not really. I was worried they'd figure out it wasn't really me. I was at work that day, my employees all saw me. Even if I could get them to lie for me—which I couldn't, and wouldn't—I worked on a studio lot. There are cameras everywhere, clocking who comes in, who goes out. There was no way to say I wasn't at work when it happened. I had been there all morning.

And then there were the phone records. That devastating incoming call that made my breakfast rise up in my throat. I didn't know what I was hearing at first. *Slow down, I can't understand you,* I told him, until I realized something horrific had happened. Then in a stern voice I said, *Hang up the phone and meet me at the house.*

The entire ride home I prayed that I had misunderstood. The words were garbled, mangled by emotion. *Maybe I didn't really hear "I think I killed him."* But then why was he sobbing like that?

The twenty-minute ride to the house was a blur. I was not in my body. My car drove on autopilot, stopping at red, cruising through green. *This isn't real. Things like this don't happen to people like me. Tragedies befall damaged people. I am healthy, hardworking, good. This can't be happening. Not to me.*

A man will go to extreme lengths to protect himself from pain. He will lie, cheat, steal, or even resort to violence in order to save himself. It's how, as human beings, we are wired. It's in our DNA.

Until we have children. Then our focus shifts from protecting ourselves to protecting them. It makes perfect sense. We are today, but they are tomorrow. Our kids are our future, our legacy, a chronological extension of ourselves.

I pulled into the driveway and opened the garage. He was already there, sitting inside the SUV. I could see the outline of his shoulders hunched over the wheel.

I parked and got out of my Porsche.

Then walked into the garage and hugged my son.

CHAPTER 30

"We need to talk," Evan announced when I answered the phone. It was late—after ten o'clock—but he said it couldn't wait until morning. "I'm coming over."

He sounded upset. It wasn't like him to show his emotions, at least not to me. I knew him to be professional, disciplined, reserved. I tried not to panic, but the possibilities scared the shit out of me. *Had someone found a piece of evidence linking us to the scene? Did Holly break? Or maybe it was Savannah, was she having buyer's remorse?*

I kissed my wife, muttered something about having to catch up on some work, and headed to my study to wait. We never talked about the incident over the phone. Only in person. It was our hard-and-fast rule. But I tried to reassure myself—just because he wouldn't tell me over the phone didn't mean it was catastrophic.

I thought about how the accident had changed my life. My son was supposed to be a freshman in college, but I wouldn't let him go, not until I knew we were in the clear. I told him he needed to stay close to home, get a job, let things settle. He wasn't happy about it, but he obeyed.

It was not a big deal to defer his admittance. I made the call to the dean of admissions myself. We had "a family situation," I'd explained. And it was done.

Kate was surprised when our son told her he wanted to defer starting college, but not disappointed. She loved having him at home. He sometimes even joined us for dinner. She cooked all his favorite meals—shrimp scampi, spaghetti carbonara, jambalaya—even though it was murdering my waistline.

My phone chirped with Evan's text announcing his arrival, and I went to the front door to let him in. Kate was in the kitchen making her nightly cup of tea. I didn't think she could hear us over the sound of the kettle humming, but I played it safe. "Thanks for coming," I said, shaking his hand. "Shall we go to my study?"

He knew this formality was just for show, and he played along. "Lead the way."

We walked to my office in silence. *This is what a man having an affair must feel like,* I thought, *sneaking around at night in the dark.* I had made the decision to hide this from Kate the day it happened, and it was too late to go back now. She had no idea I had reassigned our son's trust fund. It was Evan's idea—a way to hide the payout from both the IRS and my wife. And while losing this money surely hurt him, it was far less painful than what would have happened to him if he had turned himself in.

I opened the study door for Evan and indicated for him to sit, but he declined, so we both just stood there. He had called this meeting, so I waited for him to speak. When he finally did, his voice was raw, stripped down to pure emotion.

"I have some difficult news," he began. He looked exhausted. Whatever he was about to tell me had really rattled him. I braced myself for the worst. He looked up at me with hollow eyes.

"What is it?" I asked.

"Holly tried to kill herself today."

Shame bubbled up from the pit of my stomach. I grabbed the desk as my legs went numb. We had talked about her "breaking," but never in a million years thought we would push her to this.

"Jesus Christ," I muttered. I thought about Savannah, how happy we'd been that we'd gotten to her first. We never thought about what it might do to her mother. "Is she going to be all right?"

He nodded and said, "Yes, thank God," then sank down onto the couch. "I got her to the hospital in time to pump her stomach." I let the image wash over me. I deserved to feel the grotesque shock of it. Neither of us spoke for a long, solemn minute.

"Maybe I should talk to her?" I finally suggested. I hated hiding in the shadows like this. Perhaps the best thing to do at this point was to tell her the truth.

But Evan wouldn't have it. "Absolutely not," he said firmly. He was right, of course. My fame and popularity had smoothed many a ruffled feather in the past, but this was bigger than even me.

"There's something else," Evan said, and now I sat down, too, hoping he had led with the worst of it. "Your son came to her hospital room."

And that confused me. "He did what?" I asked dumbly, unable to make sense of it. "Why would he do that? How did he even know?"

And Evan's reply was so absurd I almost laughed.

"He's dating Holly's daughter."

I repeated his words in my head to make sure I'd heard him right, then shook my head. "Logan knows better than to go anywhere near either of them," I insisted. "He's smarter than that!"

But Evan was insistent. "They're dating. He introduced himself as her boyfriend. They were holding hands."

I felt anger rise up the back of my neck. I wasn't sure if it was meant for Evan for saying something so implausible, or for my son, because I thought there was a chance it could be true.

"Maybe it's a coincidence," I suggested, and Evan laughed out loud. "No way."

My anger turned to panic. Because Logan was smart—deviously smart. Which meant he knew exactly what he was doing. Even though I didn't have a clue.

"There could be a perfectly reasonable explanation," I offered, even though I couldn't think of one. Logan was a good kid, a varsity athlete and straight A student. I knew it was hard for him sometimes, being the son of a celebrity—never knowing who your friends are and having to share your dad with the world. But he handled the pressure of being under the public eye well—or at least he seemed to. Maybe I had missed more than I knew during all those months away shooting movies. Had I overlooked something? Was there a side of him I'd never seen?

"Where is he now?" Evan asked, and I shook my head.

"I don't know. He's an adult—" I started, by way of excuse, but he cut me off.

"You need to find him," my lawyer said. "We need to talk to him about what the hell he thinks he's doing."

Evan had never raised his voice at me before. But I let it go. Because in this fraught moment, I knew I was going to need him now more than ever.

SAVANNAH

Three months ago

There was a knock on our door at eight a.m.

We knew the police were going to want to talk to us, we just thought they would come at a decent hour.

I showed Officer Kellogg and his plainclothes sidekick into our living room, then went to the bedroom to wake up my mom.

"Mom," I said as I touched her arm. "They're here."

She blinked herself awake. She looked disoriented. But that was not uncommon these days.

"I'll make you some coffee," I told her as I handed her a bra and a pair of sweats that would fit over her brace. There was no point in asking them to come back later. The sooner we got this over with, the better.

"You can sit down if you want," I told the policemen as I returned to the living room after putting the coffee on. Kellogg looked a little winded from those three flights of stairs, but Plainclothes dismissed my offer with a stoic smile, so they both just remained standing.

It took a couple of minutes and the aroma of fresh brew to get my mom out of bed. She was bleary-eyed but not ungracious to our unexpected company as she joined us in the living room.

"Good morning, Officers," she said. "Hope you don't mind if I sit?"

"Of course," they both said in unison. In the kitchen the coffeepot sputtered, and I used it as an excuse to slink out of the room. I had to get out of there. I felt like I was suffocating. Mom was about to put the final nail in our Pandora's box of secrets. After she lied to the police about what we did, there would be no going back. I reminded myself that our hand had been forced, and that I didn't want her to tell, nothing good would come of it.

"Any details you can remember . . ." I heard one of them say as I opened the cupboard to forage for cups.

I suddenly realized I had no idea what she would say. We hadn't talked about how to handle questions from the police, or any of it, really—how else we could have survived without Dad, what we would do if we got caught. I never asked her if she wanted to go through with it, because what if she didn't? Would I try to change her mind? I didn't want to be broke. I didn't want to be pitied. And more than anything, I didn't want to go back to my old school. The thought of facing all those tears and hugs and *Oh my God, I am sooooo sorrys* was enough to make me want to hurl.

My teachers had already told me I could take my tenth grade finals at home, and excused me from all remaining assignments. So once my mom moved back home, I cleaned out my locker and said goodbye to my friends. I didn't know I'd never see them again, but even if I had, I wouldn't have cared. I hated that place. I wanted to be at a school where you didn't have to keep your head down when you walked through the halls. I wanted to go somewhere with a real track-and-field program, one that had locker rooms with working showers. I wanted to be with people who wanted something more out of school than to just get through. I wanted friends who didn't have to work every weekend and could hang out. And I wanted a boyfriend. A guy from a good family, who could afford to take me out and had a car to drive me home.

But more than all those things I wanted, there was one thing I didn't want—to be the girl whose dad died.

I didn't want people to look at me with that "poor you!" half smile. I didn't want to spend the next two years ducking Principal Price, who I'd cried all over and would never be able to look in the face again. I didn't want anyone to start a GoFundMe page or bring us hand-me-downs or a lasagna. I didn't want to be talked about, pitied, stared at, coddled, or avoided. I didn't want to have to assure people I was going to be OK, because some days I might not be. I didn't want to have to start every conversation with someone saying *sorry about your dad*, or hate them for not saying it. People would say they didn't bring it up because they didn't want to "remind" me—as if I wasn't going to be thinking about him every damn minute of every damn day for the rest of my life.

I wanted to move forward. But more than that, I didn't want to go back.

I fished the milk out of the fridge, then smelled it to make sure it hadn't turned. With just two of us in the apartment, perishables sat a lot longer now. I had already thrown out a pound of deli meat, a half dozen tomatoes, two avocados, and a hunk of moldy cheese.

"I'm sorry, but it's all just a blank," I heard Mom say as I opened the cutlery drawer. I was just about to fish for a spoon when the detective asked a question that stopped me cold.

"Do you know what this cord was for?"

Out of the corner of my eye, I saw Plainclothes pinching a power cord between his finger and thumb. The one for the dashcam. My hand hovered above the teaspoons as I waited for Mom to answer.

"Is it for a cell phone?" Mom asked.

"No, not for a cell phone," Kellogg said. "It's a barrel connector, phones use USB." Plainclothes stepped forward to show it to her. She looked at it and shrugged.

"I'm not much of a tech person," Mom said, and that was true. When Dad showed her the dashcam, she had just rolled her eyes and called it a "ridiculous waste of money." And at the time I had agreed.

"Did you have a nav?" Kellogg asked. Mom shook her head no.

"I always just used my phone." And that was also true.

"What about a dashcam?" the detective asked.

The coffee maker gurgled as the last drops of french roast dribbled into the pot. This was her chance to tell all, get justice for Dad. I squeezed my eyes shut as I waited to hear if she was going to take it.

"It was an old car," Mom said. "We never bought any fancy equipment for it." I opened my eyes to see my hand was shaking. I balled it into a fist to match the growing knot in my stomach. The dashcam was in my room, a mere ten feet from where the cops were standing. And the video was on the phone in my back pocket—it had automatically synced when the camera was in range, no password needed.

"That's too bad," Kellogg said. "A dashcam would have made our jobs very easy. But we have other avenues, don't you fret."

I suddenly realized I'd been holding my breath. I picked up the pot, then exhaled behind the swoosh of pouring coffee. A skilled detective might have sensed Mom was hiding something. But we were poor white trash, we didn't get LAPD's A-team. I didn't know whether to be relieved or pissed.

I vaguely heard Kellogg ask if we wanted to file a stolen property report for the car, and then apologize that that cord, "whatever it was for," was the only thing they had extracted before the car "disappeared."

I tried not to think about what kind of people could disappear a car right under the cops' noses.

But, as I was about to find out, they were capable of much worse than that.

CHAPTER 31

I spent the night in my mom's hospital room. *Just like old times,* I thought as I contorted my body to fit on the narrow foldout cot. They discharged her first thing in the morning. I didn't want people to wonder where I was—Calabasas High kids didn't ditch—so I went straight to school wearing yesterday's clothes and propped up by a triple espresso.

If any of my friends knew my mom had OD'd, they didn't let on. Tricia from precalc hit me up for help with her test correction like always, Nicole asked to borrow my phone at lunch again because she was grounded and had hers taken away, and my English teacher still called on me to explain how Cordelia propels the plot in *King Lear*— and still tsk-tsked me when I didn't know. I was having the high school experience I'd always dreamed about. I loved my shiny new locker, our fancy auditorium with recessed lights and padded seats, the chem lab with enough Bunsen burners so everyone got a turn. I tried not to think about how I got here, because those kinds of thoughts would have ruined the whole thing.

The bell finally rang. Butterflies twirled in my stomach as I scooped up my books and headed for the meeting place. I was relieved to see my mom was already there. She smiled at me when I got in the car, then asked about my day like everything was perfectly normal. I had told her that we didn't have track practice that day, which was a lie. I didn't want her to know I was afraid to leave her alone all day, because that would have made her feel guilty and sad, and we'd had enough of that.

When we got home, she said she needed to lie down, and went up to her room. A few minutes later, she called to me, so I went up and stood at her bedside.

"Sit," she said softly, and I sat down on the bed. She grabbed my wrist, and she held it tight like you would a child's.

"What I did yesterday," she said, "was incredibly selfish."

My throat got tight. I willed myself not to cry. I didn't want to make her feel bad, her feeling bad is how we got here in the first place.

"I want you to have a big, full life. Have everything I never had. I guess I just didn't want to get in the way of that, y'know?"

I nodded, but I wasn't sure what she meant. She was my mom, and the reason I even existed. *How could she be in my way?*

"Anyway, it was stupid, and I'm not going to do it again. I don't want you to worry."

She looked really tired, her undereyes were puffy and dark, so I nodded like I agreed, even though I was worried as shit.

"Libby came over this morning," she said. "I was afraid to try to be friends with her. Afraid to try to be friends with anybody. I don't know, maybe I thought I didn't deserve to have friends?" Her voice went up like a question, so I nodded to let her know I understood.

"Did you tell her?" I asked, unsure what I wanted her answer to be. It was risky letting even a trusted friend in on our secret. But keeping everything all bottled up had proven dangerous, too.

"Not everything," Mom replied, "but enough to feel like I don't have to pretend to be someone I'm not anymore. And you know what? It felt good."

She smiled, but I still felt uneasy. *Is she telling me I should tell someone, too? And how much could I say if I did?*

She squeezed my hand, then closed her eyes. I knew she wanted to sleep, so I swallowed my questions and went downstairs to start my homework. Shakespeare was hard enough when you could concentrate, so I didn't make much headway. As I sat there reading the same three verses over and over, I thought about what she said about not deserving friends. And I realized I felt the same way every damn day, I just handled it by shopping and pretending.

It was getting dark out. I was just about to rummage in the fridge for something to eat when the doorbell rang. I should have known Logan would stop by. He had been texting me throughout the day, funny little memes like a cat clinging to a branch *(Hang in there!)* and dancing flowers singing *(The sun will come out . . . tomorrow!)*. I was such a wreck at the hospital that I'd sent him away. He didn't need to see me all puffy-faced and crying. I wanted him to like me, not feel sorry for me, although it was probably too late now.

"Hi," I said when I answered the door. I tried to sound normal, like everything was fine now.

"Missed you at practice," he said, pulling a bouquet of yellow roses from behind his back. They were the color of sunshine and cut through the darkness like a ray of light.

"Why are you so nice to me?" I asked. I didn't deserve flowers after what I had done to my mom. In fact, they were just making me feel worse.

"Because you're my girlfriend," he said simply. I had never been anyone's girlfriend, or gotten flowers, except for from my parents at my eighth grade graduation. But they weren't the fancy kind like these were, with little vials of water on each stem to keep them fresh.

"Are you going to invite me in?" he asked. I looked and felt like shit, but those flowers looked expensive. I closed the door behind him as he stepped into the entryway.

"How's your mom?" he asked, and I clenched my teeth to keep from crying. I didn't trust myself to speak so I just shrugged. The crinkly plastic sheath around the flowers crunched against my chest as he pulled me into a hug. "It's going to be OK," he said into my hair. He let me go, then looked down at the flowers. "Let's go put those in some water."

I found a vase, and we set the flowers on the kitchen table. "I need to go check on her," I told Logan. "She's upstairs resting."

I hated him seeing me like this. I thought he would take the hint and leave, but instead he asked, "Want me to come with you?"

I didn't, but I nodded anyway. He slipped off his shoes and held my hand up the stairs. I indicated that he should wait in my room while I peeked in on her, then padded down the hall toward her open door.

I took a few steps into the room but stopped short of her bedside. Mom was lying on her back, hands by her sides, eyes softly closed. I could see her chest gently expanding and contracting—she was sleeping. I don't know what I was so worried about. She didn't have any more pills left, I'd made sure of that, and the other ways to do it seemed too complicated and messy. But I was still uneasy.

"How's she doing?" Logan asked when I returned to my room. He was sitting on my bed, trying to solve my Rubik's Cube. I didn't want to talk about Mom, so I changed the subject.

"There's a trick to that," I said, indicating the cube, and he laughed.

"Yeah, you have to be smart!" he said playfully.

The sound of his laugh made me feel tingly all over, and I felt myself relax a little. "There's a sequence of moves, you just have to memorize it." I sat down beside him, and he offered me the cube. Our fingers touched as I took it from his outstretched hand. He lifted my chin. His eyes were the color of water, clear and blue and deep.

"I don't want you to feel like you're alone through all of this," he said. "I'm here. Lean on me."

His gaze was like a drug. I wanted to look away, but I couldn't. I thought about what Mom had said, about how it had made her feel better to talk to someone. I decided to test the waters.

"There's a lot you don't know," I started, then squeezed my eyes shut. I knew I shouldn't say any more, but holding all these secrets by myself was exhausting. And I needed to be strong for Mom, now more than ever.

"So tell me," he coaxed. And I imagined how good it would feel to have it all off my chest. To tell someone, just like Mom had.

"The accident that killed my dad . . . ," I began. I would just tell him the basics, not the whole thing. Just that we were being taken care of, that we didn't see any point of anyone going to jail.

"What about it?" he asked. A piece of hair fell in front of my face, and he tucked it behind my ear. "It was an accident, right?" He leaned on the word "accident," like he wanted to make sure, but I shook my head.

"It was a hit-and-run," I announced. This was the first time that I had said the words out loud, and they scared me. Because it was a crime. My dad had been murdered. And I had played a part in covering it up.

"And they never found the guy who did it?" Logan guessed, and I shook my head.

"No, but . . . ," I started, then shut my mouth. I knew I should stop there. It wouldn't be fair to bring Logan in on this. If I told him what I knew, he'd be an accessory. Just like me.

"You've been through so much," Logan soothed. "Don't carry this by yourself."

His hand was on my thigh. It was heavy and strong. I wanted those hands to lift the horrible weight of all the guilt I was holding and carry it away. Mom said she just told Libby a little—not everything, just enough to not feel alone. *Maybe I could do the same?*

"I have a video," I announced. "From the accident. There was a dashcam in my parents' car." He suddenly retracted his hand. My leg felt cool with the sweat from his palm.

"You have a video and you didn't turn it in?" His blue eyes turned to fire. I suddenly realized I'd made a huge mistake. I shouldn't have told him that part. Now he knew I was a criminal. In a few short moves he'd crack me like that Rubik's Cube, figure out my whole life was a lie.

"It might not show anything," I backtracked. "I never even watched it."

I could see his mind spinning. I could tell he was distressed. *What kind of a person withholds evidence from the police?* I had to find a way to bring him back to my side. It was possible the video was just a blur, that this was all a big nothing.

"I was afraid," I started. My voice was shaking, but I didn't care. "Afraid to see . . . y'know." His expression was blank. I was losing him. When he finally spoke, his words surprised me.

"You need to delete it."

I had thought about that, how I couldn't get in trouble for suppressing evidence if I didn't have any. But that video was the only leverage I had. What if whoever Evan worked for decided he didn't want to pay anymore? We would lose everything. We had already lost so much. We may not have handled this perfectly, but we didn't deserve to be tossed out on the street.

"I can't," I said. "It's complicated," I added, even though I knew it would only swell his curiosity.

He thought for a beat, then made a suggestion that made my blood run cold.

"Then let's watch it," he said.

I looked into those eyes that made me feel safe and loved, that had seen me naked and never once looked away. "You mean . . . right now?"

He nodded. "Yes. Let's watch it together. Then you don't have to be afraid."

I pulled my phone from my pocket and opened the app with shaking hands.

I had no idea what was on that video, but with Logan by my side, I decided to find out.

I clicked on the footage and pressed play.

LIBBY

Three months ago

"Pick three things," Andy said as he snuggled with the girls in Tatum's bed.

"A bunny!" Tatum shouted.

"A broomstick!" Margaux offered.

"One more," Andy said. He was playing the story game, where the girls pick three random objects and he weaves them into a fairy tale—sometimes an absurd one, depending on what they picked.

"A fire truck!" Tatum said, and I knew this was going to be a fun one.

"You can come in if you want," my husband said to me as he caught me watching from the doorway.

"Well I do love the story game," I said, then joined them on the bed. It had been a long time since Andy had done story time with the girls, he was so busy writing these days. But he must have sensed they needed it, and maybe he needed it, too.

"Mommy needs to pick something!" Tatum demanded.

"But we already have three," Margaux said. She was always a stickler for rules, just like her mom.

"We can do four tonight," Andy offered, looking at me.

I thought for a second. "A banana," I finally said, and Tatum giggled.

"Once upon a time, there was a beautiful princess," Andy began. "Princess Elizabeth," he said, then smiled at me. Elizabeth was my given name, of course, but nobody had ever called me that, not even the minister at my baptism.

Andy launched into the story, about the benevolent Princess Elizabeth who oh-so-desperately wanted a banana, and I was surprised at how eager I was to find out if she would get one. My husband was a master storyteller. If creativity were a currency, we'd be rich. *If only it were that simple.*

Both my sisters married well. Cricket was the oldest. She married Gary, who worked on Wall Street and made a fortune reselling mortgages. They lived in a penthouse in Lower Manhattan and had a beachfront home on Martha's Vineyard.

Gabrielle, who we called Gator, was the youngest. Her husband, Richie, did credit card payment processing for huge retail and restaurant chains. They lived in Greenwich and had a boat.

My mother had no shame about encouraging her daughters to marry for "lifestyle." It's not that she didn't believe in love, she told us. It's just "foolish" to fall in love with a man who can't take care of you. Because, as she put it, *If you don't love your lifestyle, inevitably you will fall out of love with your man.* She told us this because she genuinely believed it. And based on the choices they had made, it appeared my sisters believed it, too.

But I was the middle child, so I had to do things my way. I had a romantic vision of finding a man with potential and shepherding him toward greatness. I wanted a man who wasn't fully cooked, so that when he bloomed into a magnificent soufflé, I could take credit for helping him rise. I confess my ego was wrapped up in this fantasy. But I also wasn't attracted to the kind of man whose idea of creating was using money to make more money. I needed someone with more interesting abilities than that.

My mother warned me that marrying Andy might not turn out like I had hoped. It's not that she didn't like him, she just wasn't a fan of unnecessary risks. She reminded me there were plenty of "established" men to love, and even schemed to introduce me to some.

But in the end, I followed my ego and my heart. Mine was the only wedding of the three where my mom cried. And I was the only granddaughter who got a diamond—and we all knew it wasn't because I was grandma's favorite.

So now, as predicted, we were dangling out on a ledge. But my husband was smart. And my kids didn't need concert tickets or a trip to Disneyland to be entertained.

"Suddenly, the princess spied something strange and magical," Andy said. "It was big and red and had three times as many wheels as any chariot she had ever seen."

"A fire truck!" Tatum bellowed, and we all laughed.

"That's right! A fire truck," Andy confirmed. As the girls hung on his every word, something stirred deep in my belly. It had been a long time, but I recognized it as desire.

And I knew—even though times were tough—I had made the right choice.

CHAPTER 32

I had to find out how he died.

Holly said that he'd been killed, and that it was her landlord who did it. I decided not to tell her who her landlord was, at least not yet. The idea that Jack Kimball was a murderer seemed positively insane. And if it was true, did I even want to know? My husband had just signed a life-changing contract with him. If I was smart, I would just keep my mouth shut and forget all about it.

But I couldn't.

So how was I going to find out how Holly's husband had died? I didn't even know his name. Solving puzzles was my husband's super-power. But I wasn't sure I wanted to tell him what Holly had just told me, not with a million-dollar contract on the line. I would have to find out for myself.

I recalled the day when Andy found out Holly was a widow. He had started sleuthing, but I had interrupted and so he stopped. I'm not the jealous type, but Holly was a bombshell, and he likely—rightfully— felt self-conscious taking an interest in her past. I trusted he had abandoned the investigation. Under normal circumstances, any wife would be relieved. But now I wished I'd let him finish the job.

I remembered that he'd been on Savannah's Instagram, so that's where I started. Andy had told me Holly's husband died about three months ago, so I logged on to his daughter's page and started scrolling backward. After enduring countless mind-numbing selfies, I finally got to her post of May 20 announcing the death of her dad.

I scrolled through the flurry of condolence messages. It was a sea of hearts (Thinking of you) and hug emojis (Sending hugs). I was about to give up when I saw a post from someone called Byline_By_Jed:

We honor your dad in this week's paper, Jed wrote. Hope I got the deets right, hang in there. He included a link. My heartbeat quickened as I clicked.

And there it was. An obituary for the departed Gabriel Monroe Kendrick in the *Valley High Times*, Savannah's Van Nuys high school newspaper. There was a picture of the happy family, arms around each other, smiling at the camera. They were dressed up—*maybe some sort of concert? Was Savannah in the chorus? The band?* Savannah's hair looked professionally blown out. Holly was in a black wrap dress. The departed husband wore a dress shirt but no tie.

I read the article, savoring every word so as not to miss any details. Our cherished classmate Savannah Kendrick lost her father in a tragic accident last week. The article was dated May 24. Four days after Savannah's post. The timeline made sense, but there was one discrepancy—Jed wrote that it was an accident, but Holly implied something far more nefarious. I continued reading.

Mr. Kendrick was struck and killed by a speeding car outside their home on Calvert Street in Van Nuys. I paused to look up the address. Holly had said they'd lived in Van Nuys. This detail checked out.

While by all accounts an accident, the budding reporter wrote, the driver fled the scene and at this writing is still at large.

I pondered the words "fled the scene." If the student reporter got the story right, it was not just an accident, it was a hit-and-run—which is both an accident and a crime. The wheels in my head started turning. Could Jack Kimball have been the driver? If his identity was unknown to Holly, why had he bought her a house? I couldn't make sense of it. I was going to need some professional help.

"Andy!" I called out. He was probably in the garage fixing something. He didn't answer, so I unplugged my laptop and headed that way. If anyone could quash this crazy hypothesis, it would be Andy. He'd figure out what really happened, and then we'd laugh at how my imagination had once again gone completely off the rails.

I opened the garage door to see Andy sanding one of Margaux's desk drawers. He stopped when he saw me. "She said it was sticky," he began, and I cut him off.

"You need to help me with something," I said, flipping the computer screen to face him. At the end of the obituary was a headshot of Gabriel Monroe Kendrick in military blues. Andy looked at it, then up at me. "What is that?"

"Holly's husband's obituary," I said. "It says he was killed in a hit-and-run."

I read him the short passage about the driver being at large, then announced, "You're going to think this is crazy, but I think Jack Kimball might have been the driver."

To my great surprise, my husband didn't laugh at me. "Because he owns her house?" he asked.

I nodded, then dropped the bomb. "Holly told me the person who owns her house killed her husband."

"When did she tell you that?" he asked.

"Just now, when I went to visit her."

"That would be a hell of a coincidence," he said. Then he asked, "She really said that?"

I nodded. "She said she lives there for free. Compliments of the man who killed her husband."

He frowned. "But she doesn't know who it is?"

I shook my head no. "Evan is some kind of middleman," I said. "What I can't figure out is, why would Jack Kimball anonymously be taking care of them?" *Could it be for karma's sake? Or is there a more diabolical reason?*

"Let me see that," Andy said, reaching for my computer. His eyes scanned the obituary. "Says he died on May 17," he said, not really to me. His hands started tapping on my keyboard. And then they suddenly stopped.

"What?" I asked. I was eager for him to find the hole in my theory that would debunk the whole thing.

"You're not going to believe this," he said, looking up at me, "but I saw Jack Kimball on May 17."

He had opened up his calendar of appointments. Sure enough, on that very day, he'd had a meeting with the one and only Jack Kimball.

"So he couldn't have done it!" I said, feeling a surge of relief. "Because he was meeting with you!" It would have put a serious damper on things if my husband's new boss was a killer. I once again felt foolish for even imagining it.

"No, he canceled on me," Andy reminded me, "because something suddenly came up. But he was there on the lot. His office is all glass, I saw him through the window."

I was getting confused now. *Does that mean it could have been him? Or couldn't have been him?* My husband was already googling again. I looked over to see he'd typed "Jack AND Kimball AND family" into the search bar.

"He's married with one son," Andy said, clicking on a photo of a younger Jack Kimball with his wife and a boy who looked about ten.

My hand flew over my mouth as I audibly gasped.

"What?" Andy asked. "You recognize them?"

"The son," I said. "What's his name?"

It was an old photo, but the resemblance was unmistakable.

"Logan," my husband said, reading the caption. "Why?"

My heart plunged into my stomach. Because it all made sense now.

"Logan," I stuttered, pointing to his photo. "Logan is Savannah's boyfriend's name."

Andy's brow contracted. I could see the wheels turning in his head. "This photo is from eight years ago," he said. "Which would make him well into his teens by now." I remembered thinking what a good conversationalist he was for such a young man, how polite and composed—like someone who grew up in the limelight would be.

"He's coaching her track team," I reminded him, "on a gap year before starting Harvard."

He clicked through more photos and finally found a more recent one. There was no denying it was the same Logan.

"The coincidences keep piling up," I said nervously, hoping my husband would agree with me.

But he didn't. "I'm not sure it's a coincidence," he said somberly.

"You think he's the one . . . ?" I couldn't finish the sentence. It was just too horrifying to speak out loud.

"It would certainly explain Jack's behavior that day," Andy said. "And his need to make amends."

"But why is Logan hanging around Savannah, then?" I asked. "You would think if he did something like this, he would stay as far away from her as possible."

"Unless he wants something from her," he replied. His expression was grim as he added, "But I can't imagine what that could be."

"We could be completely wrong about all of this," I said. "I mean, we can't just go accusing anyone."

"If he's stalking Savannah and we knew but didn't warn her mom, how would you feel?"

I thought about Holly, how she'd taken all those pills, how vulnerable she was.

And I knew I had to tell her.

JACK

Three months ago

"I only looked down for a second," Logan said. "One second. He came out of nowhere!"

I didn't doubt my son was telling the truth. He was a good boy. He didn't drink or smoke, certainly not during the day, and would never drive under the influence. He knew there was always another way to get home. He had his own Uber account, and worst-case scenario he could call me or his mom. We would always come get him, no questions asked.

"It wasn't my fault," he insisted, and maybe it wasn't. Maybe the pedestrians he mowed down in broad daylight did "come out of nowhere." It was possible. Something similar happened to me when I was a teenager. I was riding my bike down a hill, and someone in a parked car opened his driver's-side door right in front of me. My front tire slammed into the inside of the car door, and my bike crumpled into itself. *Whose fault was it?* Technically I slammed into the car, but the driver opened the door without even looking—there was no way I could have avoided hitting it. But I was on a speeding bike. And nobody died.

So whose fault was it in Logan's case? Just because the guy he hit was dead, didn't mean my son was at fault. In all likelihood, they were both culpable, the dead man and my son. But only one of them lived to talk about it.

"Traffic was bad, so I cut down a side street," Logan explained. "I looked down at the phone to see where to turn, one or two seconds max.

When I looked up a guy was opening the door for some lady. I tried to swerve out of the way, but there was a moving truck blocking the middle lane, there was nowhere to go!" His whole body was shaking. I knew he wanted me to tell him everything was going to be OK, but I couldn't. It was too late for that.

"I blew the door clean off," he said, eyes wide with fear. "I know I should have stopped but, I just . . ." His voice crumbled into sobs. I spun his shoulders toward me and held him tight.

"You panicked," I said. He was frantic, so I tried to reassure him. "That's natural, anybody would." Of course he should have stopped. Fleeing the scene was the worst thing he could have done, but now was not the time for should-haves.

"Don't tell Mom!" he begged. "Please!" This was of course an absurd request. I would tell his mother, and we would both go with him to the police station so he could turn himself in. Just as soon as he calmed down.

"It was an accident," I said, trying to reassure him. "We'll stand by you when you go to explain—"

But he cut me off. "Dad, a man died. We can't go to the police!" His eyes were wild with desperation. The thought of not telling the police was crazy talk. And the longer we waited, the worse things would get.

"Logan, don't be stupid," I said in my stern, parental voice. "We have to come clean here."

"No one saw me," he insisted. "The street was empty, and even if they did, there's no plates on this car yet, there's no way to ID it."

It was true. The SUV was almost brand-new, the plates hadn't arrived yet. It would be difficult to positively ID the vehicle. But just because he might get away with it, didn't mean we should try. I shook my head, tried to show resolve. "Logan, we can't—"

"They'll kick me out of Harvard," he pleaded. "Even if it was an accident, it's still manslaughter, that's a crime. You know I'm not a criminal."

I looked at my son. At seventeen, he was still just a boy, with barely a hint of facial hair and skin as fresh as snow. No, he wasn't a criminal. But hit-and-run was a crime, and the more time that passed, the more likely he would be charged with it.

But before I could explain this, he hit me with another argument. "You have your career to think about," he warned. "The press will have a field day with this." Of course I had thought of that. And he was right, something like this would hurt me personally and professionally. It would ruin my life, my wife's life, and my son's entire future. He had the most to lose here. The fallout would be excruciating for him. But we couldn't just pretend it hadn't happened . . . *could we?*

"I sent Evan to the scene," I said, not sure where I was going with this. "I have no idea what he's going to find there . . ." I stopped short of promising anything. *Could I really ask Evan to try to bury this?*

"It will follow us forever," Logan warned. "You'll be that movie star whose son killed a man." And then he said something that rocked me to my core. "It will kill Mom. She'd literally die."

I thought about Kate. How much she loved her son, what it would do to her to have him crucified by the press, kicked out of Harvard, reduced to a celebrity cautionary tale. Logan was right. If she found out, she'd be crushed.

I dialed Evan's number. He picked up on the first ring. "Almost there, Boss," he said into the phone.

And I said something I immediately knew would come back to haunt me.

"I need you to fix this," I told him.

There was a long beat of silence. I knew I was asking too much. I half hoped he would say he couldn't, or wouldn't. I was about to rescind the command, but he spoke first.

"I'll do my best," he said.

And I knew that if there was a way out of this, he would find it.

And I didn't know if I should be terrified or relieved.

CHAPTER 33

I had a busy day of meetings, but that's not why I was avoiding Evan's calls.

He was waiting for me in my driveway when I got home. "Jesus, Evan," I said, "you can't just hang around my house—"

"Did you talk to him?" Evan asked. I shook my head.

"Not yet."

"You need to tell me what he knows about the deal we made with Holly," Evan said a little too loud. Kate was inside, and I didn't want her to hear him talking to me like that and become alarmed.

"I told him everything," I said, trying not to sound defensive, then completely blowing it by adding, "he's my son."

Before today, I had never once worried about what my lawyer thought of me. It's not that I didn't care, I just trusted him to remain objective and do his job. But something had changed. He was no longer cool-headed and detached. Holly Kendrick's loss had become personal for him, he didn't even try to hide it anymore.

"I had to tell him," I insisted. "I didn't want him asking about his trust fund in front of his mother." Of all the things I had to be ashamed of, hiding this debacle from Kate was the most pathetic of them all. We were supposed to be a team, our thoughts and values in lockstep. I had betrayed her, and that was by far the most sickening thread in this whole web of lies.

"So he knows about the video," Evan said, and I nodded. I had considered not telling Logan. But in the end, I had thought it was important that he knew Holly and Savannah had leverage over us. Which meant his money was gone *forever*.

"I told him we got the camera, but the girl likely had a copy of the video," I said, recalling the day I had sat him down and outlined my plan to keep Holly and Savannah happy and comfortable, with their beautiful new house and bottomless black card.

"That's probably what he's after, then," Evan asserted. "He got close to her so he could find out if she has it, and what she plans to do with it."

I didn't like the implication that my son was some sort of devious opportunist—maybe he genuinely liked the girl.

"How would he even get it from her?" I asked, hoping to challenge Evan's theory. If he was going to accuse my son of plotting something, he'd better have thought this through.

But he just shrugged. "He's your son. You tell me." His voice was flat, and I couldn't tell if he was angry with me for getting us into this mess, or if I was hearing him through the filter of my guilty conscience.

"I'll talk to him," I said, hoping to end this conversation. We had been standing in my driveway for several minutes. Kate would be wondering why we didn't come in.

"He stalked and seduced this girl, even though you explicitly told him to stay away," Evan said. "We need to know what he's up to right now."

"Fine." I took out my phone and dialed my son's number. It went straight to voice mail. "His phone is off," I announced. "I'll try again later." But my lawyer did not let me off so easily.

"What if he's there?" Evan asked. And it took me a second to process what he meant.

"What, you mean at her house?"

He raised an eyebrow. I got a prickly feeling on my arms and neck. I didn't think my son would do anything to inflame the situation, but

I knew my lawyer wouldn't relent until we had tracked him down and made sure.

"Fine, let's go," I said.

I had no idea what my son was up to, or what he was capable of. I tried to ignore the growing feeling of dread in my stomach as I got in Evan's car to go find out.

SAVANNAH

Three months ago

They told me not to go, that the accident had left my dad "unrecogniz-able." But I wanted to say goodbye, and they were transferring his body tomorrow, so today was my last chance.

Mom already told me we weren't going to have a funeral. She didn't want to cry in front of a bunch of people she barely knew. Marines might come, I guess they have a habit of showing up when one of their own dies, and Mom didn't want to endure their hardened faces and somber salutes. The funeral home would pick up the body, he would be cremated, and that would be that.

The funeral director said the cremation would take a week. You would think setting a body on fire would be quick and easy, but appar-ently people's bones take a long time to burn. Mom had to sign a form saying we understood that even though they sweep the oven between cremations, they don't always get everything, so there may be little bits of other people mixed in with my dad. I wasn't sure I wanted bits of some-one's favorite aunt coming home with us, but they said it couldn't be helped. I hoped the person they burned after my dad came from a nice family, so if some of my dad's ashes wound up with them, at least he wouldn't be surrounded by assholes.

After Mom signed the forms, they gave us a catalog and asked us to pick an urn. Even the plain ceramic ones were ridiculously expensive for what they were—*$400 for a vase with a lid?* I could buy a perfectly good canning jar at the dollar store that would work just as well, but "That's not how they do it," Mom said, so I just let her pick. Some of the urns came with twin mini urns, but they didn't put ashes in those, because "Souls split in two different containers can't find their way back to God," the funeral guy told us. That didn't make much sense to me after what they said about bits of bodies being left behind, but I didn't want to make a big deal about it, so I didn't say anything.

Mom said she didn't want to see Dad's body without him in it, so I had to go to the morgue by myself. I called the hospital, and a nice lady with a fancy job title arranged for an orderly in pale-green scrubs to meet me at the hospital and escort me to where my dad was chilling.

We met in the lobby of the emergency ward, then walked in silence to an elevator you needed a special key to operate. As my escort inserted the key into the slot, I noticed there was only one button on the panel. It didn't have an arrow, but I assumed it was "down." I watched enough bad TV to know the morgue is always in the basement.

The elevator was wide and lined with metal panels textured in a criss-cross pattern that reminded me of monster truck tires. The orderly hesitated before depressing the button. "You sure about this, kid?" I wasn't, but I nodded. I had no reason to be afraid. It was just my dad. And it's not like he could yell at me for what I'd done, he was dead. For once I would get to do all the talking.

The elevator stuttered as it started moving, and I gripped my toes in my shoes to keep from lurching forward. The doors opened to a wide, brightly lit hallway, and I followed Mr. Scrubs around a corner, past a whiteboard with names neatly printed in a grid. A dry-erase marker hung from a string, and I almost laughed at the obvious metaphor of how easily a life could be erased.

My escort stopped in front of a door with a little window in it, then turned to look at me. "Take as much time as you like," he said simply, then opened the door.

Susan Walter

The room was narrow, with sterile white walls and a hard tile floor. There were two chairs along one wall, facing the gurney where my dad was resting. He was covered with a thick white sheet, and I remember thinking my big, strong, invincible dad suddenly looked really small.

The orderly went in first, and I followed him in. I noticed he was wearing thin yellow gloves, and I wondered if he'd had them on the whole time and I just didn't notice? Or perhaps they were in his pocket, and he slipped them on when we were walking.

"I'm going to pull the sheet back a little," he said, his voice rising like a question, so I nodded to let him know it was OK. I felt heat rush up my spine as he pinched the sheet between his gloved fingers. It was thick—more like a tablecloth than a sheet—and I wondered if they used special linens for viewing, or if all morgue sheets were this nice. As he peeled the sheet back with silent fingers, it folded in on itself like a gentle wave lapping the shore. I braced myself to see my dad's face, but it was covered by what looked like a dinner napkin. I noticed the napkin sat almost flat, instead of rising where his nose should be, and I tried not to think about where the strong, straight feature I'd inherited might have gone. The orderly flipped up the bottom corner of the napkin, revealing a sliver of Dad's chin, then retracted his hands and took a step back. He didn't say anything, but I understood he would stop me if I tried to move that napkin, and to my surprise, I felt a flood of gratitude that he was standing guard.

I looked at my dad's two swatches of exposed skin—smooth shoulder and sculpted chin. They were so white, more like the color of chalk than skin, and I realized that without blood running through it, a body was just an empty shell. Everything that made this ghoulish white vessel my dad was gone—his opinions, his thoughts, his warmth. This body was just Dad's temporary shelter, which he made his own through workouts and haircuts and silly smiles, but now had no purpose at all. *So where is my dad? Where did he go? How could a lifetime of thoughts and wisdom vanish into nothingness?*

I had come here to talk to him, but standing there, I realized I had nothing to say to this matrix of bones and decomposing organs. My dad's body was just like this room—hollow and soulless, with nothing to grab on to. I had already told him everything that needed to be said in my prayers, things I couldn't say with that orderly standing there. *I did a bad thing,* I'd confessed. *I betrayed everything you ever taught me about being a good person. But I know how the system works, how rich people buy cops and juries and judges. Someone was going to get bought. It might as well be us.*

If he could've talked back, he'd have told me some things were more important than money. Like dignity, honesty, and honor. And of course he'd have been right.

To move forward with the arrangement we'd agreed to, I had to let my dad go. Not the stiffening mass on the table in front of me. I had to let go of what he'd stood for.

"I'm sorry, Daddy," I whispered to my dad's dead body. Pain crept up my throat, but I choked it down. I took a slow, deep breath for strength, then took a step back.

"I'm done," I announced.

My orderly nodded and pulled up the sheet.

And that's how I said goodbye to my dad.

CHAPTER 34

He told me that he loved me.

Nobody ever said *I love you* to me except my mom and dad, and at first I didn't believe him. But he just kept saying it like it was the most natural thing in the world, and after the third or fourth time, I figured he really meant it, so I said it back.

To be fair, I wanted to believe he loved me. Because I loved him. I loved the way he smelled, I loved how his laugh made me feel light as a feather, I loved the way his hand felt holding mine. I felt happy when I was with him, and anxious when we were apart. I thought *Romeo and Juliet* was stupid when we read it in tenth grade, but now that I knew what it felt like to want to die for someone, I totally got it. That's how I felt about Logan. And I was pretty sure that's how he felt about me.

Which is why I had to tell him everything. I wanted to know I was his Juliet, who he would love no matter what I did or where I came from. I needed to prove to myself what we had was real, which meant we couldn't have secrets from each other. My parents argued sometimes about who had the car keys last, or how we would pay for my dance lessons, but they never kept secrets from each other. My dad always said love dies in dishonesty. *If you can't share your true self with someone,* he once told me, *you're wasting your time.* I didn't think I was wasting my time with Logan, but I wanted to be sure. I wanted to know everything about him. And I was ready for him to know everything about me.

It all started with the video. If I had given it to Officer Rice Krispies instead of to Evan, things would be very different. I wouldn't live in this big house or be at a new school. I wouldn't have a Louis Vuitton bag, an en suite bathroom, or friends with bright futures. And I wouldn't have met Logan. Our relationship wasn't real if he didn't know how I got here. So I had to tell him the whole story. And that video was the key.

At first I was surprised that he wanted to watch it. But then of course it made perfect sense. He loved me, no matter what. And he knew that if I didn't watch the video, I would never know what happened that day. He wanted to help me find closure. He wanted to watch it with me so I didn't feel scared and alone. That's what you do when you love someone—you stand by them, even through the ugly stuff. That's what he wanted to do for me.

"Are you sure you want to see this?" I asked him as the video started to play. I knew from the concave silhouette of my dad's face under that napkin that something gruesome was coming. I had tried to bring myself to watch the video at least a dozen times since my trip to the morgue, but so far hadn't been able to bring myself to do it.

"Are you sure *you* want to see it?" Logan asked me. It was already playing. Mom and Dad were driving home from somewhere, I recognized the neighborhood, they were close to home. They would be on our street in less than a minute. I thought about asking him to watch it first, or even for me, but I wanted him to be my partner, not my protector. We loved each other, we would do this together.

"Yes," I said simply. I wanted to show him I was brave, that I could handle it. He reached for my hand and held it tight, and I knew I'd made the right choice.

"If you need to look away, just put your head right here." He patted the smooth nook between his neck and shoulder, and I nodded. I remembered watching *Halloween* with my dad when I was a little girl, how I had buried my head in that exact spot during the scary parts. But Logan wasn't my dad, and I wasn't a little girl anymore.

"I'll be OK," I told him, and believed it—that's how safe he made me feel. Our eyes were glued to the phone as the Cherokee turned onto my street. Only a matter of seconds now.

The car stopped. My head felt floaty as I held my breath. The dashcam didn't have a mic, so there was no noise to drown out the thumping of my heart. For several seconds, we stared at the street I once called mine. It was eerily quiet, and for a hopeful second I thought nothing was going to happen, that we'd be spared.

But then there was movement. A man stepped in front of the car. I could see clear as day that it was my dad. He was wearing the shiny Adidas warm-ups we gave him for his birthday. He was rounding the front of the car to open my mom's door. He always opened the door for her, and she always waited for him. I used to tease her about it, but she insisted she only let him do it so he could feel like her "knight in shining armor," that he liked it. Maybe if I had teased her more insistently, she would have stopped letting him do it. But I didn't, and now it was too late.

"Maybe you should look away," Logan said, and I shook my head no. There was urgency in his voice, like he wanted to protect me from what was about to come. I didn't realize I was crying until I felt tears slide down my chin and onto my chest. No point wiping them away, there were surely a lot more coming.

My dad was out of frame now. The camera was not positioned to see the side of the car, only the front, so I could only guess what he was doing—opening the door, coaxing my mom out of her seat—she was always slow to get out of the car. She had to unplug her phone, gather her purse, get her water bottle or coffee cup out of the cup holder. The seconds passed like hours. My head felt so light I thought it might fly off.

And then the waiting was over.

The first thing we saw was the image rock, like an earthquake shaking the car.

Then snow was falling as window glass rained down on the hood in an angry blizzard.

Then a car—a black SUV—sped through the left side of the frame like a silent freight train.

I heard myself gasp as a person that must have been my mom bounced off the hood and down out of sight.

Brake lights lit up as the SUV stopped.

A bright-red car door danced and spun on one edge, then skidded to the ground.

A limp body in shiny warm-ups peeled off the front of it and flopped to the pavement.

The SUV was frozen in the distance, brake lights lit, like it knew it should stay.

I stared at the back of the car that killed my dad.

Black SUVs were a staple of Southern California. There were literally thousands of them, and I couldn't tell a Toyota from a Tesla.

But this car I knew.

Because it was exactly the same as one I had ridden in dozens of times.

"Oh my God, he has the same car as you," I blurted, the shock of recognition prickling up my spine. I had no idea the danger this innocent admission had just put me in, how I would come to wish I had kept my mouth shut.

The brake lights went out. Sunlight illuminated the back of the SUV like a spotlight. That's when I saw it, in that split second between the brake lights going dark and the SUV barreling away.

A bumper sticker that said Devils.

Except it didn't say Devils. Because it was upside-down. Someone had drawn a vertical line through the upside-down *V* to make it look like the letter *M*, spelling the word Slimed. It was so small in the frame, if it wasn't so familiar to me, I might not have even noticed it.

But I did. And there was no denying it. That car was one of many, but that sticker was one of a kind.

And they both belonged to Logan.

He clicked off the phone. I couldn't speak. I couldn't breathe. It was impossible that the car in the video was his. But it was more impossible that it wasn't.

My hand holding Logan's went limp. I wanted to cry out, but terror had a choke hold on my throat. I should have taken his advice. I should have looked away. I wished I hadn't seen it. Because now I knew this boy who came out of nowhere to love me had worse secrets than mine.

"Well," Logan said, "now you've seen it."

I should have looked at him. I should have pretended that I didn't recognize the car, or the sticker, or the double meaning in his words. I should have acted like I was so overwhelmed by seeing my dad get run over that I couldn't possibly have noticed anything else.

But I didn't. Because I was terrified. Not by the accident, or by seeing my dad's dead body. I was terrified of the impossible coincidence that of course wasn't a coincidence at all.

I was terrified of *him*.

"I need to go check on my mom," I said, trying to keep my voice from cracking.

I slipped out the door and down the hall toward my mom's room. I pushed open the door to see her sitting up in bed, reading on her phone. As she looked up at me, I put a finger over my lips.

"How are you feeling?" I asked her, careful to keep my voice calm and steady, even though I could feel my eyes bulging with fear. She furrowed her brow but answered the question.

"I'm good," she said, trying to match the brightness in my voice, not the alarmed expression on my face. "I was just playing Scrabble."

"Oh! Can I see?" I held out my hand, and she put her phone in it.

I closed the game and typed a note with shaking hands:

PUT ON YOUR SHOES WE NEED TO GET OUT OF HERE NOW

I passed her the phone. Her eyes flickered with surprise, but she didn't flinch.

"I think I need to go out for a bit," she announced. I nodded almost imperceptibly, but enough so she knew she was on the right track, and to say more. "I'd love your company."

She swung her legs off the bed and leaned over to slip on her boots—steel-toed Timberlands I'd picked out for her online, perfect for the drizzly winter nights that would soon be upon us. But before she had the chance to put them on, Logan appeared in the doorway.

"How's everybody feeling?" he asked. The question was meant for my mom, but he was staring at me.

"Hungry!" Mom responded without missing a beat. "I was just going to drag Savannah to the grocery store."

"Yeah . . . ," Logan replied. "I don't think so."

He stepped into the room and closed the door behind him. He had something in his hand. He saw me looking at it, so he raised his arm to show me.

It was a kitchen knife. The one meant for cleaving meat. The blade was wide and razor sharp.

"Logan, what are you doing with that?" I stammered. The sight of my boyfriend standing in the doorway flashing a knife as long and thick as my arm made my head spin. I tried to tell myself this wasn't really happening, that it *couldn't* be happening.

"Oh, come on!" he belted. He sounded annoyed, like *wasn't it obvious?* "We all knew this charade wouldn't last. You with my money, living in this house like you belong here."

Mom looked at me. Her expression was a mix of bewilderment and terror. "I'm sorry," I whispered, and she suddenly got it—why Logan had pursued me, that he was the one Evan was protecting, that we were in deep shit.

"Let's all just calm down," Mom said. "Nobody took your money, Logan. The money to buy this house was a settlement—"

"It wasn't my fault!" he spat back, then turned to me. His face was red with rage. "Your dad was stupid. What kind of moron steps out in front of a speeding car? This was a setup, he set me up!"

I shook my head in stunned disbelief. *Does he really believe my dad died on purpose?* The suggestion was as absurd as him standing there waving that knife.

"We don't want your money," Mom said. Her voice was steady but tight with fear. "You can have it back. All of it. We didn't know it was yours."

"It's too late," Logan said. "Don't you get it?" He suddenly looked exhausted. His lips puckered with frustration. "My dad doesn't give a shit about you. All this . . ." He waved the knife in the air, indicating the room, the house, all that had become ours. "It isn't a gift meant for you. It's a punishment meant for me. You got all this so I would have nothing."

I raced to put the pieces together in my mind. He killed my dad. So his dad took his money and gave it to us. That's why he came to my school—to find me and make me fall in love with him. He was never into me. Not even for a second. I couldn't believe how gullible I had been, believing his compliments and *I love yous*. He didn't love me, he despised me. The realization ripped through my heart like a bullet. My disappointment and shame poured out in sobs.

"We didn't know," I insisted. "We never would have taken it if we'd known."

"Why'd you have to keep that video?" Logan asked, eyes boring into my tear-streaked face. "You already had the money, he wasn't going to give it back to me."

Mom jumped to my defense. "She had no intention of showing it to anyone—"

"She showed it to *me!*" Logan snapped back, then raised the knife and shook it at me. "I knew you were weak," he seethed. "I knew you would show someone. I was never safe from your squealing little fingers."

"I'm sorry," I mustered, because he was right. I was weak. Because I did show it to someone. Someone I thought loved me. I cried harder, and Mom squeezed my hand.

"Because she trusted you," Mom said. "She's not going to show it to anyone else. We'll delete it right now." She snuck a glance at me, and I nodded that I would. "We have nothing to gain by telling anyone it was you," she reasoned. "Nobody else has to know."

But he ignored her and laid into me. "You did it to yourself," he said, his blue eyes boring into mine. He reached behind him and locked the bedroom door, then waved us toward the closet. "Get in the closet."

"Logan, please . . . ," I begged. *Why does he want us to go into the closet?* Dad used to keep guns in his bedroom closet, but we weren't at our old apartment, and I had no idea where they were now.

"GET IN!" He pointed the knife at me and charged at my throat. Mom grabbed me and pulled me out of its reach.

"OK, OK," she soothed, one hand outstretched like she was commanding a dog to stay. "We're going."

She stood up, then looked at me and squeezed my hand. *We're in this together,* the gesture telegraphed. *Two are stronger than one.*

"Hurry up!" Logan commanded, and Mom made that *OK, OK* hand gesture again, then slowly led me toward her closet. As she opened the closet door, full of her things and God willing those guns, Logan barked, "Wait!" He peeked in the other closet—the empty "his." "This one," he ordered.

Mom's face twitched with disappointment. And I knew I was right about the guns, that she kept them tucked on a high shelf, between her sweaters and jeans, just like Dad did.

"If it's the money you want, we can work something out," Mom said, but Logan just laughed.

"You made it really easy for me by taking all those pills," he said through the crooked smile I once adored but now made me sick. "When they find your dead bodies, they'll see there was a history and won't be suspicious."

My head felt light as my blood waterfalled into my feet. He was not improvising. He had planned this. Ever since the day he'd taken me out for tacos.

"You're right," Mom said, trying one last time to bargain with him. "No one would question if something happened to me. But Savannah, she had nothing to do with this. She's a smart girl, you could work it out—"

"Stop it!" Logan shouted. "Stop talking and get in!"

He pointed at the closet with his knife hand. His arm muscles flexed rock-hard, his knuckles were white. He was strong, but I was fast. I suddenly thought, *If I can get by him, I might be able to run for help.*

I felt a surge of determination. The hallway between the two closets was wide, I could definitely slip past him. *But then what?* He had a weapon and I didn't. If he threw that knife at me, I'd be toast. But he said he was going to kill us anyway, so what did I have to lose?

Like a sprinter in the starting gate, I readied myself to spring. I twisted my back foot in the carpet, hoping my mom would see the signal that I was going to make a move. She showed me she did when she shifted her weight away from me to give me space.

"Move back," Logan ordered. My mom glanced at me as she stood firm. "I said move back!" Once again she defied the order. He raised his free arm to push her. She grabbed it and shouted, "Go!"

She yanked his arm with all her might, widening my path just enough to streak through.

I exploded off my back foot.

Adrenaline surged through my body as I lunged for the door. I had a solid jump on him, plus the element of surprise. By the time he turned around, my hand was on the door handle. I pulled on it, hard.

It didn't budge. I forgot he had locked it.

"Savannah, watch out!"

I turned around. Logan was lunging for my throat. He swung the knife. I ducked, and it connected with the door.

Mom's arms were around Logan's neck in a flash, but he was too strong for her and he quickly shook her off, then body-slammed her to the ground. Her head bounced off the wall, then rolled to one side.

"Mom!"

I sprang to standing. The knife was still in the door, but Logan was between it and me, there was no way I could get to it. I scanned the room for a weapon—anything that could even the fight. My eyes combed the furniture, the walls, the floor.

That's when I saw them.

Mom's steel-toed boots.

I stumbled back toward the bed, groping for a boot as Logan grabbed the knife and yanked it free.

My hand found the boot, and I plunged my fist into the shank and raised it like a claw. All that love I'd felt for him swirled into a vortex of rage and hate. If this was a fight to the death, I was ready.

As the knife came at my chest, I swung the steel-toed Timberland at Logan's outstretched arm. It missed his arm, but slammed into his hand, springing the knife from his fingers and sending it clattering to the ground.

"You little bitch!" he growled as he shook his hand, then lowered his shoulder and came at me like a battering ram.

I cried out as I slammed the boot down on his back.

It sank into his flesh but was not enough to stop him.

My lungs burned for air as he slammed my back against the floor.

He was on top of me now, the full weight of him across my chest, using his knees to pin my arms to my sides. I bucked and flailed my legs, but they were as useless as kite tails in the wind.

"I should have slit your throat when I had the chance," he hissed, then grabbed me by my hair and yanked me to my feet. Pain shot across my scalp. I cried out.

"Shut up!" he barked as he dragged me toward the open, empty closet.

My mom groaned and tried to grab his legs, but he kicked her aside. My screams turned to sobs as I watched her body wilt back down onto the carpet.

"This is your fault," he hissed as he pushed me into the closet. He raised my arms above my head, then took off his belt and used it to bind my wrists to the clothing rod. He gripped the knife and floated it under my nose. "I should gut you like a fish," he rasped.

Fear surged through me as he held the knife under my chin. For a second I thought he might actually do it.

"Fuck it," he said, pulling his arm back and letting the knife drift down by his leg. "You're not worth the trouble."

He walked away, then a few seconds later returned, dragging my mom by her shoulders. Her eyelids fluttered as blood caked on her hairline.

"Momma," I whimpered. The leather belt pulled at my wrists as I strained to get to her, to touch her, to hold on to her, love her back to life.

The door slammed shut, and we were plunged into darkness.

I heard the thump of something heavy landing in front of the door. Then silence.

"Momma? Can you hear me?" My voice was high, like a warbly bird.

She whimpered softly. She was concussed but she was alive.

My wrists burned against the thick leather tether as I tried to work them free. The bind was tight, but I felt a little flicker of hope as I realized I could move them. It might take a few hours, but I was pretty sure I could stretch the leather enough to wriggle them out.

I pulled on the belt, sliding it back and forth against the rough wooden bar. My shoulders ached already, but I knew from my track workouts that I could push through.

I settled into the pain, taking slow, deep breaths. I felt a tiny bud of confidence, a swell of hope that gave me strength.

And then I smelled it.

Smoke, sour and pungent, like a smoldering campfire.

It was seeping in under the door.

This house that was so carefully chosen for my mom and me was burning.

And barring a miracle, we were going to burn with it.

LIBBY

Three months ago

Shopping at Home Depot made me feel like a boss.

I loved wandering the aisles, looking at all the tools and fixtures, discovering the secrets of how a house became a home.

Today I was in the garden center. I knew flowers for our front yard did not qualify as "essential," but they made my heart happy, so I decided to indulge. The prettiest ones were the perennials. I couldn't carpet my lawn like in *The Wizard of Oz*, but a few strategically placed clusters could go a long way, and the optimist in me insisted by this time next year we'd have enough money to plant twice as many.

I pushed my cart through the wonderland of lilies. I loved their long, slender necks and starbursts of color. I chose some Stargazers for their zingy fuchsia petals. I would put them by the mailbox so our mail carrier could enjoy their tangy-sweet smell.

They say home is where the heart is. It's a romantic notion, but not a terribly realistic one. There are plenty of days my heart is on a beach on the French Riviera with a good book and a bottomless martini. Doesn't make it my home.

No, a home is not where your heart is, it's where your effort is. It's where you cook and eat and sleep and take pains to decorate. It's where your memories are made and kept. It's the photos on the mantel, the artwork on the walls, the blankets that you snuggle under, the trees and flowers that you plant and care for.

A home is not a faraway place that lives in your heart. It's where you are today and every day. It's an extension of who you are.

As I loaded some playful peonies into my cart, I wondered, *What does it say about me that my home is falling apart? Am I a reflection of my crumbling home, or is it a reflection of me? Did I drive it to ruins, or did the ruins corrupt me? Which one is the chicken, and which one is the egg?*

When we bought our house, with its aging cupboards and sagging floorboards, we were full of optimism and grand ideas. But over time, we became the home we had bought—tired, worn out, and sad.

We were a total mismatch from the start. For years we were engaged in a struggle over whose aesthetic would prevail. The house knew what it was, and what it wanted to be.

And it was winning.

I had no idea if my cheery purple peonies would help close the gap. But I was ready to fight back. For my husband, for my children, and yes—for me.

If I was going to manifest a bright future, it was going to start right here, in the garden center at Home Depot. If there was a better metaphor for reinvigorating my marriage than dumping a twenty-five-pound bag of fertilizer on our dull, tired soil, I couldn't think of one.

My commitment to support my husband was renewed right then and there.

And I would tend to our homelife until those wilted flowers bloomed again.

CHAPTER 35

Margaux's room was at the front of the house.

It had a big circular window overlooking the street, with a padded window seat for all her dolls. Because the window curved like the inside of a spoon, we couldn't put a shade over it—which was fine with her, she liked the rising moon as her nightlight.

But that night her room was lit by a different light. It wasn't cool, blue, and steady—it was hot and danced angrily on her walls. It scared her. And so she came downstairs.

"There's something outside my room," she said, twisting her nightie between nervous fingers as she came into the family room where Andy and I were both on our laptops.

"What is it, sweetie?" Andy asked, opening his arms to give her a hug. At seven she was just on the outside edge of being a little girl. Her hair was losing its bouncy curls, and her first grown-up teeth were starting to sprout through her gums.

"I'm scared," she said. Margaux often had trouble sleeping and needed a second or third tuck-in, we'd gone through this drill hundreds of times.

"I'll go," I offered, taking her hand in mine. "Let's go get you all tucked in."

She let me pull her out of her daddy's lap, and we walked up the stairs hand in hand. She had a million reasons to come get one of us—*I heard a noise, I saw a bug, my room is cold.* They were all just excuses to get one of us to tuck her in again. I figured this was just another one of those times.

Until I walked into her room.

"Oh my God!" I gasped, pulling Margaux toward me and peering out her window.

Flames were curling out of the upstairs windows of Holly's house, lapping the roof, sending funnels of smoke up into the sky.

"Andy!" I shouted as I hoisted Margaux onto my hip and backed away from the window toward the door.

Andy thundered up the stairs. "Holy shit!" he exclaimed from the threshold of her room.

"I'm calling 911," I said, clutching Margaux to my breast as I ran for the phone.

I put Margaux down and dialed with shaking hands.

"911, what's your emergency?"

Margaux sobbed into my leg as I spat out our address. "The roof of the house across the street is on fire," I stammered. "It's burning out of control!"

The operator was eerily calm as she asked, "Are the occupants of the house at home?"

I dropped the phone. "Andy!"

Andy burst out of Tatum's room, clutching our four-year-old. "Get in the car, take the girls. I want you out of here!"

"What if they're in there?" I demanded. It was eight o'clock at night. He didn't answer, so I asked again. "What if Holly and Savannah are trapped inside?"

"What's happening?" Tatum asked, rubbing her eyes. Andy handed her to me. Margaux was clutching my leg.

"Go with Mommy," he coaxed. Margaux grabbed on to his shirt and held it tight.

"What are you going to do?" our seven-year-old asked, and I wanted to know, too.

"I'm going to go make sure Savannah and her mommy are OK," he said. I shook my head.

"You're not going in there!" I commanded. "No way!"

"I'll meet you at the bottom of the hill," he said, running into our bedroom, pulling on his shoes on the way out.

"Andy, please," I begged. My husband was capable, but he was not a firefighter. I didn't want him anywhere near there.

"I won't do anything stupid," he promised.

He kissed Margaux, Tatum, then me. "Now go!" he commanded. Then he ran down the stairs and out the door.

JACK

Three months ago

It was time to wash the car.

I could have taken it to a drive-through place, but, for obvious reasons, I opted to do it myself.

It was a bright-blue, sunny day, but my mood was so overcast I barely noticed. Scrubbing the bumpers with the stiff yellow sponge, I had a bit of a Lady Macbeth moment *(Out, damn spot! Out!)* as I attacked not just any physical remnants of our dastardly deed, but my guilt and shame along with them. As I swirled the soapy liquid across the hood, I tried not to think of how things ended for the troubled lady, or how my fall from grace might be equally inevitable.

Newton's third law of motion *(What goes up must come down)* certainly had ominous implications. You see it all too many times in the movie business. Young actors coming into sudden fame, then a few short years later overdosing, slitting their wrists, sucking on a tailpipe.

We blame the media, for prying into their lives. We blame their families, for failing to support and love them. We blame their so-called friends, for glomming on to their newfound fame, asking too much, making them feel used.

But maybe it's simpler than that.

Maybe these poor souls implode because they are thrust into a realm that's not meant for them. Maybe they were meant to live modest lives. Maybe they were meant to spend their lives striving but not arriving. Maybe fame and fortune was not their true destiny, they just don't belong, like land animals thrust into the sea.

Do people have a destiny? And what happens if their intended path is interrupted? Upset by an unintended gift? Or the loss of a gift meant for them?

As I flipped the wipers up to squeegee the windshield, I wondered if I was making a terrible mistake, thrusting Holly Kendrick into a realm not known to her. *Does she belong there? Is her soul meant to be suddenly and unexpectedly thrown into lavishness?*

I thought about what I was doing to her, forcing my brand of comfort and riches upon her. *Am I upsetting the natural order of things? And how will it end?*

And what am I doing to my son by abruptly severing his trajectory, and putting him on a vastly different path than he was destined to follow?

I thought I would never know the answers to these questions. I thought they were machinations of my guilt and doubt.

But I was wrong.

The answers were coming.

And they were exactly as bad as I feared.

CHAPTER 36

We smelled the fire before we saw it.

I assumed it was a distant brush fire, we had so many this time of year. I even said a silent prayer that it was minor and that no one had been hurt.

But then Evan turned onto Holly's street, and panic pierced a hole through my heart.

"Good God!" I heard myself say as Evan leaned on the accelerator and we shot up to the curb.

"Stay in the car!" he barked as he jumped out of the driver's seat and ran up the lawn.

There was a man already at the front door, shouting and banging on it with both fists. Evan called to him as he whipped out his phone and used it to open the garage. As they ducked under the lumbering door, I saw Holly's Lexus SUV—the one Evan had picked out and hand-delivered to her—parked inside.

If her car was here, she was home.

I felt a surge of panic as I unclicked my seat belt and ran in after them. It was unthinkable that my son might have had something to do with this. *So why am I thinking it?*

"Holly! Holly!" I heard Evan calling from somewhere ahead of me.

I had seen pictures of this house but had never been inside it. I didn't know the layout. For a moment I was frozen, unsure where to go.

"Savannah!" It was a different voice—the man from the front porch. He was coming out of what looked like an office, then ran ahead of me and disappeared from sight.

I jogged straight ahead. A staircase appeared in front of me. Smoke curled down it like a snake.

"I'm going upstairs!" I called out, not waiting for a response as I covered my mouth with the inside of my collar and took the stairs two at a time. It was hot below, but upstairs it was sweltering. If I died here today, I wondered if I'd be remembered as a hero or an idiot. I shook off the thought as I peeked into the girl's room, then the bedroom next to it. Both were empty.

"Jack! Wait!" Evan called after me, and I could hear his heavy footsteps coming on hard. I could see flames now, licking the walls of the bedroom at the end of the hall. Against all self-preservation instincts, I lowered my head and charged toward it. Evan caught up to me at the threshold. I had no idea what I would find, my head spun with the possibilities. *Where is my son? Has he been here? Is he still here? Am I too late?*

Smoke burned my eyes as I scanned the room. The fire was everywhere, devouring the drapes, the bedframe, the walls. It was literally hell on earth. I was about to turn back when Evan grabbed my arm.

"There!" he shouted, pointing to a door with a nightstand pushed up against it. It took me a second to understand what a nightstand was doing in front of a closed door. I got a sick feeling as I realized—it was barricading it.

Someone was in there.

And someone wanted to make sure they didn't get out.

Evan and I bolted toward the barricaded door. Above and all around us, wood beams and drywall were crackling and buckling into themselves. Embers swirled with rage. I was already so hot I didn't notice a smoldering ember had landed on my arm.

"Your sleeve!" Evan yelled as he clamped his bare hands around the burning cloth. I shook him off and dropped to the ground, extinguishing the flames with my body weight.

I crawled to where Evan was pulling at the nightstand, then rolled onto my back and used my legs to help push. The nightstand slid clear of the door, and in a few seconds we had it open, and I saw the inevitable result of what I'd done to this family. The shame I felt was as suffocating as the smoke-filled air.

"Holly!" Evan cried out, then fell to his knees. I watched as his two fingers probed her neck for a pulse. "She's alive!"

I had to step over Holly's legs to reach the girl, who was hanging off a clothing rod by her wrists. I forced myself not to ask myself what kind of monster was capable of this, because the answer would cripple me.

"Oh my God, Savannah!" a stranger's voice called out. And in an instant he was beside me. I did a double take when I saw his face. *Do I know him?*

"We need to lift her up to unbind her wrists," the man said. I took in his dimpled cheeks and pale-blue eyes—he was definitely familiar, but I still couldn't place his face. I wrapped my arms around the girl's slender midsection and hoisted her up on wobbly legs. As the man loosened the leather belt around her wrists, I glanced down at his shoes—shiny Chuck Taylors. And I immediately knew, this Good Samaritan helping save not just this poor girl but also my rotten soul was the investigative reporter whose script I'd just optioned.

"Almost got it!" he said, working the supple leather belt with determined fingers. Of course I knew that belt, too. Because I had bought it for my son. His name was engraved in the buckle. The bill of sale was probably still in my wallet. Tears welled up from the deep recess of my heart, mingling with the ones caused by the stinging smoke and heat.

"Mom?" the girl murmured, and I held her tight.

"Your mom is OK," I soothed. "We're going to get you out of here."

Evan was carrying Holly fireman-style out the door as the belt dropped to the ground and the girl's arms flopped free.

"Let's go!" Andy barked, as I remembered his name. He lifted Savannah in his arms. "Jack! C'mon!" And of course he remembered mine.

I looked down at my son's belt, with its monogrammed buckle, clearly linking it to him.

"Don't," Andy said sharply, and I spun to look at him. "You've held the secret long enough."

My breath caught in my chest. I didn't have time to wonder what my shrewd new investigative reporter colleague had pieced together. I couldn't ask how and when he'd figured it out, or what the hell I would do about that. Answers to those questions would come later.

What I did know in that moment was that he was absolutely right. That secret had ravaged all our lives. It was time to set it free.

I looked back down at my son's one-of-a-kind belt.

And I left it there.

EPILOGUE

Three months later

HOLLY

I woke up to see snow falling, sifting down onto emerald-green grass.

The first and last time I saw snow was on our family trip to Big Bear. Savannah was three, and she was absolutely charmed by it. As it swirled down from an infinite gray sky, she turned her little Kewpie-doll face up to greet it, opening her mouth to catch it on her tongue, then flapping her arms like a bird as if inviting it to play with her. Seeing her so completely delighted is one of my favorite memories of our time with Gabe. I was too caught in the moment to take any pictures that day, except in my mind, where the memory lives swirled with feelings of sadness and loss.

I remember thinking snow-covered trees were the most beautiful thing I had ever seen. I loved how the fluffy white confection balanced on the branches, like thick frosting on coffee-colored ladyfingers. Everything dark and dirty was hidden—at least for the moment—and the blur of pure, white heaven made me feel peaceful and free.

Evan saw me staring out our bedroom window and touched my face. He said it was a good thing I liked snow, because it snowed a lot here in New Hampshire. He had bought Savannah and me poofy parkas and cozy, fur-lined boots even before we had decided to move here, and they quickly became our daily uniform. It took some getting used to, having to bundle up every time we went outside, but it made coming home to the warmth of our cabin in the woods that much nicer.

I never thought I would love again, but who does when they marry their high school sweetheart? My feelings for Evan were not that urgent, hungry kind of love, but they anchored me, and my heart felt full and safe. I never in a million years imagined I would move all the way across the country to escape my past, but now that we were here, it made perfect sense.

I would never forget my husband and the life we had shared. But the woman who married him was gone now, like a tiny boat swept away by a storm.

I still carried her memories, of course. And her secrets. They jangled around in the pockets of my new life, gently reminding me that not all debts can be paid with money, but taking someone's money always leaves you in debt.

They also reminded me to go forward in gratitude. Because I got my second chance, my emerald forest, with the one man who could know the real me—secrets and all.

And I wasn't going to waste it.

Evan

The first thing I did was quit my job.

My letter to Jack was short and to the point. "Effective immediately, I will no longer serve as your personal attorney." I wrote it on my phone, from a chair next to Holly's hospital bed, where I stayed until I convinced her to come live with me by the beach.

It wasn't romantic, not at first. I worked hard to win her love. I knew I couldn't do it with things—she'd had enough of shiny, new things. I would have to find another way.

I started by giving her the spare room in my condo for her and Savannah to share—no frills, and no strings attached. I no longer worked for Jack, so I made it my job to tend to their needs, getting up at five to drive Savannah to school, keeping the fridge stocked with their favorite foods, then leaving them alone to eat when they pleased.

About a month into our arrangement, I came home to a table set for three. Holly often cooked—a lasagna or beef stew, which she would cover with tinfoil and leave on the stove—but until that day, she had never invited me to sit with them, and I'd never asked. But that night they waited. We ate family-style, which I hadn't done since I was a kid, passing clear bowls of salad and vegetables back and forth across the table, serving ourselves until we were full.

After dinner she asked me to go for a walk with her. As we stepped into the cool night air, she reached for my hand, and as I wrapped my fingers around her palm, I was careful not to squeeze too hard.

As we walked, she told me she had never been with anyone but her husband. She said it like an apology, and I told her we could take it slow, or not at all. She didn't owe me anything. And then she turned to face me, wrapped her hands around my neck, and went on tippy-toes to kiss me. I tried not to seem too eager as I kissed her back, putting a gentle hand on her waist but resisting the urge to pull her in to me. That would come later that night, after she came to my room wearing nothing but a T-shirt, which she left by the door as I pulled back my sheet and made room for her beside me.

She apologized for not knowing what to do next, so I showed her. She cried a little after, and apologized for that, too. I thought she might leave, but she didn't. I didn't hold her as she slept, but she was touching my arm when I woke up, and when I kissed her good morning, she kissed me back. Then she asked about New Hampshire and said she would like to see it sometime. I didn't know if she wanted to go to learn more about me, or escape what she knew about herself—I imagine it was both. We flew across the country on Savannah's Thanksgiving break and never left.

We don't tell people the story of how we met. "Through friends" is our go-to response. She forgave me for subjugating her life to protect another, and I would spend the rest of my life working to forgive myself.

Susan Walter

I know from the outside it may look like I saved her. And in some ways I did.

But she also saved me.

ANDY

I got my million dollars.

Two weeks after the fire, Jack Kimball exercised the option on my script, and by Thanksgiving the full amount had landed in my bank account.

A start date for filming was set for spring. Once people heard that I was in business with Jack Kimball, my phone started ringing and still hasn't stopped. Hollywood is funny like that. I didn't become a better writer after selling a script to Jack, yet suddenly all the producers who had passed on my scripts were lining up to buy one. Getting my name printed next to Jack's in the trade papers transformed me from outsider to insider, and any door I wanted to walk through was opened for me with a hearty "come on in."

I'm a little embarrassed to admit the scandal around Jack's family turned out to be the best thing that ever happened to my career. What is it they say about publicity? That it's all good, even the bad stuff? After Jack's son got arrested when "young love turned to fiery rage," Jack's name was everywhere, and mine along with it. You'd think being linked to arson and attempted murder would scare people away, but this is Hollywood. Being talked about is more marketable than being decent. And Jack Kimball was suddenly the most talked about man in town.

But that's not why I never wrote the story. Because of course I knew the truth. The look on Jack's face when my fingers found the tender engraving on his son's belt confirmed everything I had come to suspect—that it was Logan all along, and Jack had done what any father would do to protect his son. A search of public court documents confirmed what I suspected about Evan—he was the attorney of record for Jack on more

256

than a handful of cases. I never did buy that he and Holly were lovers, though I wasn't surprised to learn that's how they wound up. Tragedy has a way of bringing people together, especially when it's born from a treacherous secret.

And I guess I carry that secret, too, now. But keeping secrets is not new to me. As an investigative journalist I'd kept lots of secrets—torrid affairs, identities of whistleblowers, evidence that would have put many a man in jail had my sources allowed me to disclose it. Perhaps that's why I wanted out of that sordid business. I was good at keeping people's secrets. I had to be. Having tight lips was a job requirement. And many of those secrets were orders of magnitude worse than the one I was holding now.

Of course there were reasons to tell, but there were more reasons not to. After many years of suffering, my wife was happy. Going public with the story would expose our family to all sorts of unwanted attention, and, like Jack, I had a duty to protect Libby and the girls. Plus I had compassion for Holly. Outing her would rip her life apart, and she did not deserve that. Logan had been incarcerated and was no longer a threat. I had nothing to gain by exposing them. But I did have something to lose.

I'll never know why Jack put my movie into production—if it was worthy, or if he feared what I'd do if he didn't. But I didn't agonize over it. Because I was in the club now, and would have plenty of chances to prove I belonged there.

Would the story come out? A good investigative reporter could surely write a dazzler.

But I'm a big-time screenwriter now.

So it's not going to be me.

SAVANNAH

They blamed it all on me.

Jealous Boyfriend Burns Down Girlfriend's House, the headlines read. Apparently Teen Romance Erupts in Flames explained everything. Anybody who's read *Romeo and Juliet* knows that young people in love do crazy-ass shit. Nobody suspected there was a whole 'nother layer to this tragic tale, and (hopefully) never would. Logan was already staring down indictments for arson and attempted murder, no way he would want to add hit-and-run to his rap sheet. And I sure as hell wasn't going to tell anyone.

My room didn't burn, but all my stuff stank so bad like smoke I had to throw it away. Which was fine because I didn't want it, not anymore. I'll go to college, get a job, and buy my own Louis Vuitton. That's the way Dad would have wanted it. Because that's the only way it would ever be truly mine.

I deleted the video. Now that police were digging around our house, a.k.a. the "crime scene," I didn't want any loose ends around for them to find. Mom got the insurance money—it wasn't the same as having a bottomless bank account, but we wouldn't starve. Honestly, after nearly being set on fire, I was happy just to still be alive.

After it came out that my track coach tried to burn my house down with me in it, school got a little awkward. I never really liked that school anyway. I wasn't a Calabasas girl, with bouncy hair and rounded edges. But I wasn't a dark-eyed *chica* from Van Nuys either. I didn't know if I would find my tribe in New Hampshire, but at least I wouldn't be "the girl whose dad died," or "the girl whose boyfriend tried to kill her." I could, for the first time in my life, just be me. And I liked that idea.

Moving to New Hampshire was a chance to start over. Again.

Hopefully for the last time.

LIBBY

Obviously, we had to move.

I couldn't have my daughters staring out at that charred tangle of two-by-fours across the street from us every day. Margaux was already nervous at night.

I started looking the second the check cleared. We would get new construction this time, something closer to the studios so my husband could get to his meetings without any stress.

I had reservations about Andy staying in business with Jack after what his son did to that poor family, but the script was under contract, and we had bills to pay, whether or not the family was crazy.

And the fact is, we don't know what happened, not really. I liked Holly and tried to be her friend, but whatever bizarro arrangement she had made with Jack Kimball was none of my business. It was wrong of me to poke around in her private life. It's not like I had been living in integrity myself!

I would have gone to see them, but Holly and Savannah never came back to the house, not even to retrieve their things. As I peered out Margaux's window at the house, with its sunken roof and black-ened walls, I wondered if my house burned, what I would take? Surely I'd come back for my jewelry—not just because it's valuable, but because it's meaningful to me. Much of it was inherited, it connects me to my ancestors, my past, who I am today. I'd want my wedding dress—not to wear it again, but for the memories woven into the fabric. I'd want my favorite books, for the notes written in the margins that show the evolution of my thoughts. And of course I'd take anything framed—photos, diplomas, awards, babies' footprints—to remind me of the milestones that had shaped our lives.

I hate when people dismiss the loss of an object because "it's just a thing." Things are important. They give comfort, shelter, style, identity. The sum total of your things is a road map of your life. They show where you've been, what you accomplished, who you loved, who loved you back. They are an expression of who you are. You can learn a lot about a person by their things. Material things are not what's most important in life, of course! There is nothing that makes me happier than my child's laughter or her hand holding mine. But anyone who says they would not cry if they lost their childhood blankie or their wedding ring or the house they grew up in is either lying or a saint.

I remembered Holly's suicide attempt, and the cocoon of sadness that followed her around that house. It suddenly occurred to me that maybe she never wanted a Bosch oven or a Baccarat chandelier. They certainly didn't make her happy. I thought about how I contorted myself to live in this crumbling house, how unhappy I had been without things that were familiar to me, how far away from myself I had felt.

Perhaps Holly and I were the same after all. Both of us had been living a lie.

And now we both were where we belonged.

JACK

Acting is all about finding truth in made-up situations. I know that seems like a paradox, that's why it's hard. An actor's job is to be completely honest while pretending to be someone else, in a place that's dressed up to look like somewhere else, while telling a story that isn't true.

A good actor is a master of deception. Sometimes we get lost in the role, and the line between what's real and what's imagined gets blurred. I've never fallen in love with a co-star, but I understand why it happens. If you're really good at pretending to be in love with someone, sometimes you fool even yourself.

My son was not an actor, but when the press decided that he burned that girl's house down because he was mad with jealousy, he played the part. They made it easy for him, because even his denials were seen as proof that of course it was true—*the boy doth protest too much!*

But there was one person who didn't believe the narrative—his mother. She knew our son too well. She had felt his indifference about the girl. She didn't buy what the press was selling.

"I don't think he was in love with that girl," she told me as they hauled him off to jail. "He didn't act like a boy in love."

She asked me if I believed it, or if there was more to the story. I was tempted to lie. But I knew that, even with all my acting training, I couldn't, not to her. I didn't know how to play myself in a made-up story. She knew my process. She would see my tells. There was no way to hide the truth, not from her.

I told her on a Sunday, and she was packed and gone by Monday. My son was in jail, Evan had resigned, and for the first time in my life, I was completely alone.

I didn't have a big bottle of Vicodin lying around, but there were other ways to do what Holly had done, and if I'd had the courage, I might have tried them. I thought about Holly a lot those first few weeks as I slept anywhere but in my bedroom and ate standing at the kitchen counter to avoid seeing Kate's empty place. I was mortified that I'd tried to bury this woman's grief by gifting her a dream house. I knew now it was preposterous to think a princess would want to live in the castle without her prince, and that I was cruel to have suggested it.

A week into my sequestration, a man in a suit came to my door. I assumed it was the law and readied myself to get carted off to jail. But it wasn't a policeman. It was the attorney Evan had hired to represent my son. I nearly wept at the kindness of the gesture. After everything I'd put him through, he still had my back. In that moment, I knew definitively I hadn't deserved him, and felt genuinely relieved that he'd finally left me.

I had thought the press would drag me through the mud, but in the end, they probably saved my life. Because they wrote their own version of the story—that my son was ill, my wife was heartless, I was the victim. My fan base was energized. People all over the world sent messages of love and support. Rather than plummet, my star rose to new heights. The studio begged me to make a movie. I had a script that I liked under option, written by an investigative reporter I'd be wise to keep busy, so I agreed.

My days are a whirlwind of prepping and scouting and putting the movie together now. I am as busy as a shovel in a blizzard, but thoughts of Holly still leak through. The nights are the hardest, but whiskey helps, and I have something stronger when the whiskey's not enough. And when the time comes to shoot the movie, I'll get to pretend to be someone else for a while, just as Holly did, with borrowed costumes, a new haircut, and a fake backstory to complete the masquerade.

The movie will end, as all fake lives do, and, like Holly, I'll return to myself. And, like Holly, I will continue to grieve. Yes, Holly's grief reeks with the permanence of death, but mine carries the stench of shame and regret, which is just as relentless and tastes just as sour.

If loss could be measured, I think Holly and I both got our fair share. Death is worse than divorce, but Holly's daughter—a willful accomplice—roams free, while my son sits behind prison bars. And my most trusted friend has defected from my home to hers.

Has justice been served? Have we been returned to equilibrium and balance restored? If the dead man could speak, would he say we all got what we deserved?

I look to my tattered heart for the answer.

But like my life, my heart has been ravaged. I peer inside only to find it is barren, broken, as good as dead.

ACKNOWLEDGMENTS

It takes courage to say yes when a friend or family member asks you to read her first book—especially when you know she's going to ask you all sorts of questions, including the dreaded "Did you like it?" I want to thank my brave early readers, Libby Hudson Lydecker, Selah Victor, Aimee Simtob, Miranda Lewin, Maria Schneider, Wanda Frodis, Lena Rotmensz, Irene Ornovitz, Avital Ornovitz, and Jenny Smith for diving in, and Debra Lewin for being the very first (and encouraging me to keep sharing it). I am indebted to Margaret Howell for daring to scrutinize my verb tenses, and Jonathan Groff for teaching me a new word that I get to pretend I knew all along. Karen Glass and Andy Cohen made introductions that changed my personal narrative, and I owe them each a parade. Victoria Sainsbury-Carter lent her special brand of magic to lure me into the unknown, and Alethea Black was the ever-reliable compass that helped me find my way through. Thank you, Dr. Martin Bennett, for telling me what a doctor actually would say, and literary genius David Walter, for always pushing me to say it better. To all my friends and supporters who offered a heartfelt "You go, girl," thank you, it helped more than you know. This book is dedicated to my mother, Maila Walter, who let me be a moody artist long after it was hormonally appropriate, and my father, Edward Walter, who, by his example, taught me the value of never giving up.

I hit the jackpot with Lake Union's Christopher Werner, whose warmth and intelligence kept my creative fire lit, and editor extraordinaire Tiffany Yates Martin, who asked the best questions at every turn. This book would not have taken flight without the skillful piloting of my brilliant agent, Laura Dail, who finds the most sublime destinations and leads me toward them with dexterity and joy. Thank you to all the talented professionals at the Laura Dail Agency and Lake Union Publishing, I am humbled and honored to work alongside you.

Through it all I had the best cheerleaders in my daughters, Sophie and Taya, and husband, Uri, who endured at least a thousand "What would she do nexts?" (and often had the best ideas!). I am so grateful for their loving support and for allowing me to indulge this incredibly rewarding but terribly impractical calling of being a writer. Thank you for putting up with me and keeping me steady, I love you and I'm sorry but I am going to do it again.

ABOUT THE AUTHOR

Photo © 2020 Maria Berelc

Susan Walter was born in Cambridge, Massachusetts. After being given every opportunity but failing to become a concert violinist, Susan attended Harvard University. She had hoped to be a newscaster, but the local TV station had different ideas and hired her to write and produce promos instead. Seeking sunshine and a change of scenery, she moved to Los Angeles to work in film and television production. Upon realizing writers were having all the fun, Susan transitioned to screenwriting, then directing. She made her directorial debut with the film *All I Wish* starring Sharon Stone, which she also wrote.